You Had Me at
Good-bye

You Had Me at Good-bye

A Novel

Tracey Bateman

FaithWords

New York Boston Nashville

Scripture quotations throughout are from the King James Bible (public domain).

FaithWords
Hachette Book Group USA
237 Park Avenue
New York, NY 10017

Visit our Web site at www.faithwords.com.

FaithWords is a division of Hachette Book Group USA, Inc.
The FaithWords name and logo is a trademark of Hachette Book Group USA, Inc.

Printed in the United States of America

First Edition: February 2008
10 9 8 7 6 5 4 3 2

Library of Congress Cataloging-in-Publication Data
Bateman, Tracey Victoria.
    You had me at good-bye / Tracey Bateman. — 1st ed.
        p. cm.
    Summary: "Aspiring editorial diva Dancy Ames must find a new life when she's fired by her publisher. Could this be the time to risk it all on her writing career—and maybe even love?"—Provided by the publisher.
    ISBN-13: 978-0-446-69894-8
    ISBN-10: 0-446-69894-6
    1. Women journalists—Fiction. I. Title.
    PS3602.A854Y58 2008
    813'.6—dc22   2007033302

You Had Me at
Good-bye

girl has every right to stand up for herself. To insist that she be treated with, at the very least, a modicum of respect from her employers. Doesn't she? I mean, seriously. Is it too much to ask that I not be humiliated every single day by the powers that be? I've given my heart and soul to Lane Publishing for the past nine years. And I've gone high enough on the ladder that there's nowhere to go until someone leaves or gets fired.

I don't know—maybe I'm just bitter. But it does seem like there are an awful lot of menial tasks for someone at my level in the office. An editor should not be doing the job of an editorial assistant, should she? Tell that to my boss. It's always: Dancy, make copies. Dancy, get coffee. Dancy, clean the bathrooms. Well, no. Not that bad. Except there was that one time when the custodians were on strike, but that didn't last more than a couple of weeks. Anyway, I might as well be the janitor, for all the respect I get around there.

Forget the fact that I would be a great senior editor. Much better than Jack Quinn! Forget the fact that Jack, who is co-incidentally my brother's best friend from NYU, swooped down with his stupid English accent and charmed his way into my job. Forget that Jack is devastating to look at—wait, actually, *do* forget that. I didn't mean it at all. "Pretty is as pretty does," my mother always said, and Jack doesn't *do* very pretty, let me say. So by those standards he's a big ugly troll.

With dimples. And a cleft in his chin. And you should see his eyes . . .

No. Stop it! I will not be distracted by that man's looks, charm, or accent—which may or may not be fake! It's all his fault that Mr. Kramer, the publisher, gave the job away. It should have been mine. I was robbed.

I jerk to my feet in Nick's Coffee Shop, all bad attitude and determination. Jimmy Choos planted, knees locked, hands resting on the table, I make a fast decision. It's far past time I made it clear how serious I am about this. The opportunity is upon me. It's now or never.

"Mr. Kramer," I say in an extremely professional manner, using all my training as a debutante to give me that special air designed to make the other guy feel intimidated. "I truly feel that my talents are not being utilized to their full potential. I'm dissatisfied with the direction of my career at Lane Publishing. And if changes aren't made, I will be turning in my resignation shortly. There are, as you know, many opportunities for a young professional with my abilities in New York."

The emotional exertion of making that kind of threat is just too much, and my wobbly legs revolt, refusing to hold me up for one more second. Exhausted by my feeble attempt at the whole "I am editor, hear me roar" game, I drop back into the wooden chair. I'm actually panting. "How was that?"

Tabby and Laini, my two best friends in the world, cheer me on like I just won the Tour de France.

"Hear, hear!" Tabby says, raising her gigantic latte mug in my honor. "I especially like the part about the opportunities for a young professional. Don't you, Laini?"

"Bravo!" Laini pipes in, lifting her own mug as though she's toasting the queen. "Do it just like that and Kramer will realize, once and for all, that you mean business."

"I don't know." I can feel the frown lines making permanent etches in the non-Botoxed skin between my eyes. Something that mystifies my mother. Thirty years old and haven't had Botox? Oh, the horror.

"What do you mean, you don't know?" Tabby demands. "Take a stand already. That guy works your tail off for all these years, then hires someone else for the job he promised you. And then proceeds to upend the entire staff. It's no wonder you're ticked off. You have a right to ask some questions about his intentions. That Kramer guy has fired eight office staff members in the last six months, for crying out loud. Don't take it sitting down. Find out if you're next in line, and if you are, make him sorry to let you go."

"I know, I know." I push my fingers to my temples to rub away the knots forming there. "I'm going to do it. Only, probably not next week because there's this huge thing with the Paris office and he's going to be up to his elbows in bagels and baguettes . . ." My voice trails off as my friends shake their heads at each other.

"What?" I demand. "I *am* going to do it."

"Um-hmm," Tabby grunts out around a swig of chai latte. Laini snickers. Real ladylike, both of them.

I'm completely outraged by their lack of understanding. "I should disrupt his focus when all these bigwigs are in town? What if he fudges the entire meeting and we lose a major distributor, all because I want more respect? I'll lose my job for sure, and then where will I be?"

"Well, there are all those other opportunities," Laini says—not to me, to Tabby.

Tabby gives her a nod, keeping her expression stoic. "Right, especially for a young professional in New York City—such as our friend Dancy here."

Laini gives an exaggerated sigh, clasping her hands—which

would benefit from a little lotion, by the way—to her chest. "Oh, but she'd hate to bother Mr. Kramer, the boss from you-know-where. I mean, what if he gets distracted or something?"

Tabby clearly can't hold her laughter any longer. She snickers, which of course sets Laini off, too. "Well, wouldn't that be horrible for the poor man?"

Funny. Very, very funny.

Tabby turns back to me. "Don't worry, Dancy. If your head is next on the chopping block, you can always move back in with your mom or dad. Although Fifth Avenue would be a comedown after cramming into our spacious apartment all these years."

I roll my eyes. "Whatever."

"Just do us a favor, Dan," Tabby says, her face suddenly devoid of humor, her tone somber.

"What?"

"When you finally break the news to Kramer about how you're not going to take it anymore, be sure he's actually in the room so he gets the message." The girls break into laughter, even though I see nothing amusing about any of this.

"Shut up." I toss a napkin at Tabby, which she easily bats away.

"Hey, you three," Nick calls from across the room where he's taking care of customers. "Knock it off or I'm tossing you out of here."

Tabby's not even slightly intimidated by the shop's owner. The two of them have had this special bond ever since her fiancé, David, sort of made his move right here in the coffee shop and asked her out over cheesecake. She turns to the counter. "Hey, Nick. How about another round for me and my friends here? Dancy, the cowardly lioness, needs courage."

"And brains," Laini calls.

"And you two need a couple of hearts," I grump.

The Italian fiftysomething mobster (allegedly) behind the counter lifts a hand. "Hold your horses, girlies. What do ya think this is, a whiskey bar?"

"Sorry." Tabby grins.

"We have to go anyway," Laini says, before guzzling the rest of her latte.

For the first time I notice that Nick's looking a little frazzled. Unusual for him. "Hey, Nick, where's Nelda?" The line's backing up to the door, and Nick's all alone. His wife of thirty years is usually right there in the trenches with him, but she's conspicuously absent this morning.

"Well, she ain't here, now is she?" Nick barks, taking his gruffness to a new level. I mean, he's always a little rough around the edges, being that he is probably a Mafia mogul, but I'm almost positive that's just a front for his tender heart.

"We can see she's not here," I bark back, because I'm not in the mood for any more dissing today. I mean, I do have my limits. "Where is she?"

"That's my business, ain't it?"

"Wow, I've never seen Nick so freaked out," Laini says. "That article in the *New York Times* calling this shop 'one of Manhattan's best-kept secrets' really made the business pick up today. Weird that Nelda's MIA."

I'm more focused on Nick than on what Laini's saying, so the rest of her comments go over my head—except the part about Nelda being MIA. "You don't think she left him, do you?" It's an honest question. Marriage isn't exactly sacred in my family, the way it is for Tabby's parents.

"No way," Tabby says, without taking her eyes away from Nick. "If anyone's in it for life, those two are. She must be sick or something."

A man in a very smart black suit that may or may not be Armani gives an unsophisticated bang on the counter. "I don't have all day."

Nick swings around from the latte machine, and I swear I see actual steam shooting not only from his ears, but from his eyes and nose as well. He's like a bull snorting at a red scarf. "Buddy, one more word outta you and you're gonna be drinking this thing with a fat lip."

I flatten my palms on the table and push myself up from the chair. "I'm going to help him." I move across the shiny wooden floor with as much grace as I can muster in three-inch heels. My shoes *click* with one step and *clack* with the next, a sound that always fills me with confidence—something I need right now—as I slide behind the counter before the customer recovers from Nick's bad attitude. I smile at the guy. "Your order is coming right up, sir." I send him a dazzling smile, one that seems to do the trick. "Thanks so much for your patience."

I may not have any actual hands-on experience at customer service, but how hard can it be to pour coffee and smile at idiots who have no idea that dressing for success means nothing if you can't be civil? In my book anyway.

I snatch an apron from the hook next to the swinging kitchen doors. I'm actually feeling positive and ready to get into the trenches with this big galoot, for whom I suddenly feel a huge surge of affection.

"What can I do, Nick?"

"You can get your behind back out front, princess. This ain't no self-serve joint."

My face warms under his admonishment as my glass goes from half full to a little on the empty side. "I'm just trying to help."

"Help what?" he asks, distracted as he makes change. A frown burrows into the fleshy skin between his eyes.

"I thought I'd give you a hand with this crowd. But hey, if you're not interested, I'll just have another iced green tea. Hold the whipped cream, please. I'm watching my weight." That was a little mean, wasn't it? But it wouldn't hurt the guy to be a nicer to the help.

He slams the register shut and glances over at me. "You wanna help ol' Nick? No kiddin'?"

Does he not notice the green apron wrapped twice around my body? Not exactly my usual style. I give him a shrug. "No kidding."

He looks me up and down. Dubiously, I might add. I've never been more ashamed of wearing designer labels. Why didn't I just grab a pair of Levis and a sweatshirt, like a normal person would have? It's only morning coffee with the girls, for heaven's sake. And on a day off, yet.

It's not often I get a weekday off, but it was pointed out to me—*pointedly* pointed out—that I haven't had a day off, other than mandatory holidays and deathly-sick days, in years. Not even a vacation. So I made a bet with a fellow editor that, yes, I am capable of taking a personal day on occasion, and today was locked into the calendar. I woke up dreading today. I knew I had the day off, so why did I dress like I was going to the office?

"You wearing those shoes?"

"Yes. So?"

We leave the obvious unsaid. Three-inch heels. I'll be lucky if I don't break my neck. But truly I've had a lot of experience wearing these things. If anyone can pull off a shift in high heels, it's me.

"Whatever. They ain't my feet." Nick shrugs. "At least you're smart enough to put on an apron. Can you run a cash register?"

As much as I shop? *Pulease*. In my sleep.

"Sorry, Nick," Tabby calls. "Wish I could stay and help too, but I'm shooting a love scene in Central Park. Blythe'll kill me if I'm late again."

People turn and stare. I hold back a grin because this happens all the time. Laini tucks her hand inside Tabby's arm. "She's a *famous* actress," Laini explains, but I don't think they believe her.

Laini's telling the truth, though. Tabby is an Emmy-nominated, bona fide leading lady on *Legacy of Life*, the number one soap on TV. She's marrying the father of Jenn and Jeffy, the twins who play her children on the show.

Laini calls over her shoulder, "I promised to help my mom clean out the attic today. She's having a garage sale next weekend."

He pushes the button on the latte machine and waves them away. "Don't worry about it. The princess and me are gonna be fine."

F*ine* might be a bit of an overstatement, considering the register-tape incident and the multiple spills, not to mention the three-thousand-dollar latte (the lady completely overreacted, by the way, so Nick gave it to her on the house and then told her to take a hike), but we made it through. A full three hours later, I'm only a little sweaty and, thanks to the apron, my clothes have been spared. My shoes, though . . . let's just say they've seen better days, as have my feet and calves. Oh my goodness, I'm dying. I hobble to a chair and slide out of the toe torture chambers. My feet are splotched with red, angry places that will most likely be blisters by the time I get home. But at least my feet look better than the shoes themselves.

I was seriously thinking of donating these Jimmy Choos to Goodwill, considering they're last year's style. But of course they won't want them now, with the chocolate stains, so I guess I won't bother. Which is a real shame, actually. I always envision some half-starved, just-out-of-college girl landing a fabulous job while wearing something I've donated to Goodwill. I guess that's a bit prideful—not to mention presumptuous—of me, but it makes me feel . . . useful. Like I'm good for something more substantial than arm candy for the latest fix-up date. Like I'm more than just an editor, working under a British senior editor with a smile that screams veneers and a cleft in his chin that he probably bought from a plastic surgeon.

But I refuse to think about him on my day off.

I'm definitely not worth much to poor Nick. As a matter of fact, I couldn't even blame the guy when he sort of yelled at me—well, not the first time, anyway. I venture a glance at the clock. I can't believe it's already two! I've been working for hours.

Thankfully the shop is completely free of customers, except for one girl in the corner, long stringy hair covering her face, glasses resting way too low on her nose. Plus, her clothes are too baggy and not in style. I mean, do you have to spend a lot to at least wear something close to fashionable? What's wrong with today's girls? Even thrift shops have designer clothes. I know because, as previously mentioned, I donate some every season. And she's exactly the type of girl I have in mind when I do so.

She glances up as though she feels me staring. My face warms and hers goes red, and we both look away, I to my final swipe of the counter, she back to her book, which, I have to say, shows great taste in literature. *Pride and Prejudice*. My favorite.

"Okay, princess. What'll you have?" Nick asks. "Anything you want is on the house."

"You don't have to do that, Nick."

He shoots a huge grin from behind the counter. "You got me out of a jam, kid. Now, what's it gonna be?"

Nick's praise and fatherly show of affection weaken my resolve. "How about a meatball sub?" I shrink inside a bit. "Or is that too much?"

"It ain't enough. You stay there and rub those toes while I go rustle up something to put a little meat on your scrawny bones."

I gulp. Meat on my bones? I'm barely down to an acceptable size 2 as it is—well, as far as my mother knows. I'm really a 4, but if I suck in and lie down . . . but then, that only works if I've had less than two hundred calories all day. If I eat anything between now and tonight's dinner party, Mother's going to know as soon as I walk in the door. She's got calorie radar, I swear. She'll look me over, give a long-suffering sigh, and announce my BMI and percentage of body fat with alarming accuracy.

"Wait, Nick . . . maybe just a green tea." Increases the metabolism and promotes weight loss, so they say. "And a tuna salad on wheat—hold the mayo."

He stops and stares at me. "You sure?"

"No. Wait." I shake my head, thinking of that itty-bitty skirt taunting me from my closet. "Never mind the sandwich. Just the green tea."

"You kiddin' me? You need food." He scowls as though I've insulted the entire family, and for a second I picture myself sleeping with the fishes. "Wait right there. I'll fix something you'll like. Trust me. You fill out a little, and maybe you'll catch yourself a man, like your friend Tabitha."

Heat rushes to my face. "I don't want to catch one. As a matter of fact, I'm trying to throw one back." He's looking at me like I have chocolate on my nose, so I think I'd better explain. "There's this guy at work giving me a hard time."

"You mean sexual harassment? He can't get away with that. I got some friends, if you need someone to have a talk with him."

Okay, that's a little more than I wanted to know about Nick, but I do appreciate the offer. I don't like to talk about my life at the office, especially since it always makes me feel like a failure, but then, I *am* wrapped in a dirty apron with chocolate-covered shoes on my aching feet. Who am I to pretend I have a smidgen of pride left? "Not sexual harassment. Trust me—that I could deal with."

I tell him all about Mr. Kramer and how he's ruining my life. "Every time he looks at me, I think I'm doing something wrong. It's like he's waiting for me to step up to the table. And he allows the new senior editor to walk all over me. Jack Quinn has taken every edit I've done in the last month and completely rewritten the critique I was planning to send to the author."

Nick works and talks. "Is this Jack Quinn bein' a jerk, or is he right about stuff?"

I give a shrug. "I don't know. I guess he's right sometimes."

"It don't seem like you like the guy very much."

Astute observation.

"It's not so much about like or dislike. The question is, can I work with him?"

"Well, can you?"

"I don't know." I shift and, with a defeated sigh, prop my feet on the chair across from me. "I love Lane Publishing. But Kramer's made so many changes lately, I'm afraid I'm the next one he's going to shove out the door."

Nick shakes a spoon in my general direction. "You know what your problem is?"

Just what I need. Someone else telling me my faults.

He doesn't wait for me to answer. "Your problem is that you ain't got no confidence. You're a pretty girl and smart with all them books. Ain't nothin' wrong with you a little backbone won't fix."

"Yeah, sure. Sorry. I'll just roll right into his office like I'm Everywoman and tell him how it's going to be from now on. I'm sure he'll just move aside and offer me his job."

He scowls like only Nick can. "You can demand respect without being disrespectful, can't you? Didn't your mother raise you to have any gumption?"

I give a snort, because if anyone "raised" me, it certainly wasn't my mother. "Do you want to discuss my mother, Nick? Or the women who raised me? Let's see, there was Nanny Elizabeth, who took the shift from birth to kindergarten. She quit when she found Prince Charming among my parents' cronies, married him, and hired a nanny of her own nine months later. Then there was not one but *two* Nanny Marys. One retired to Florida, and I never knew what happened to the other one—she just vanished one day. Next there was Nanny Frieda. Mother hired her straight out of high school and fired her when she caught her dipping into the liquor cabinet. And last but certainly not least, Nanny Carol, who stole a pair of diamond earrings from my mother and claimed she got them from my dad for favors rendered. Dad played dumb and Mother could never prove it, so she eventually let it go."

I stop to catch a breath, arching one eyebrow at Nick. "Shall I continue? Because really they all did a bang-up job of making me the woman I am today."

Do I sound bitter? I do, don't I?

His scowl deepens as he slips my meatball sub onto a paper plate. "You havin' your woman time or somethin'?"

The girl in the corner looks up and gasps. I shoot a frown at Nick. "Could you be less subtle?"

"Well, you ain't acting much like yourself. I never seen you this grouchy." He shoves a fat, diamond-ringed finger at me. "And let me tell you, princess, it ain't pretty."

"I know. Hyde has returned." I drop my forehead into my palms.

"Thought you said this fellow's name was Kramer."

"I meant Dr. Jekyll and Mr. Hyde."

He nods. "Oh. I get it." Nick peers closer. "Something else wrong besides work?"

Am I that transparent? "My mother's giving a dinner party tonight for my aunt, and I have to be there. I dread her parties. She always forces me to sit next to Floyd Bartell and be nice to him."

Floyd Bartell. A creepy guy who has lived with his mother all his life—and he's thirty. His family is blue-blood rich and very well connected. If Mother could have arranged our marriage, she'd have done it a long time ago. Forget the fact that her grandchildren would likely be mutants, like their father. Thank God it's the twenty-first century, or the banns would have been read and I'd have become Mrs. Bartell before my sixteenth birthday.

"I get the willies just thinking about it. He's so gross."

"So tell him. No self-respecting guy's gonna want a girl that don't want him, anyways."

I give him an eye roll, accompanied by my trademark pursing of the lips. "My mother's been forcing me to sit next to him at every dinner she's thrown since junior high, and he's never even gotten to the batter's box, let alone to a base. Do you really think Floyd has any self-respect left?"

"Okay, look. You practice on me." He drops the gooey, cheesy meatball sub—made as only a true Italian can make it—on the table in front of me.

My mouth waters at the sight and smell of it. But my resolve is strong. "Nick, I can't eat this today. I have to fit into a size 2 Versace skirt in"—quick glance at my watch—"three and a half hours."

"So what? You can't eat?"

I shake my head and suck in at the very thought of that skirt. "It has a side zipper, and cheese bloats me." I look at the delightful mess with more than a little longing, and the look isn't lost on Nick.

"So wear a different skirt."

To anyone else, that might seem like the simple solution. However, nothing is simple when my mother is involved. The truth? She bought it for me and had it sent over to the apartment with instructions to wear it tonight.

Do I realize how pathetic I am? Yes, I do. That's why I'm not going to admit anything to Mr. Mafia. Instead, I use the old standby. "This one makes me look skinny."

The aroma of beef and sauce floats upward, tempting my taste buds and making my mouth water even more. Maybe just a little taste. I'll just sort of lick the melty cheese. "Mmm, Nick. This is wonderful."

His face lights up. "Now that's more like it." Looking around, he takes note of his one customer. "You doin' okay over there, honey?"

The poor girl's eyes widen in terror. She swallows hard and nods. From the way she's eyeing the door, I sort of get the feeling it's all she can do not to bolt.

Nick doesn't seem to have a clue how badly he terrifies young girls and little old ladies. He just gives her a nod. "Okay, then. I'm gonna have a seat and talk to my friend, here. You need anything, you let me know. Got it?"

She ducks her head. I'm not sure, but she may have fainted.

Nick plops his two-hundred-fifty-pound bulk into a chair that I'm not positive will hold the big guy, and wipes his brow with a towel. "The way I see it, you got two men in your life making you unhappy: one you gotta sit by at dinner, and one giving you trouble at work."

I'm amazed at his brilliant powers of deduction.

I'll just keep that little sarcastic remark to myself. I will not bite the hand that is feeding me this marvelous sandwich. But he's right. Why do I let people roll right over me? I can be strong when my friends are in trouble, so why can't I stick up for myself? I really don't want to sit next to nasty Floyd and hold my hand over my chest all evening to keep him from ogling. It's awkward and embarrassing and I'm—yes, I am—*sick* of it.

I'm contemplating this, along with a gooey string of cheese, when Nick scowls and snatches away my plate.

"Hey!" I say around the huge bite. "You said I need to eat."

"You can have it back after you practice on me." He yanks a napkin from the holder and shoves it at me.

"Practice what?"

"Telling the guy at dinner to take a hike."

Taken aback, I stare at the big guy for a second. The thought never occurred to me. I mean, I've dreamed of simply getting up and walking to a different seat, but I never actually considered it a viable option. I just wasn't brought up that way. "I don't think I can do that. Can I? I mean, wouldn't it be rude? And Mother would be mortified."

"You want this sub back?"

Desperately.

"Okay, fine." I wipe my mouth and gather a breath. I look at Nick and do my best to pretend he's Floyd. "Shove off, Floyd Bartell. You were a troll in junior high, still a troll in high school, not to mention college, and if I'm forced to marry you, I'll jump off the Brooklyn Bridge and bury myself in a watery grave." I hold out my hand. "How's that?"

He shoves the plate back across the table. "Pathetic," he says. "You been dating this guy all your life and you don't even like him?"

"I despise him." I'm a bit ashamed of my lack of control, not to mention my complete lack of grace, as I talk with my mouth full. "And I'm not dating him. He just escorts me to dinners and things a few times a year."

He shakes his head at me. "No wonder you can't find yourself a husband, if you let this guy sew up all your time. What kind of a weenie are you?"

"The worst kind," I admit.

"I gotta say, I'm a little disappointed, princess. I know you dress like a hoity-toity, but I sort of thought you was the hot dog of that group of girls you hang around."

It's true. In every other area of my life I am strong. I mean, last year I even coerced an ER nurse to get Tabby into the exam room ahead of everyone else right before her appendix burst—and you know how intimidating those nurses can be. (I mean that with the utmost respect for how busy they are, saving lives and all. Still, it's a fact. They scare me).

Anyway, back to my weenie ways. Usually I can hold my own. "It's only where men are concerned, Nick. I think I might have father issues because I don't have a good relationship with my own."

He gives a snort. "You been watching that *Mr. Philip's Neighborhood*?"

Is it just me, or is it a little scary that he just said that? "I think you mean *Dr. Phil*, and I don't watch it every day."

Usually I TiVo it and watch a week's worth of shows on Saturday. But that has absolutely nothing to do with my sudden revelation, and I'm disappointed that Nick is discounting my theory so firmly when he's the one who wants me to develop a backbone in the first place.

"There ain't nothing to it, sweetheart. Just tell this Floyd character to take a long walk off a short pier. He'll get the picture."

See? Comments like that are what make me think Nick's family might be pretty "well connected" themselves. Maybe I should just ask him to make old Floyd an offer he can't refuse. My lips go up at the thought of it. Then I look down at my plate and sober up real fast. It's scraped clean. Not even a glob of stuck-on melted cheese remains. In my desperate desire to become the woman I've always wanted to be, I'm suddenly feeling the need for a roomy size 4 skirt.

2

Valerie Orion might not have had time for friends, and maybe she had no time for a relationship, but one thing she had always prided herself on was having a lot of spunk. Her daddy had always told her to stand up for herself. So at two minutes to three on January second, she stormed into her boss's office and tossed her list of demands on his sleek mahogany desk.

His brows pushed together as he lifted the eight-by-ten sheet in his overly tanned hands. "What's this?" he asked, his frown marring what might have been handsome features if he'd smiled.

"I think it should be perfectly clear." Her lips tipped upward at the corners in a rueful smile. This man did not intimidate her in the least, and she couldn't have cared less if he knew it.

Valerie walked back to the door, keenly aware that his eyes followed her every move. She twisted the doorknob and turned her body halfway, looking over her shoulder at the bewildered face of her boss, John Quest. "You have until five o'clock to decide whether I give my two weeks' notice or not. It's really your choice."

—An excerpt from *Fifth Avenue Princess*
a novel by Dancy Ames

T here is no point in going back to the apartment I share with my two best friends after leaving Nick's full of cheese and green tea. (I broke down and took the whipped cream.) And since I had already eaten too many calories anyway, and Nick insisted, I ate half a slice of chocolate cheesecake, too. I shoot a glance at my watch. Three thirty. Mother expects me at six, so I have just enough time to implement my deception: buy another skirt exactly like the one my mother bought, only one size larger—which is honestly the size I needed in the first place. I pray they have the skirt in size 4. Otherwise, I will have to face Mother's questions, and quite possibly her anger, that I'm not wearing the Versace. The thought doesn't appeal to me at all.

I'm almost positive Cate Able would never put up with being squeezed into a skirt she can barely breathe in. She writes about strong women who can face down anyone for the cause of right and justice. I could never be a Cate Able heroine. Shoot, I couldn't even be the heroine in my own pathetic attempt at writing a novel, which is unbelievably sad.

I hail a cab and head straight to Saks, where I find the Versace jersey skirt with front pleats in a 38 (don't panic; that's Italian sizing and equals an American size 4). I charge the $900 skirt on Daddy's credit card. But I figure I'll return the ridiculously unrealistic size 2 tomorrow and recoup. Thank goodness Mother always leaves on the tags just to prove she didn't buy it off the sale rack.

I slip the cabbie the fare plus five when he pulls up to Mother's building. It's only five thirty, so I'm hoping she'll be in the throes of preparations and won't even notice I'm here until I make myself presentable.

I gather a deep breath, partly for support, partly from nostalgia. Every time I come home, I can't help but wonder about all the people who have lived in this building over the last century.

I grew up in a prewar high-rise condo my parents bought for a few hundred grand—twenty-five years ago. A few years later, my plastic-surgeon dad moved out, and Mother kept the apartment, the Lincoln, and the kids. Dad got us every other weekend, holidays, and whenever Mother went away for a weekend with the newest boyfriend.

I'm not sure why, but Mother has recently had the apartment appraised. The staggering value: over fourteen million dollars—and Dad was the first person she shared the happy news with. Mother is fabulous at rubbing it in. A true master. The epitome of the scorned woman.

Anyway, Dad can't even *almost* hide his irritation with the whole thing, which naturally delights my mother. My folks have always had a love/hate relationship. They both love money and would hate to give any of it up, so they refuse to get a divorce and risk the other coming out on top.

But they'd never live together in a million years. Dad has his bachelor pad a few blocks east of here. And I do mean a bachelor pad. He lives in a swanky loft apartment in a co-op. My brother, Kale, says Dad thinks he's Don Johnson (the guy from *Miami Vice*—the series, not the movie). The apartment is decorated with appalling animal prints. Leopard-print sheets and comforter. I can't imagine why he thinks that's a good idea. At least one of the bathrooms has zebra-skin decor, complete with black-and-white-striped toilet cover and bath rug.

I find his taste in interior design especially interesting, considering the reason he finally moved out of Mother's apartment once and for all. She was going through her "pagoda" stage and dared to decorate the library with religious art befitting the most devout Buddhist. And, no, she will not be found in the lotus position, humming to herself. The phase had absolutely nothing to do with religious fervor. It was nothing more than another example that my mother is a slave to the latest trend. As a matter of fact, Mother claims to be an Episcopalian, although I must admit I've never actually witnessed her going to church. Anyway, Dad was so disgusted with the "idols" that he demanded a return of his (revolting) bearskin rug and deer heads. Of course, no self-respecting feminist (which is what Mother was that year) is going to let a man tell her what to do. Besides, she'd already sent the gold-trimmed invitations for a tea to be held in this room, and woodsy, dead-animal decor simply wouldn't do.

My mother's rebellion was Dad's last straw. He packed up his dead-animal things, and that was the last time he called this Fifth Avenue apartment home. My secret theory—and hope—is that he knows how horrid his apartment is, from the perspective of anyone with good taste. Or even mediocre taste. Personally, I think he decorated with all things animal only to show Mother that he won't be bossed around. Childish, but not out of the question. And it's the theory I prefer to stick to until Dad proves me wrong. In all other areas, such as dress, jewelry, and music, he's the epitome of good taste, so the good-ol'-boy decor just doesn't add up.

Anyway, I love the Fifth Avenue condo. It's perfect, and I hope my mother will resist the urge to sell, despite the fact that the appreciation is incredible and most people would kill to have a panoramic view of Central Park like Mother's.

I think it's the whole *Sex and the City* syndrome. Everyone wants to live in Manhattan and buy six-hundred-dollar shoes. But I was "city" before "city" was cool. I *am* New York City. It's my town.

Norman the doorman (yes, my brother and I have always had a field day with that rhyme) smiles and opens the door as I step under the awning. "Good afternoon, Miss Ames."

"Hi, Norman. How are you?"

"Fine, miss."

Norman doesn't look like your typical doorman. He's at least six-foot-five with orange red hair and a beard that is streaked with gray. He looks like a Viking. I have no idea how old he is. He could be anywhere from forty-five to sixty-five. I'd ask him, but I have a feeling he'd never tell me, so what's the point?

In all the years I've known him, Norman has never crossed the line of "place." He knows his, and he knows mine, and no matter how curious I am about his life or how much I'd like to be buds, he's having no part of it. A gold band encircles his ring finger, so that leads me to believe he either is married or wants everyone to think he is. I suspect my parents know his history, but they won't budge either. So short of hiring an investigator to give me the scoop, I guess I'll never know. Which is devastating to the curious-writer part of me. But the logical editor in me knows that sometimes you have to cut and move on.

I push the button for the elevator, which always takes forever, and turn back to Norman. "Am I the first guest to arrive?"

His red mustache twitches, so I'm guessing that if I could see his mouth, it would be turned up in a smile. His eyes are unmistakably twinkling. I love twinkle-eyed smiles. They feel so . . . real. And real is something I rarely get from anyone when I come to this apartment. "Your father arrived hours ago."

I stare at him, slack-jawed. For two reasons. One, because it's typically futile to ask questions. Two, because when was the last time Dad showed up at Mother's?

"Hours ago? And the police haven't been called?"

He frowns. "Why would they?"

"It was a joke."

He nods. "I see."

Boy, tough crowd. I literally thank God when the elevator bell dings and the doors open.

"Well, see you later, Norman."

I travel up to the tenth floor, the slow elevator giving me plenty of time to wonder why in heaven's name Dad is suddenly showing up at one of Mother's unbearable dinner parties.

I'm confused even further when Dad is the one who answers the door.

"Princess!" he says rather jovially, and I suspect he's been nipping into the Captain Morgan. The close proximity of his mouth, and therefore breath, as he kisses my forehead and both cheeks confirms my suspicion. "A little early, isn't it, Daddy?"

He swishes the amber contents of his glass. "Don't be a party pooper. We're celebrating."

"Funny, I didn't realize Aunt Tilly's birthday was so special to you." As a matter of fact, the two have never gotten along, and I've heard my dad on more than one occasion refer to her as a pelican because she's all legs below the waist and all breasts above. Even at eighty years old, those ladies are practically to her chin. Methinks she's had some work done—not by my dad, of course. That would just be . . . odd.

But I digress.

Dad raises the glass in his hand and gives it a tip when it reaches his mouth. He completely ignores my attempt to bait him into telling me what he's doing at my mother's.

"If I'd known you were coming, I'd have brought my black-and-white cap and whistle," I say with a grin.

Still, he remains disturbingly cheerful. "You always did have my wit."

I hear the *click-clack* of Mother's heels thirty seconds before she finally makes her appearance. She's beautifully dressed in a silky white shirt, a black skirt, and a lovely red scarf.

I do a double take. Isn't that the scarf . . . I turn to Dad and he's grinning like a doofy sixteen-year-old geek who just landed a date to the prom with the head cheerleader. That confirms my suspicion about the scarf. It's the one Dad bought her the Christmas before he moved out. I was about seven.

"Nice scarf, Mother," I say ruefully.

She reaches for me and gives me the socialite kiss-kiss, never getting even close to actually smudging her lipstick. "It's vintage."

"Yes, I remember." I frown, stare from Dad to Mother. "Is there something I should know about? Who's dying?"

"All in good time, princess," Dad says with a chuckle. He winks at my mother. She touches the scarf ever so delicately and blushes. Something is definitely going on here.

Mother looks me over as if she just realized I lack proper attire. She nibbles her lip. "Honey, why aren't you dressed?"

I lift the garment bag and show her the carrying case where I have my hair products and makeup—also new, and charged to Daddy's Visa. I'm not proud of it, but, given my meager salary, it was a necessary evil, and I'll pay him back. Not that he'd notice if I didn't. But I will.

"Well, do go on and change. People will be arriving soon."

"Okay, but after I come down looking fit to make an appearance at a social party, I expect to be let in on whatever this little secret is that the two of you have going on."

Mother's eyes are twinkling suspiciously. "We'll be making an announcement at dinner tonight. You'll just have to wait until then to satisfy your curiosity."

I head for the stairs, filled with foreboding.

"Oh, Dancy." Mother's voice whips me around. "I'm sorry to say that Floyd's come down with an abominable sinus infection. He sends his apologies that he can't attend tonight."

Finally, some real proof there is a God.

"I think I'll survive one night without a dinner partner, Mother. Truly, I don't mind going stag."

"Really, Dancy. Such a vulgar term." She clicks her tongue. "Besides, I've replaced him with another date for you."

"*Mo-ther.*"

"Whining isn't attractive, darling. And will you please trust me?"

Need she ask?

"Fine. What rock did this one crawl out from under?"

"I've half a mind not to tell you, unless you stop being so sarcastic."

"Well, then. I suppose I'll have to wait to find out." I spin on my toe and head up the steps. What do I care who she's roped into sitting beside me and boring me to tears all evening? It's two hours out of my life, and besides, no one can be as bad as Floyd.

I have a bigger problem on my hands, anyway. Dad's sudden desire to be back in my mother's life. I hate to even think it, but I suspect his interest has less to do with a sudden need for Mother's arms (yuck) and more to do with the enormous check pending should she decide to sell the condo. And that makes me nervous. The woman who gave me birth is definitely a challenge from time to time, but she's not all bad, and I love her. I don't want to see Dad take her for a ride and then drop her off at the first sight of a sexy hitchhiker—metaphorically speaking.

I enter the room where I slept every night from kindergarten until college. I'm filled with that sense of nostalgic dread. Like, I would love to have the good ol' days back, but would rather not have to relive the bad days. Of which there were more than good.

"Hi, Beemer." Beemer is the forty-five-pound beagle that joined the family when my grandmother passed away five years ago. She's a fat, moody dog with an affinity for pizza and pancakes. We all agree she needs Jenny Craig, but no one has the heart to look into those adorable puppy-dog eyes and refuse her a crust.

She looks up at me and closes her eyes without one tail thump of acknowledgment. Beemer's depressed. Mother's considering therapy for her, but so far the first opening is something like three years away. And the dog is already ten. So is there really any point? "I know how you feel, girl," I say, giving her ears a scratch as I pass by on my way to the sliding glass doors. I push back the drapes and drink in the sight.

My bedroom looks out across the glorious Manhattan skyline, from the George Washington Bridge to the awesome landmark buildings of Midtown. The terrace slings around two sides of the corner apartment. On the lower level, the living room overlooks Central Park. It's truly an amazing place. If I could afford it, I'd buy it myself. But editors for New York publishing houses, even huge ones like Lane Publishing, don't do well enough to afford much of anything, let alone fourteen-million-dollar condos. Even my trust fund would barely cover the down payment. Maybe if I'm really nice to Aunt Tilly tonight . . . No. Bad idea. I don't beg, borrow, or steal. Well, I don't beg or steal anyway, and I only borrow from Daddy—and only in an emergency. Besides, I love living with Laini and Tabby in our cute, if cramped, apartment.

I step onto my terrace and sigh. Nothing compares to the view of the Manhattan skyline at dusk.

What's *he* doing here? At the sight of Jack Quinn, I stumble on the steps and nearly break my neck in these ridiculously high-heeled slingbacks. The guy shoots up the steps like he's Clark Kent and grabs me—unnecessarily—as I steady myself.

"Are you all right?" He's on the step below me and is still several inches taller. I hate my reaction to this guy. Every time he gets close like this, my heart beats faster and I feel like an absolute idiot. Why does he have to look so great? And the smell . . . understated aftershave and scent of man. It's especially embarrassing when he's leaning over my desk at work and all I want to do is close my eyes and drink it in.

"I'm fine." His fingers are still wrapped around my bare arm and, quite frankly, he's cutting off the blood flow. "Do you mind?"

"Hmm?" He follows my gaze to his mammoth grip and turns loose instantly. "So sorry."

"So, Jack. What brings you here tonight? Did Kale invite you to Mother's little soirée?"

A frown mars his oh-so-perfect face. "Oh dear," Jack says Britishly. No self-respecting, straight American guy would dare use a phrase like "oh dear." But Jack can get away with it because of his accent.

"You don't know? I was told you wouldn't mind. Your mother . . ."

"Oh, did she invite you to dinner?" I shouldn't be surprised, I suppose. Jack has been charming my mother since the first time Kale brought him home for Thanksgiving during their freshman year at NYU. I was sixteen, so that was—oh, boy— fourteen years ago. He's been yanking my hair and teasing me as mercilessly as Kale ever since. Only recently, since he's come to work for Lane Publishing, has he started treating me differently. Not like a colleague. More like an employee. And not a very good one at that. But at least he's stopped pulling my hair and poking me in the ribs.

"In a manner of speaking."

I give a shrug. "Oh well. She didn't tell me, but she doesn't typically discuss her guest lists with me." I'm trying to be polite, but I'm nervous, and I feel sweat under my arms. So unlady-like to perspire in polite company. "Don't worry. I'll make sure we're at opposite ends of the table, so you can't be accused of fraternizing with the staff." I give him a flippant smile and expect him to move so I can make my way down the steps.

Instead he leans forward ever so slightly and whispers in my ear. "This is rather awkward, but I believe I'm your escort for the evening."

I swallow hard. "Wh-what?"

"Your mum asked me for a little favor. How could I refuse?"

"It's easy. All it takes is one little two-letter word."

He gives me a rueful smile and moves aside, offering me his arm. "Yes, I'd be willing to wager you could give enthralling lessons on how to refuse your mum's requests." He is, of course, being sarcastic.

Heat slides up my neck. Since Jack is Kale's best friend, he knows the ins and outs of our family dysfunction and is fully aware that I can't say no to my mother unless it's through e-mail, and even then I usually give in. It's disconcerting.

"Come along," he says, taking my hand and tucking it through his arm. "Don't be difficult. Let me escort you to dinner and I promise to provide stimulating dinner conversation. Would you like to hear about the time I met the queen?"

Okay, the word *stimulating* is probably extremely appropriate here, given the way my stomach has just dropped at his touch. I clear my throat. "I'm not worried about the conversation," I say, freeing my hand from the comfortable warmth of his elbow. "Just refrain from slurping your soup, and I'll be happy." Why does he always reduce me to acting like a ditzy teenager?

He gives a low chuckle and stays fixed to my side. The man

is nothing if not persistent. "And you must refrain from cutting me with your barbed—not to mention extensive—vocabulary while I'm doing a good deed."

I stop. Will there be no end to my humiliation this evening? "Are you saying you agreed to this 'date' out of pity?"

"Hardly pity." His gray eyes pierce me. "Let's call it a pleasant favor for my best chum's mother. Why are you so offended, anyway? Would you prefer Floyd?"

I'd love to have the nerve to slap that smug grin right off his gorgeous face. Why should he know how relieved I am that Mother replaced hideous Floyd with extraordinary Jack? I jerk my chin at him, feeling sick of the entire exchange. "Actually," I say, "I do prefer Floyd. As a matter of fact, I was very sorry to hear he isn't feeling well. I-I'd been rather looking forward to seeing him tonight."

"Indeed?"

I give a jerky nod. "Indeed."

"Well then, you're a very lucky young lady." Jack motions over my shoulder and I turn, dread sinking into every pore. Floyd's standing there, listening to every word and, judging from the look of rapture on his face, feeling secure in my love for him.

"Hello, honey. Sorry I'm late."

Oh no. Oh no. How stupid am I? Okay, he's not unattractive. I mean, he's not gorgeous like J— well, you know. But he's got that Greg Kinnear kind of appeal. If only he had the personality to go along with the looks. "Fl-Floyd? I thought you were sick."

He pulls out a hanky and makes disgusting noises as he clears his sinuses. "Don't worry," he says, stuffing the thing—and oh, it's hard not to visualize—back into his jacket pocket. "I'm not contagious."

Well, that's something, isn't it?

"B-but I thought you told my mother you weren't coming. She—um—replaced you with another guest."

"Oh, I know. When I called her an hour ago, she said she could easily invite another girl for your other date."

I follow his hostile gaze to Jack's face, and I swear, my own hostility rises at the British smirk lying there under the guise of thoughtful acceptance.

"Who did Mother find at the last minute?" As if I don't already know.

"Someone named Sheri."

"Did I hear my name?" A sugared tone sets my teeth on edge and makes me cringe inside. It's not that I don't love my cousin. I do. Sheri is everything my mother wanted in a daughter. Painfully thin, poised. Your typical former cheerleader and class valedictorian. Beautiful, smart, and a classical pianist to boot. And she adores my mother. Genuine niceness is the only reason I don't hate this woman. And I don't mean my genuine niceness. I mean hers. Plus, guess what? She's a senior editor for a rival publishing house. "Isn't it lucky for me I showed up without a date for Grammy's birthday party?"

Aunt Tilly is, as Sheri mentioned, her grandmother, my great-aunt. My granny and Aunt Tilly were twin sisters, identical in all ways except on the inside. Granny was the sweet, spiritual one. Aunt Tilly worked in publishing for fifty years. She's a salty character—smoked cigars in the fifties, burned her bra in the sixties, got a tattoo in the seventies, and finally married her lover of thirty years in the eighties, only because her grown children—all four of whom are Christians—begged her to stop living in sin, and she figured she might as well give in. She's recently gone so far as to start attending church with her oldest son. She's a little softer, but still rough around the edges.

And I adore her. I'd give anything to be just like her. Sheri, on the other hand, is more like my mother than I can stomach most of the time.

I force a smile as I turn. "Sheri. So nice of you to come." I can only pray I sound sincere as I'm drawn into a cozy embrace.

"It's wonderful to see you again, Dancy. You look beautiful."

Sheri calling me beautiful is like a Mercedes-Benz calling a VW Bus classy. You just can't help but feel patronized.

"Thanks," I mumble. "You do, too." I sound insincere, but it really is the truth. She does look amazing. But then, she could dress in a potato sack and not bother with makeup and she'd still be beautiful.

"How are things at work?" I ask, because it's the one thing we have in common.

Her smile brightens and she gives me a wink. "Wonderful. I'm about to be promoted, but who can talk about work when I smell scallops and sea bass?"

Jealousy is such an ugly trait, and I admit that I struggle with it from time to time. However, the way she moves right up the publishing ladder just irks me. I know she works for the same publishing house as Aunt Tilly did for all those years, so obviously they love her. And Sheri is great at her job. But you know, if she gets a promotion she'll be two steps above me. Associate publisher is a huge step up from editor. Big big. But then, if she moves up to associate publisher, that would mean . . .

"They'll be looking for another senior editor?"

Jack swings a quick glance my way, and I realize I blurted it out with him standing right there.

Sheri laughs. "I suppose they will. But you would never leave Lane Publishing," she says, as though it's unthinkable that I'd rather have a promotion than stay in a place where I'm completely undervalued.

I clear my throat. "I just know someone looking to move up." Someone like me, for instance.

I refuse to even look at Jack. I'm sure he doesn't believe for one second that I'm asking about the job opening for any other reason than my desperate ambition to move up myself.

Sheri looks past me and sends Jack one of those smiles that beautiful girls can't help but send to the best-looking man in the room. I've seen similar smiles from her undo more than one male since we were kids. "Hi, Jack. Looks like it's you and me tonight. I hope you don't mind."

His Adam's apple goes up and down, and I'm pretty sure I see sweat beading on his forehead. I swear, I never thought I'd see the day when Jack Quinn would lose his composure. He smiles, never taking his eyes off the blond bombshell as we descend. I find myself hoping he'll trip over his feet and fall flat on his face (only not hard enough to do any damage to his handsome features). Instead, he recovers his composure in record time.

"I confess, I'm the lucky chap." He offers her his arm. I want to huff, truly. Does he realize he's just insulted me?

Toad.

Sheri sashays close to him and tucks her hand inside his arm. My brother, Kale, pokes his head out of the dining room. "Are you four coming? Mother says we're going to start without you."

I watch the world's best-looking couple walk toward the dining room.

"Shall we, my love?" Floyd asks. Only it sounds like, "Shall we, by lub?" I look into his watery eyes and wish like crazy this was nothing more than a terrible dream.

3

Valerie walked into her parents' Fifth Avenue condo at precisely five minutes before six. Her mom greeted her with a warm hug and an equally warm kiss to her cheek. "Sweetie," she said, "you look beautiful. I just love the way those extra pounds have softened your face."

Pleased, Valerie returned her mom's affection. "You noticed! I'm so glad you like the results."

"Is that my baby girl?"

Valerie whipped around at the rich baritone of her daddy's voice. He held out his arms and smiled. "Come here and give your old dad a hug."

A contented sigh escaped Valerie's lips as she became enveloped in the strong, wonderful arms of her favorite man on earth.

The sound of barking interrupted her homecoming, and she turned as her mom laughed. "Looks like Mercedes has missed you, too."

Valerie stooped and gathered the faithful old beagle in her arms. She smiled. It was good to be home.

—An excerpt from *Fifth Avenue Princess*
by Dancy Ames

ightmare to end all nightmares. Did I really think listening to Floyd chew all evening was the worst thing that could ever happen to me? Listening to him blow his nose and chew, respectively, is infinitely worse. For an hour and a half, I fight not to squirm against the excruciating need to escape. Even with my charm-school training, nothing could have kept me glued to my seat except the impending announcement from my parents.

Jack leans over and says in a low voice, way too close to my ear, "It's not polite to be so obvious." Why my mother seated me between Floyd and Jack, I'll never know. It's almost like she did it on purpose, just to watch me squirm.

"I don't know what you mean."

"Really? Because anyone with a properly working set of eyes can see you'd likely sacrifice your last quid for the opportunity to bolt."

"Like you wouldn't?" Oh, brother. I said that, didn't I? I give a sigh and turn to him, staring him firmly in the eye. He chuckles, which of course ticks me off. "And FYI, we don't use 'quid' in the good ol' US of A. How long have you been out of the mother country now?"

He chuckles. "Quite right, of course."

I sniff, a complete highbrow imitation of my mother, intended to dismiss the annoying person to my left. "Shouldn't you be paying attention to your own date?"

The thing about Jack is, he isn't easily put off. "I would, but I'm afraid she's paying attention to someone else. Not that I blame her. Rumor has it I'm a frightful bore." He grins. "Besides, you're quite amusing to watch. Heart on the sleeve and all that."

I wish he didn't have that accent. I find myself fascinated and often—like now—watch his mouth as he talks. But I cannot, *will* not, let my brother's best friend know how hot he is. As if he didn't already know. "Fine, you caught me."

Thankfully, the tinkling sound of knife against crystal spares me the necessity of expounding on the statement. All eyes focus on my dad, who has, disturbingly, taken Mother's place at the head of the table for tonight's festivities.

"We've asked you all here tonight because we have an announcement to make."

Aunt Tilly gives an obnoxious old-lady snort. "Funny, I thought we were here to celebrate my birthday. It's not every day a lady turns fifty."

"Just once every August for the last three decades," I whisper, eliciting a snicker from Jack.

"What's the announcement, Dad?" Kale asks.

Mother reaches up and takes my dad's hand. "Stuart and I," she says—I hold my breath; here it comes—"have been keeping something from all of you."

No kidding.

"We—uh . . . well, we've been back together for the last few months." Dad looks down at my mother in a sickeningly love-sick way. I mean, if they're in love, that's great. But do I really have to look at it? Shock fills the air, but only Aunt Tilly has the guts to speak up.

"Oh, Caroline," the old dowager says, "why do you have to be such an idiot?"

"Aunt Tilly, please," Mother says, but who can blame the old woman? As much as I love my dad, he's sort of your love-'em-and-leave-'em type. Hasn't Mother ever heard of "Fool me once, shame on you," etc.?

"I think it's wonderful!" Sheri breathes, her eyes all aglow. "I'm so happy for you both."

She would be. As I said, she's the daughter my mother never had.

I catch my brother's eye and see that he's having about the same reaction as I am. We exchange a "can you believe this?" look.

You see, it's not that we don't love our dad and wish our parents could be happily married forever. It's just that we don't want to see our mother hurt again. Our family is not your typical nuclear family with dad, mother, and two-point-five kids. We're our own brand of dysfunction, with years of Dad's indiscretions and Mother's forgiveness, accompanied by expensive jewelry and a string of "second" honeymoons. Tropical beaches where they could reevaluate their relationship and start over—wiser and more committed than ever to "making it work." And it usually did work, for about two days after their return. Once, I think a week went by before all you-know-what broke loose.

Mother finally decided enough was enough, and my parents went their separate ways. But it's okay. Kale and I are all grown up now. We're both strong and working in fields we love—I'm in publishing and Kale is an ER doctor at New York Presbyterian Hospital. We're way past the illusion of family dinners (and this kind doesn't count). Way past the Waltons fantasy. We're simply not going to stand by and watch our dad take advantage of our mother, just because she's about to come into a few million dollars.

"Uh, Mother," I say, mindful of the fact that there are non-family members at this little dinner party. "Are you sure you want to do this? The whole 'let's try again' route hasn't worked out well in the past."

"Darling," Dad says with a rueful twist to his lips. He flattens his palm against his chest. "I'm hurt."

"Sorry, Dad. Forgive me if I'm dubious." I stare him down, and I'm slightly disconcerted by his smile, which borders disturbingly on being genuine. I straighten my shoulders to bolster my resolve.

Kale gives him a stern look and says what I don't have the nerve to say. "This wouldn't have anything to do with a little fourteen-million-dollar price tag on the old digs, would it?"

"Kale Ames!" Mother's eyes are flashing, and the look she gives him slides around to include me in her admonishment. "Do you children take me for some kind of fool?"

Do not answer. Do *not* answer!

"I know your father better than anyone. Don't you think I'd recognize any attempt on his part to manipulate me out of money?"

"Okay, you two," I say, tired of the whole charade. "What is it you'd like to tell us?" I would give just about anything to be sitting at home eating a gallon of Chunky Monkey ice cream. "If Mother chooses to trust you again, who are Kale and I to stand in your way? But just for the record, I can't help but worry that history might repeat itself."

"Your concern is duly noted," Mother says, tight-lipped.

I think I may have overstepped a little. But is it truly none of my business? Then why the elaborate announcement?

Dad swishes his glass of wine and looks from me to Kale. "I understand why you feel the way you do. But regardless of our history, or perhaps because of our history, I'm more devoted than ever to your mother." He leans over in a gentlemanly fashion and presses his lips to her hand.

Kale gives a snort that, from her pleased look, makes Aunt Tilly proud. "I'm sure all that cash you two will get from the condo won't hurt your commitment. For a little while, anyway."

"All right, young man." Mother stands, drops Dad's hand, and leans over the table. Her angry gaze flashes, taking in every one of us except, of course, Sheri, Jack, and Floyd (who incidentally is making short work of his scallops and making me a little sick to my stomach in the process). "I'm a grown woman. I'm tired of how little faith you have in my ability to see through this man I've been married to for thirty-five years."

"Muffin," my dad says, his face red. "That's a little insulting."

She smiles affectionately and pats his cheek. "Sorry, darling. But the children have valid concerns based on our history. However"—she pierces us once more with her gaze—"we have always loved each other. Your father just had some . . . issues . . . that only time and maturity could fix. He's proved himself to me, and it's my choice to believe in him."

"Mother—" I begin, only to be cut off by an upraised hand with long, French-manicured nails. I shut my mouth and listen.

"Furthermore—and this was your father's suggestion, not mine—we are not selling the condo." She smiles and holds out her hand to my dad. Slowly and with dramatic flair, he removes a document from his coat pocket and slips it to her. She walks over and stands between Kale and his fiancée, Brynn, then slides the document onto the tablecloth. "Our wedding gift to you two." The deed to my childhood home, handed over to my brother and a girl who has only been around for a couple of years?

I'm as flabbergasted as the rest of them. "You're giving Kale the condo?" I can't believe I blurted that out. Can anyone say, "smacks of injustice"? I mean, if I had known the condo was up for grabs to the first kid to walk down the aisle, I'd have smiled at Floyd a little more often.

I do my best to sit through the rest of the meal, but I forgo coffee and dessert and head up to my room. Beemer has finally roused and looks at me, begging to be taken out. The distraction will do me good. "Okay, girl," I say. "Let's go."

She slowly descends her three-step doggie stairs from the bed and sighs when she reaches the door, which I haven't opened yet. She follows me down the stairs and past the dining room on the way to the front door. "Dad, I'm taking Beemer out, so she shouldn't need to go out again tonight."

"Thank you, princess. That's sweet of you."

"It's okay."

"Thank you for the lovely dinner," I hear Jack say as I head to the door. "If you'll excuse me, I'll be going now."

I give an inward groan. There's no way to avoid walking out with him. And normally that wouldn't be a bad thing, but not tonight. I just want to walk the dog, then go home and find that Chunky Monkey ice cream. And maybe cry a little.

I'm waiting for the excruciatingly slow elevator to arrive when Jack saunters down the hall. Beemer lifts her head from where she's resting on the floor and thumps her tail as he walks toward us.

"I hope you don't mind sharing an elevator ride with me," he says with a self-deprecating smile.

I give a nonchalant little shrug. "Why would I?"

"I'm glad to hear it." He bends over and gives Beemer a scratch behind the ear. She actually sighs.

The elevator finally arrives with a ding, and we step aside as Floyd's mother and father exit. Floyd is a replica of his dad. In every way. The man blows his nose and stuffs the handkerchief back in his breast pocket as he steps out. I may be ill.

The Bartells own a condo on the same floor as my mother's. I'm not sure my mother honestly enjoys their company, but she has most definitely enjoyed the social interaction and introductions to the "who's who" of New York climbers that the Bartells provide.

"Dancy?" Mrs. Bartell says with that tone that means, "Why aren't you with my son?"

"Good evening," I say, including them both in my nod. "You remember Jack Quinn, don't you?"

Mrs. Bartell looks down her old-money nose. "Of course. Hello, Mr. Quinn."

Jack takes her manicured hand. He smiles warmly into her pinched face, and the ice slowly begins to melt. "So lovely to see you again, Mrs. Bartell." He looks past her to Mr. Bartell. "And you, sir. You're looking well."

Floyd's father preens before the compliment. "Well, I have been walking the course instead of riding in the golf cart lately."

"Very good, old chap." Jack gently releases Mrs. Bartell's hand and turns to me. "Shall we go walk the dog?"

Dumbfounded at how he had those two fuddy-duddies eating out of his hand, all I can do is nod and allow myself to be escorted into the elevator. His hand at the small of my back feels warm and cozy. Almost like we fit. But, of course, we don't.

We say our good-nights to the blue-blood couple as the doors close. Silence shrouds the inside of the elevator. Finally the bell dings us past the ninth floor.

"This lift must be the slowest one in New York City."

I give him a nod. "I wouldn't doubt it."

He turns to me. "Listen. This is going to be an incredibly awkward ride if we don't speak."

"Fine. Speak."

Beemer gives us a bark. The one command she still responds to. I catch Jack's gaze and we share a laugh.

He leans in toward me. "Will Kale and Brynn inherit the dog, too, or will your mother take her?"

Just when we were starting to get along, he had to bring that up.

I feel my shoulders tense. It's impossible to keep that tension out of my voice. "I really don't know."

Jack peers closer, as though he is just getting the picture. "I'm so sorry you were blindsided by the news."

"Yes, well. That's my parents for you."

"Odd, isn't it? Their giving the apartment to Kale instead of you?"

I'm dreadfully close to tears, so I'd just as soon he stop speaking. "Well, I suppose it's because Kale's getting married and I most likely never will."

"Never?" His brows push together. "How can you make that prediction at so young an age?"

A short laugh bursts from me. "I'm nearly thirty-one years old, Jack. I've never even had a third date, unless you count all the dinners Mother forces me to attend with Floyd. The prospects are pretty slim."

I suppose my extreme vulnerability tonight is to blame for that little admission. But I can't help myself.

"Don't give up on the institution quite yet," he says. "Thirty is the new twenty."

"Tell that to my biological clock. It's been ticking so long, it's about to wind down." Oh. My. Goodness. Did I really just say that?

My cheeks go hot as he smirks.

I give him a hard look. "Don't you dare repeat that."

His palm flattens against his chest. "My word of honor."

Just as the elevator dings the second floor, he turns to me. "I'm sorry you didn't get the condo. You know Kale doesn't want it."

"I know," I say glumly. "But who could turn it down? It's the most wonderful apartment in the entire world."

Finally, the elevator reaches the first floor.

In the lobby, Norman opens the door for us and I lead Beemer, who may or may not be grateful, outside to do her business.

"Well," I say awkwardly, because I don't want him to think I expect an escort.

"If it isn't too much trouble, I'd like to walk with you."

"You would?"

His grin reminds me of the Jack I met fourteen years ago. "Well, I couldn't let my best friend's little sister walk the dark streets of New York all alone, could I?"

Figures.

I lift my chin. "I'm not alone. I have Beemer for protection."

Beemer is sniffing around trying to find just the right spot to go. The very last thing on her mind is keeping me safe.

"Really, Jack," I say with a wave. "I'm standing in front of my mother's place, and Norman is watching from the door. Beemer and I will be back inside before you know it. She doesn't need to go far."

"Well, then," Jack says, "it appears as though my chivalry was misguided."

"I appreciate the thought, though."

I wish I could decipher the look he gives me. It might be relief. On the other hand, it might be disappointment. One would think that after all these years I'd be able to gauge his expressions. But Jack is an enigma.

I decide to end this and let him off the hook completely. "Good night, Jack. I'm sorry you were brought into our family dysfunction tonight."

He reaches out and tweaks my nose. "I'm used to it, aren't I?" A quick smile touches his lips and he walks away, leaving me without a single thought in my head that isn't filled with him.

The girls and I rehash over one of Laini's divine chocolate mint tortes. So much better than Chunky Monkey, any day of the week.

"Wow, I can't believe your parents gave the condo to Kale," Laini says, serving up the torte and setting a gallon of chocolate milk in the middle of the table so we can all have equal access.

Like a true friend, Tabby pours the first glass for me. "That's rotten luck, Dancy. I know how much you love that place."

I nod glumly and shove a tasty, soft bite of torte into my mouth. It helps for the couple of seconds it takes to chew and swallow. "Kale never liked growing up there." I frown and stomp my foot. "He wanted to live in the country and raise chickens. Why should he get the double view?"

Tabby swigs down some chocolate milk. "Yeah."

"Yeah," Laini adds.

"Even Jack knows Kale doesn't want the apartment, so why didn't my parents ever pick up on that small detail?"

Laini gives Tabby a look. "Jack, huh?" Tabby says.

"Yes." I frown. "He was a stand-in for Floyd, but then Floyd came anyway. I swear, if I catch his cold, I'm suing. My cousin Sheri showed up without a date and the numbers were even again."

"The numbers were even?" Laini's grinning.

"You know. You have to have an equal number of men and women at a dinner party; otherwise it's—"

"Uneven?" Tabby asks.

"Very funny," I say.

She laughs. "So, what did Kale's fiancée say about the gift?"

"What do you think? She was all smiles and happy tears." And why shouldn't she be? She'll be Cinderella, marrying the prince and inheriting the kingdom. "Brynn's from a farm in Oklahoma. It's all been uphill for her until now."

"Hey, I had a friend from Oklahoma once," Laini says. "She was nice. I could hardly understand a word she said. You remember her, Tabby? She was in our freshman comp class. Her name was Jodi."

Tabby frowns.

Jodi? Focus, girls. We're talking about me.

"Oh, yeah," Tabby says, completely not picking up on my vibe of discontent with this line of thought. "I remember Jodi. Only she wasn't from Oklahoma. It was Arkansas."

Inside, I'm twisting. I mean, does it really make a difference where Jodi came from?

"Hmm. I knew it was down south. Remember that accent?" A smile taps Tabby's lips. "Loved it. Didn't you?"

Laini laughs and nods. "And smart. Remember how she always made A's?"

"Okay," I say. "But what about my brother getting a condo he doesn't deserve?"

They look at each other, and I swear they roll their eyes.

"Oh, never mind." I give a little huff, even though I know how ridiculous I am.

"What are your plans this weekend?" Laini asks.

I shrug. "I have some editing to do. I'll probably do that after we get back from Nick's."

"Come to church with David and the twins and me on Sunday," Tabby says. "You'll feel better if you go to church."

Tabby loves her church. It's made up of this eclectic group

of actors and singers, with a few average people like me thrown in for good measure, so it's truly laid-back and unusual. But when I start going on a regular basis (and I truly will—eventually), I need something more traditional. Something like Kale's church.

"Maybe," I say, and we both know that means "thanks, but no thanks."

Laini clears her throat. "Did Jack mention anything about the office?"

I give a quick shrug. "He's better at separating work and personal life than anyone I know. Besides, we didn't talk that much before Dad clinked the glass and made his announcement. And afterward it was all about the condo. He was pretty nice, actually."

I shake my head and flop my arm over the back of the chair I'm slouching in. "If I'd had any idea that my folks were getting back together, or that Kale would get custody of the condo, I'd definitely have missed the dinner tonight."

"You would not have," Tabby says. She's right. And so is Nick. I am a weenie.

"So, where do your parents plan to live?" she asks. "The bachelor pad?"

I picture my mother in that animal-printed monstrosity, and laughter shoots to my lips. "Not in a million years. Actually, they're selling the love shack and moving to Florida right after Kale's wedding. I have to start cleaning out my things next Saturday, as a matter of fact." I dread what is sure to be a long and tedious task. My mother kept every pom-pom, every yearbook, every—well, let's face it, every memento from my first blankie to my graduation gown. And guess what? I have to be the one to get rid of them. Because Mother was only keeping them "for me." Personally, I don't think that's fair.

I shove up from the chair and turn to my friends. "Thanks for the food and sympathy. I'm going to run an aromatherapy bath and read Cate Able's latest book again." I've read it twice already, but my love of this author's work borders on obsession. I wish she'd write one book a year instead of every eighteen months to two years. I hate waiting so long between novels. But Tony Kramer, my boss, is the only one she'll communicate with at the publishing house, and he can't entice her to speed up the process.

Tabby does a lazy stretch. "I need to go over some lines for Monday. David's parents are coming in tomorrow, so I'll be too busy this weekend to do anything but impress the future in-laws."

"Which you could do in your sleep," I say.

The two of us look at Laini and wait for her to announce her intentions. She pretends not to notice for a second, then scowls. "I have an exam on Monday. And I have to help my mom all weekend with that attic."

"Then shouldn't you have been studying tonight, instead of eating and watching TV?"

"It doesn't matter," she says dejectedly. "I'm going to flunk."

"What?" I can't believe Little Miss Sunshine is putting negativity into the atmosphere.

"It's a color thing. I'm horrible at color schemes. What's wrong with blue and black together?"

"Nothing," Tabby pipes up, "if you're a bruise."

"I know that in my head," Laini says. "But when it comes to reasonable understanding of why it's not a good idea, the whole concept escapes me."

"Well, you only need to know it cognitively to pass the test." I hate to be glib, but real learning comes from experience, not books.

"I know, but I stopped doing accounting because I was tired of being good at something I had no passion for. Now I have passion for something I'm apparently no good at."

"No good at?" Tabby's outrage fills the room. "You're great. Look at this place."

And we do. Blue and black abound, as do brass and wood. My mother's nightmare. "Look, Laini. A good designer is like a good piano teacher."

My friends stare at me like I've lost my mind. "No, really. Some teachers have classical flair, some modern, some jazz. It's all about personal taste. Your taste is . . . different."

Her expression drops further and Tabby gives me a "nice job" look. I rush on before either can speak. "No, not *different*. That's the wrong word. I meant *unique*. And there's probably a whole market out there waiting for your style. I mean, who would have ever thought Crocs would be in fashion?" I look to Tabby for help and she picks up the ball.

"Yeah, Crocs. Good analogy, Dan." Tabby clears her throat. Searching . . . searching . . . and her eyes light. Eureka! "Have you ever seen Dancy here in a pair?"

My mother would die.

"Her mother would croak."

See?

Tabby continues. "But your mom has a pair in every color, and so do I."

Laini's face remains creased with confusion, but her eyes soften as she reaches forward and gives me and then Tabby a quick squeeze. "Different strokes for different folks. I get it." She sends us a smile that doesn't quite reach her eyes, so I know we haven't done a thing for her. Ah, well. "I'm going to bed. I have a bit of a headache."

"Me too," Tabby says.

I say good night to my friends and do what I do best . . . sink myself into a bubbly aromatherapy bath. My favorite things in the world—a Cate Able book in my hands and Ella Fitzgerald playing in the background. Why is my mind filled with swirling thoughts?

Various candles lit, I close my eyes, trying to shut out the disappointing evening. For the record, I'm not jealous of my brother and his wife-to-be. At least, not very jealous. But I do think it's a little unfair. If my parents were going to get rid of the condo, shouldn't they have at least given us the opportunity to talk about it, and maybe asked if I might want it, too? I mean, what if I were the one getting married? Would I be the one getting the condo?

My cell phone is beeping when I get out of the tub and get back to my room. A message from my mother.

"Darling, you ran out so fast tonight, I didn't have a chance to invite you for lunch tomorrow. Come around noon if you're available. But do call and confirm."

No, Mother! Not on Saturday! It's simple. I'll politely but firmly explain that I need my Saturdays to do laundry and work on editing. I will not under any circumstances be bullied or guilted into accepting this lunch invitation.

I dial her number.

"Dancy, what are you doing?" she asks sleepily. "Do you have any idea what time it is?"

I'm guessing somewhere around . . . "Ten?"

"Try midnight."

Whoops. "Sorry, Mother. Just returning your call."

"My call?" I hear rustling on the other end of the line as though she's sitting up—probably grabbing her glasses—something she'd rather die than admit. She wears contacts. Too vain to wear her glasses out in public, even if they are fashionable these days. I'm not sure why she doesn't just get Lasik surgery and be done with it. It's not as though she's afraid of surgery above the neck. I don't suppose I should mention how many procedures she's had done, but let's just say it's more than three, less than twenty.

I hear her click the lamp switch. "I called earlier for something. . . . Oh dear. What was it? Oh, yes. You ran out so fast tonight, I didn't have a chance to ask. Are you free for lunch tomorrow?"

Be strong. You cannot be at her beck and call all weekend. You must get your laundry done, editing accomplished.

"Really, Dancy. It's not a trick question. Are you free or aren't you?"

Say no, say no, say no. I despise my weakness where this woman is concerned. "Thank you, Mother. I'll be there."

"Come by at noon. I'll have Amanda whip us up a light lunch. Plan to stay for a few hours."

"Yes, Mother," I mutter again, after the call is disconnected. I throw myself across the top of my covers with a groan and stare into gloomy darkness until my eyes grow heavy and I can't stare any longer.

When Laini knocks on my door at six thirty the next morning, I decide to pass on coffee with the girls. I'm wrung out emotionally and need to sleep away my depression. I'll ply myself with caffeine and sugar after the early morning rush at Nick's, when I can have the place virtually to myself and continue my third reading of Cate Able's most recent book.

That's my plan.

But by eight o'clock my phone is ringing off the hook, pulling me from a crazy dream about Jack Quinn. I hate it when I have Jack Quinn dreams. Especially because I always seem to have a British accent, but unlike his, mine sounds like Eliza Doolittle's.

" 'Ello?" I say in groggy Cockney.

"Dan!" Tabby hollers against background noise. "Nick needs your help."

"What's wrong? Is he sick?"

"Sure, Nurse Dancy. He's sick and needs your medical expertise."

Sarcasm isn't becoming this early in the morning.

"What, then?" I growl.

"Nelda is still out of town, and that article in the *New York Times* hit yesterday morning."

"Wait. What article?"

"The one about Nick's place, remember? Laini mentioned it yesterday. They said it's better than Starbucks. The best-kept secret in New York. Ring a bell?"

"Vaguely. That explains the four-hour line to the door."

"Yeah, and it's looking to be more of the same. We've been helping since we got here, but I have to meet David and the kids and Laini's mom'll have a cow if she's not there soon."

"So that leaves me. . . ."

"What do you say?"

"Tell Nick I'll be there in twenty minutes, but I have to be at my mother's by noon, so I can't stay all day."

"Okay. I'll tell him. Thanks, Dancy."

"No problem."

Sleep is nice. But helping out a guy like Nick—so much better.

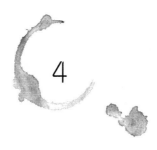

4

Valerie stared at the deed to the family condo and then back at her parents. "Are you sure you want to do this?"

"Honey, you know we've always wanted to move to Africa and feed starving children," Mom said, her eyes misting. "We feel now is the time for us to make that move."

Dad laughed to cover his own emotions. "We're not exactly getting any younger, you know."

"I'll just miss you guys so much." Valerie's eyes filled with tears she never meant to show. "Five years seems like forever."

"Oh, sweetie," her mom said, "those years without us will simply fly by. I promise. Now, let's talk about how you want to decorate. It's on Daddy and me. A going-away present."

"But I'm supposed to give *you* the going-away gift."

"Pumpkin," her dad said, placing a gentle arm around her shoulders, "knowing you'll be safe and sound in our family home is all the gift we need."

—An excerpt from *Fifth Avenue Princess*
by Dancy Ames

'Ey, princess. You wanna get the lead out already?"

I swear if that man yells at me one more time . . .

"Anyone ever tell you you're ungrateful, Nick?"

"I should be grateful you're so slow?" he hollers from the kitchen.

"You should be grateful I don't dump mocha latte all over your head," I mumble. I poise the pen over the order pad. "What'll it be?" I ask without looking up.

"I didn't realize you were moonlighting."

The husky male English accent draws my eyes upward as dread knots my stomach. "Just helping out a friend," I say into Jack Quinn's bemused face, "on my day off."

He holds up his palms. "I'm not accusing you of anything. You have a perfect right to spend your day off however you choose."

I roll my eyes. "That's big of you." I smile to let him know I'm kidding.

He winks, and his eyes twinkle beautifully.

"'Ey! You wanna catch up with your boyfriend on your own time?"

I'm beginning to realize that Nick can really be a pain in the neck.

"He's not my boyfriend, Nick. He's my supervisor, and *he* never yells at me."

"Not that I don't want to." Jack offers me a slip of a grin. "Most of the time."

Gathering a deep breath, I look him in the eye. "What can I get for you, Jack?"

The bell bing-bongs as the door opens and the last three people in line head outside and across the street to Starbucks.

"You're losing Nick customers. Either order something or—or—" I was going to say, "just leave," but I can't bring myself to do it. "Would you please just order?"

"I do beg your pardon."

The twentysomething brunette behind him in line tosses her hair over her shoulder and gives a red, waxy smile. "I don't mind waiting."

Jack flashes her that toothpaste-commercial grin. "Thank you, love." The girl blushes to the roots of her highlighted hair.

"All right, fine. Give me your order," I say.

He does, and in no time has his coffee. A smirk curls his lips as he pays and leaves a five-dollar tip in the jar on the counter. He only does it to bait me. I know it. And he knows I know it.

I glare and he walks away with a laugh. The girl behind follows him with her eyes. Good grief. I slap the counter as irritation shocks through me like a hundred volts. She jumps and swings her attention back to me.

I give her a fierce frown. Suddenly my charm-school training flies right out the door, just like those disgruntled customers.

"You want coffee or what, sweetheart?" Nick's bad influence is undoing all of my upbringing. I'm glad Mother wasn't here to see that. The girl looks a little scared but meekly gives me her order and off we go.

Two minutes later, Jack's standing at the counter again. Off to the side, not in line. He's lost the jacket and is rolling up his sleeves.

"What's wrong?" I ask. "Did you spill coffee on yourself?"

And I missed it?

He shakes his head. "Sorry, no."

"What, then?"

The guy at the counter huffs. I know I'm not up to another confrontation so I give an offhanded wave toward Jack. "Hang on a sec, Jack."

I take the man's order, and when I turn to find Jack again,

he's gone. Oh well, Mr. I Can't Wait a Sec can just take care of himself. Which I guess he did.

"What's that guy think he's doin'?" Nick asks, coming up behind me and nearly scaring me half to death.

"What guy?"

"There." I follow his finger and nearly drop to my knees at the sight of Jack Quinn busing tables.

"I have no idea."

Jack walks back to us, his Italian leather shoes making a squishing noise on the floor, and I have a feeling he's stepped in someone's spilled latte. I grin at the thought, and he thinks I'm smiling at him. He smiles back. My heart can't take it.

His arms are filled with dirty latte mugs and pie plates. "Where shall I set these?" he asks Nick.

"In the sink," Nick says, and that's the closest to speechless I've ever known him to be.

Jack nods. "Right, then. Would you be so kind as to point the way?"

Nick steps aside and motions to the kitchen. "What's that all about?" he whispers.

I shrug. I've stopped trying to figure out why Jack does anything. But I must say, I've never thought of him as the busboy type. When he comes back, he's wearing an apron. "I hope you don't mind. I thought I'd slip this on whilst I work."

"You volunteerin' like the princess here? Or you lookin' for a job? I can't pay much."

Jack smiles. "I believe I'll keep my day job. I'm volunteering like the lovely princess. Do you mind?"

"I'm obliged."

He yells at me, and he's obliged to Jack? Talk about your glass ceiling.

It takes Nick and me a good two hours to knock out the

coffee rush. Thank goodness he only serves muffins and microwave biscuits for breakfast, or there's really no telling how backed up we might have gotten.

Sweat is trickling down my back by the time Nick calls the all-clear. Sometime during the madness, Jack quietly folded his apron and hung it over a chair in the sparkling dining room. I'll admit I'm a little disappointed he didn't say good-bye. But I suppose he didn't want the gratitude, of which there would have been a lot, considering how swamped we were.

In desperate need of some green tea, I pour a fresh pot of water through the machine. Nick comes in from the dining room, carrying a towel. "Where'd your boyfriend go?"

"First of all, you know full well that Jack is not my boyfriend. He's my boss. And second of all, I have no idea. I suppose he finished what he was doing and left."

"Not your boyfriend, huh?" He purses his lips into a smirk, which quite frankly looks odd. "He seemed to me like he wanted to impress you."

Suddenly I'm interested. "You think?"

"You care?" I see a definite challenge in the way he squares his shoulders and stares at me.

I shrug. "Maybe."

"Well, I'm no love expert, but I thought I saw sort of a spark when he looked at ya."

My optimism plummets a little. A "sort of a spark" could have been the way the light hit him. I'm not getting my hopes up based on that.

I glance at my watch. "I have to go, Nick. I'm sorry I can't stay and help clean up. I'd better get my tea to go."

"You don't want something to eat?" Nick looks a little insulted.

"Another time. My mother's expecting me for lunch." I'm going to be late as it is. I snatch my purse from under the counter and slip my raincoat from the rack. By the time I'm buttoned up, my tea is ready to go.

"You done real good, princess. Worked hard and never got rattled."

I laugh out loud. "Never got rattled? Did you see me slap the counter when that airhead was watching Jack instead of ordering?"

He shrugs. "Nelda woulda given her what for."

"Come on, Nick. What's going on with Nelda? She didn't leave you, did she?"

His eyes narrow and he shoves his finger in my face. "Don't you never say such a thing."

My face goes hot and I avert my gaze, unable to look him in the eye. "I'm sorry, Nick."

He nods. "I mind my own business, and I expect others to give me the same respect."

I just about choke on my tea, because isn't he the one who sat with me for thirty minutes yesterday giving me all that unsolicited advice about telling Floyd to "take a long walk off a short pier"?

That's when I decide my business association with Nick must come to an end. I rise, sling my Prada bag (for which I do not apologize) over my shoulder, and head for the door.

"Good-bye, Nick. You'd better hire some help next week." I mean, it was a nice little change of pace, but, boy, am I ever glad my coffee-making days are behind me. Monday morning, it's back to the real me. The me I was created to be. An editor working my way up to senior editor, and eventually publisher, at Lane Publishing.

I walk into Mother's condo after the customary impersonal exchange with Norman the doorman. I'm a little suspicious, I must say. To invite me over for lunch a mere day after one of her dinner parties is odd, even for my mother.

"Hello, darling!" she says as I step into the foyer. I find it difficult not to hold my mouth agape at the sight of her. My mother is wearing a derriere-hugging pair of black yoga pants, a body shaper that shows a slight amount of cleavage—which is disturbing on more than one level—and a red button-down shirt with three-quarter sleeves.

"Interesting outfit," I murmur. "Is the first lady coming to dinner?" Sarcasm, yes. But you have to understand—my mother wears silk shirts and three-hundred-dollar dress pants, and never leaves her room without control-top panty hose. She does *not* do yoga, let alone wear yoga pants. This is just weird. I wait for an explanation, but she simply waves away my sarcasm. "We have work to do. What did you expect me to wear for manual labor? Jimmy Choos and Anne Klein?" One eyebrow goes up. Okay, that was low. I never should have told her about yesterday at Nick's.

Wait a second. We have work to do? "I thought we were having lunch."

"I've already eaten." She glances at her watch. "It's after twelve thirty. I assumed you had changed your mind. But if you're hungry . . ." She trails off, just like that, but not before giving me that once-over I know so well. The one that reminds me that she knows good and well these jeans are not the size 2 she expects of me, and thus I've disappointed her sorely.

My stomach responds to my predicament with a loud sympathy growl. But I know without a doubt that I can't ask for food. "No. I guess I'm not hungry. I had a grande green tea on the way over."

She gives me a nod. But I'm afraid I'm unable to bask in the silent approval. I'm too busy kicking myself for passing up Nick's chicken salad wrap.

I rub my palms together and take a look around, noting for the first time that there are moving boxes cluttering the floor.

"Let me guess. The work we're talking about here involves packing?"

"Of course. Really, Dancy, we discussed it last night before you left."

"I know, but I thought I'd have a couple of days, at least. They're not getting married until Valentine's Day." Which, besides being a little hokey, is six full months away.

"Yes, but Brynn will want time to decorate to her tastes, so I'm redecorating your father's hideous apartment and we'll move in there next month." She gathers a deep breath while handing me a box. "Therefore, we don't have much time to move our things out."

Okay, fine. I snatch the box from her hand. "You do know how unfair this is, don't you?"

Mother's brow creases as much as her Botoxed skin will allow. "I thought you'd want to pack up your own things, so you can take what you want. But I suppose I can hire movers to do it if you don't want to."

You know that V-8 commercial where everyone gets smacked in the head just as a revelation strikes? I'd love to see a moment like that happen for my mother.

"Never mind." I head up the steps. Hungry, dejected, a little bitter.

Mother's voice trails after me. "Beemer's sleeping on your bed. She's having one of those days, so don't bother her, okay?"

When *isn't* Beemer having a day?

The beagle shifts only slightly when I enter my room, and I

can see exactly what my mother means. Beemer has depression written all over her. Her head stays resting on my pillow, and I don't get so much as a tail thump. The dog sighs and closes her eyes.

"Don't worry about me, Beemer. I'll just work around you. Really." I drop the box on the floor in front of the closet. "Don't get up on my account." She moans, sighs, gives a little stretch, and settles back into sleep. Seriously, that dog needs an intervention. She has good days when she's frisky as a pup. Other days . . . well, quite frankly, a little puppy Prozac might not be a bad idea.

I begin pulling boxes of memories from the shelves in my walk-in closet. It's all here. Everything from my kindergarten uniform to my high school pom-poms to my college diploma. Even my baby book, for heaven's sake! It's as though my mother is washing her hands of my entire existence. Like she's planning to move to Florida to begin this new, fabulous life on the beach at Destin and forget she has a daughter.

As much as I'd like to toss them into the garbage—in protest for so many of life's flaming darts—each article pierces my sentimental heart in a new place, and I slip my childhood piece by piece into keepsake boxes.

My mother pokes her head in the door about six o'clock, just when I'm knee-deep in my beauty-pageant scrapbooks.

"Darling, your father and I are going out to dinner. Shall I have Amanda whip something up for you?"

"No. Give her the night off." I slip the scrapbook into the box and stretch my arms over my head.

She steps into the room and looks around, bewilderment replacing her typically stoic expression. "Are you keeping all of this?"

I shrug. "It's hard to decide what to toss out."

Her gaze sweeps the floor. "That apartment you live in is terribly small. Do you really want to keep it all?"

"No." I grab my eighth-grade report card and stuff it into the garbage. "See?" Who cares about old grade cards? Although that was a straight-A year. In seventh grade I got a B—actually a B minus—and about had a nervous breakdown. In eighth grade I buckled down and made sure I didn't get below an A. I was a straight-A student from then on, but not without effort. Try being a cheerleader, president of student council, captain of the girls' soccer team, and a member of the drama club, which meant a role in every school play. I'd like to snatch that grade card back and place it in the keepsake box, but Mother is still watching, so I let it go.

"See? I've thrown several things away."

Clearly not a bit convinced, she gives me a patronizing nod. She sits on the edge of my bed, lifting the scrapbook from where I just placed it in the box. Then something happens that I haven't seen in quite some time. There's actually a crack in that statuelike exterior. "You were always our little princess." She turns the scrapbook and allows me to take a look. A photo of ten-year-old me, dressed in a clingy, baby blue sequined gown, much too old for me—big brunette hair, shiny lips, and blue eye shadow that makes me look like Barbara Eden from *I Dream of Jeannie*.

"Adorable." As much as I appreciate my mother's sentimental journey, I'm not impressed with the look back. Little does she know about all of my old diaries filled with preteen disdain for the itchy, uncomfortable fabrics, the fake eyelashes that drove me crazy, the three-inch-high heels that I personally feel are responsible for my frequent visits to the chiropractor. Lecherous male judges that shouldn't be thinking about how beautiful little girls are. I mean, really. Should they?

But most of all, I hated the mean girls. Oy. Other contestants. Girls I saw at every pageant for years. I knew them each by name. But we weren't allowed to be friends. Our mothers hovered over us, making sure we didn't become distracted from our rivalry by things as silly as girlish giggles and sleepovers.

Some of us broke out of the chains as we grew into our teenage years and established a sort of honor-among-thieves attitude. But for the most part, I had friendless childhood and high school years. It wasn't until college, when I joined a summer theater program, that I met Tabby and Laini and finally learned about friendship.

I take the scrapbook and slip it back into the box. "What time is Dad coming?"

"Any second." Her face immediately brightens, and I remember this look. Mother loving Dad. I have to admit I'm just a bit ashamed of my skepticism. Maybe there is hope for love in the twilight years. "I'm glad you two are happy, Mother," I say in a sudden rush of generosity.

Rising to her feet, she does the unthinkable. She cups my chin in her palm and bends, pressing a motherly kiss to my cheek. Against my better judgment, I close my eyes and surrender for just a moment to this new Mrs. Cleaver brand of motherhood. She smells of Chanel. I remember that smell up close. I fight back tears at this, the merest of touches. It's all just too emotional. This little trip down memory lane, my lonely childhood. I don't know. I guess I'm just a baby.

"Baby," Mother says, like she's reading my mind, "are you going to be okay doing this all by yourself? I can stay and help, if you'd like me to."

I pull my chin away—subtly, under the pretense of a sudden and desperate need to check out something in the box—and shrug. "Don't be silly. You have a good time with Daddy.

Actually, it's sort of fun seeing all of my old stuff again." Fun like a bikini wax.

I spend the next two hours alone, sorting, tossing, and keeping memories, all to the sound of Beemer's snoring. Only the occasional snort and head lift breaks the rhythm. Honestly, the snoring makes me feel better. When she stops, I can't help being afraid the sleep apnea has finally gotten the best of her and she's not going to draw another breath. And, after all, she's all I have left of my granny. Beemer and—oh, wait, where is it? Furiously I begin digging in the boxes I haven't touched yet. Where? Where is my Bible? My Granny Bible. I inherited her worn, marked-up jewel when she died. I haven't looked at it since, but it's mine, and for some reason, I'm hungry for the sight of that worn black book. Hungrier for it than food, even though I haven't had a morsel all day.

My heart races like a wannabe marathon runner.

I spend the better part of thirty minutes searching for that one specific drink of water. Relief, much like a dip in the pool on a hot summer day, floods me as I lie back on my bed next to Beemer, little Bible in hand. I pull my knees up and stretch my arms in front of my eyes as I open the pages.

Granny took me to church every time she visited from Connecticut, but those times were too few and far between to make anything really stick, especially since my parents usually used Sunday mornings for sleeping it off, and Sundays were typically Nanny's day off. My spiritual training was sparse at best until last year, when Tabby really got serious about things. I've gone to church with her a few times to keep her from agonizing over the state of my soul, mostly to special events like concerts or drama performances. I like it. But if the truth be told, any organized religion sort of makes me cringe. I don't know, maybe I just don't like being told how to worship God. I don't like confinement. It's fine to attend with a friend. But to become a card-carrying member of any particular church? I'm not sure that's a good option for me.

But this . . . let's see. I'll just open it for a second. I'm adamant about starting a book on page one and never peeking at the end until I actually get there, so it seems only natural that I start in Genesis.

"In the beginning, God . . ."

I'm just getting to Sodom and Gomorrah—and I have to say, the Bible is a pretty interesting book—when Beemer rolls up against me, just like old times. She lifts her front leg to give me access to her highness's belly—a habit Granny started when Beemer was just a puppy. I laugh and oblige. "Oh, Beemer," I whisper. "I know how you feel. I miss Granny, too."

I don't know if Beemer's getting senile or if she really understands my words, but the dog actually sits up, bends her small head—small in proportion to the rest of her—and licks my face, not once, but twice, before settling back down. Something about that show of affection makes my heart absolutely soar. I think we've had a moment.

I give the beagle a pat and pick up a stack of photos from the bed. I'm about to toss the photos into a box to take home and look through later when I notice the one on top. Stopping, I lift it for a closer look. My breath catches. I remember this photo. It was the first Christmas Jack couldn't make it home to England, so he came to our house. Don't ask me why, but the guys actually included me, a sixteen-year-old, in their plans that day. Jack, Kale, and I rode the subway to Rockefeller Center for a day of ice-skating and fun. As the photo reveals, I wore a white coat with a rabbit-fur-lined hood.

The memory of that day returns as though it were yesterday. I kept falling down on the ice. Kale thought it was hilarious and snapped pictures of me on my behind. But Jack skated expertly to where I was sitting, very near tears. He helped me to my feet. The photo shows me in his arms as he looks down at me. I'm looking into his eyes adoringly.

I press my hand flat against my chest as my heart races—just like it did that day. Hmm.

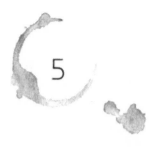

5

Valerie's black-spotted Manolo Blahnik stilettos announced her every move as she followed the maître d' through the dining room at Alfama, a five-star Portuguese restaurant that boasted sardines flown in fresh from Lisbon. She could feel all eyes turn to watch her as she made her way to her seat. This evening she was eating alone, and she truly didn't mind. No less than three successful, handsome, eligible bachelors had called her this week to ask for her company tonight, but Valerie didn't need a man to feel complete. Her own skin was quite enough, thank you very much. Tonight she was free to order the clams in white garlic sauce without the worry of that obligatory kiss good night.

She looked up from her menu as chair legs scraping on the wooden floor demanded her attention. Her heart caught in her throat. Across from her sat John Quest. His dark, Rhett Butler eyes pierced through her.

"May I join you for dinner?" he asked.

She tried to form a no, but her traitorous lips smiled instead. "I'd be delighted."

—An excerpt from *Fifth Avenue Princess*
by Dancy Ames

After a long weekend, I'm anxious to get to work today. I wake up thirty minutes before the alarm and jump out of bed. I feel like one of those characters at the beginning of *The Devil Wears Prada*, dressing for work. I can almost hear the happy music filtering through the air.

I breeze into the kitchen, which is filled with the glorious aroma of whatever Laini is cooking for breakfast. She turns to me. "You look happy."

"Of course I am. It's a workday."

"Are you going to confront Mr. Kramer today?"

A smudge of gray threatens to cloud my joy, but I shrug it off. "The Paris people are coming tomorrow. It wouldn't be nice of me to blast him with my problems."

"Coward!" Tabby calls from somewhere down the hall.

"Who asked you?" I call back.

Laini offers a sympathetic smile. She grabs a mug from the cabinet and fills it with coffee. "Here, sit down and drink this while I finish up breakfast."

I place my cloth napkin on my lap and shake Splenda into my coffee. "What's on the menu today, Chef Laini?"

"*Oui, madame*, we have a delectable veggie egg white omelet with just a touch of low-fat cheddar cheese."

"Sounds heavenly."

"Ah, but that is not all," she says, and sets a small bowl to the right of my plate. "Also, for your palate's delight, a creamy yogurt topped with fresh blueberries."

"Mmm. The perfect way to start my day."

"Good grief, you sound like a commercial." Tabby staggers in, grumpy and frazzled. One good thing about having an acting job is that you don't have to dress up for work, because they have a wardrobe for you when you get there. You don't even have to do your hair and makeup.

"Early shooting today?" I ask, because I rarely see Tabby in the morning.

"Yeah. Blythe is a sadist. And I think she hates me."

"Eat your breakfast," Laini soothes. "That'll make you feel better."

"Don't you get tired of cooking for us all the time?" Tabby grumps as she takes her omelet and heads to the table.

"Don't you like it?" Laini asks.

"Well, of course I do. But—" Tabby doesn't cook much better than I do, so it's hard for us to identify with Laini's obsession. But I think Tabby realizes she was a little hard on our friend. "Sorry, Laini. You're the best, and I think I speak for Dancy and me both when I say we appreciate you keeping us fed in such style."

"No thanks necessary. I enjoy it." She gives Tabby a small bowl of yogurt identical to mine. "Cooking is fun."

"To each her own," I say. "But I agree with Tabby. I'd be a lot thinner without you—which would make my mother happy. And that would never do." I grin.

Laini and Tabby laugh. Having their own mother issues gives them complete understanding of my plight. "You got home late last night," Laini observes, spooning sugar into her mug.

I groan. "Don't remind me."

"Must have been some long lunch with your mom."

I shrug and recount my day and evening.

"No wonder all the leftover shrimp linguini from last night is gone," Laini says as she sits at the head of our little table.

"I was starving. That was wonderful, by the way."

Her eyes sparkle with pleasure. "I made it from scratch. Even the noodles."

"Wow. Impressive."

"Tell her why," Tabby pipes up around a bite of blueberry-laced yogurt.

"Leave me alone," Laini shoots back.

I stare at Tabby. "What did I miss?"

"She bombed her test." Cooking is to Laini what eating is to most of us. She takes the concept of comfort food to a whole new level.

Laini settles back against her chair, her shoulders slumped. "I just don't know what I'm going to do. This class is vital to passing the program. My professor thinks I might be slightly color-blind."

"That's just silly." I spear a piece of my omelet and hold it up for show. "What color is this?"

She grins. "Yellow."

"Case closed." I slide the forkful into my mouth.

"Too bad it's not that easy," Laini says, sobering.

"Well, I don't know anything about interior design. But you can cook circles around everyone I know," Tabby says, hopping up. "I have to get going. Early makeup call. My children-to-be have a skating exhibition this afternoon, so we have to be done shooting early. It's at three o'clock at Rockefeller Center, if you have time to drop by. Shouldn't be more than an hour."

"I'd love to, Tabs," I say, genuinely regretting not being able to make it. "But after taking Friday off, I'm sure my to-do pile is going to be a mile high. Which is exactly why I hate to take time off."

"It's okay. As long as you don't miss the city competition next month."

I nod, sipping my coffee.

"We wouldn't miss it," Laini promises for us both.

I turn back to Laini after Tabby rushes out. "Hey, can you make that test up?"

"Nope. But if I don't bomb too badly on the next one, I should be able to pass the class. It's just . . ."

"What?" I prod.

"I don't know, Dan. I love it, but I'm not that great."

I just don't know what to say. Because honestly, I couldn't recommend her skills to anyone but male college freshmen. (Any help, even from a slightly color-blind designer, would be an improvement for most frat boys.) "There are different tastes for different types of people," I say carefully, trying hard not to patronize. "You just have to tap into the right market for you."

She looks at me askance and hops up, taking our plates from the table.

"Look," I say after her. "Maybe you should think about going back to accounting. You're good at that. More than good. And you can do interior design as a hobby."

She nods slowly, as though she hates to admit it, but she's thought of it herself so it doesn't come as much of a blow. "That's probably what I should do." She scrapes the plates into the garbage disposal. "Mom would be thrilled. Maybe she'd stop with the guilt trips every time she sees me."

We generously call Laini's mom melancholy. Depressed and desperate is how I'd actually describe her. Also selfish, manipulative, and always trying to make Laini feel guilty. My friend never would have become an accountant if her dad hadn't passed away right before college and her mom hadn't pushed her with comments like "Your father would be so proud if you'd follow in his footsteps. Don't you want him to look down from heaven and be proud?" And with Laini's knack for math, it didn't seem like that much of a stretch to think that might be the way to go. So she did, until she got let go from Ace Accounting after one of the Aces was caught embezzling, sending the company into bankruptcy.

Laini finally switches off the disposal, and I take the opportunity to lend some verbal support. "Do what makes you happy, my friend. Nothing else matters."

Laini frowns. "Are you happy? Really and truly? I mean, you have your work, but are you happy with everything? What about the book you started writing last year?"

I stare at her, slack-jawed. "How'd you know about that?"

"You left your laptop open on the coffee table one night while you went to the bathroom." She gives me a sheepish grin. "I couldn't stop myself."

My mind shifts between irritation and curiosity. Curiosity wins. "What did you think of it?"

"Well, you weren't gone very long. But I definitely didn't want to stop reading."

My heart swells at the praise.

"When are you planning to finish it?"

"Maybe someday." I grin. "When I retire to my beach home in the Bahamas." I drain my coffee.

She laughs and takes my cup. "Well, you'd better get to work so you can keep building up that retirement fund, then."

"Thanks for breakfast." I stand, towering over her five-foot frame, especially in three-inch heels. Still, I slip my arm around her shoulders and give her a squeeze.

"My pleasure," she says. And I know she honestly means it.

Jack walks by and grins in a way that says he's not going to keep on walking. That would be too easy. He stops at my desk. "Did you make that coffee? Rumor has it you make a truly wonderful cup."

"Very funny." I grin back. "Did you clean up the break room? Rumor has it you bus a truly wonderful table."

"Touché," he says.

"You left without giving Nick a chance to thank you."

He looks away, and I can't believe it, but he's blushing. Which is sort of sweet. "There were no thanks necessary."

"Well, it was very kind of you to help out my friend. And greatly appreciated."

"The way you two were sniping at one another," he says in his oh-so-British accent, "I wouldn't have guessed you to be friends at all." Only it sounds like "atall." One word. You have to hand it to the Brits. They have the coolest way of putting words together. Like adding a question to the end of their sentences. "That's the way it is, isn't it?" Things like that. I don't know—maybe it's just me—but I find it an incredibly soothing accent to listen to.

"He starts it," I mutter, and Jack laughs. I love the sound of his low, throaty laughter. It's the main thing I remember about the days when Kale brought him home on holidays. His laughter filled the house and made my heart leap.

I venture a look into his eyes, and he's staring at me, like he's waiting for . . . I can't guess. I glance at my to-do list. "Do you need something?"

His face goes stoic. "Not at all."

Heat rushes to my cheeks in the awkward silence that ensues. I clear my throat. "So, what's on the agenda for today?"

"Meeting with Tony. The Paris people will be here tomorrow, so we're going over strategy."

Anthony Kramer, the publisher. It's always a little tense when he's in the office. And when I say a little, I mean *a lot*. He's been in frequently over the last few days, because of the Paris people coming. Which explains the scurrying, tension, and downright terror of the office staff. I don't know why everyone is always so upset when he comes by. It's not like he ever actually speaks to anyone but those in command, like Jack and the other senior editors—and Fran, and I won't even say what rumors are floating around about those two. Being simply an editor, I barely get a nod from the mogul.

"Is this a meeting I need to attend?"

Jack shakes his head. "Senior editors and higher only, from what I understand."

Which doesn't really bother me. As much as I like having the 4-1-1, I have enough manuscripts and proposals piled up to keep me busy for weeks. Who needs to take the time for a meeting?

Okay, this might sound petty, but if the meeting is not for anyone below a senior editor, then what is Fran Carson doing walking in there, right next to Mr. Kramer? As if I didn't already know. Fran Carson—the editor who was in line with me for the job Jack Quinn swooped in and stole last year. The woman I'm constantly competing with. Or being forced to compete with because of her own low self-esteem. I swear, it's like those beauty-pageant days all over again. Senior editors only, my eye. Did Jack know Mr. Kramer was going to bring his girl-toy into the meeting with them, or did he blatantly lie to me?

"Are you all right?" he asks, obviously unaware of my scrutiny.

"Yes, I'm fine. Just really need to get to these proposals."

He squints at me for a second while I practice that wide-eyed innocent look (another talent left over from pageant days).

He straightens and taps my desk with the file he's got in his hand. "While you were out Friday, I took the liberty of looking over your edit on Virginia Tyne's latest book. There were a few things you missed that I thought pertinent. You might want to take note of some of my suggestions before sending it to her for revision."

The Virginia Tyne book? That's my edit. My author. He had no right! And this isn't the first edit he's stuck his highbrow English nose into either. I can feel steam rising. I ball my hands, a little technique I've always used when I need to keep my cool. A few things I missed, indeed.

"I'm sorry," he says. "Is there a problem?"

"Problem?" I ask through clenched teeth.

"Your face is red." His lips twitch.

"It is not."

"It most certainly is. Extremely so, if I may be so bold as to mention it."

"Well, you just did, so . . ."

He smiles. "So I did. I'll take my leave. Excuse me."

I watch broad shoulders in a perfectly tailored suit walk away from me. Frustration shoots through me as I grab the edit with his "suggestions." I'm all set to shoot him down, argue about how stupid his thoughts are. Only, every single comment he made is . . . right. Disturbingly so. Embarrassingly so. What is wrong with me that I missed her overuse of the word *plethora?*

I fight back tears as I type his comments and mine into one unified e-mail to the author. His comments add another three pages to the six I've already written, which Virginia is going to be upset about. But I've had to talk more than one author off the ledge after a particularly long edit. And I'm sure this one will work out fine. I hope.

The day goes from bad to worse. The tension in the office is off the charts because of Tony's visit and preparations for the Paris people. Plus we get calls from five agents, checking on submissions and getting huffy about the postponement of a committee meeting that will decide the fate of the manuscripts they're hoping to sell for their clients. I hate days like this. I never, ever should have taken a day off.

To compound things, just before I'm about to call it a day, Virginia Tyne slams into my office. I hate authors who live in

New York and barge in any time they want, instead of calling or e-mailing. Only the A-listers have the nerve to do it. My assistant, Claudia, looks absolutely white as she follows her in. "I'm sorry," she mouths behind Virginia.

"It's all right, Claudia. Close the door behind you, please."

Virginia has written thirty books in twelve years. She's a publisher's dream. Writes fast, writes well, and meets her deadlines. Plus, her books sell respectably well. Not like Cate Able, by any means, but respectably enough that the publisher wants to keep her happy, which is why she's been with Lane Publishing for so long.

My hormone headache is at an all-time high when she barges in, flings a printed-out copy of what I know instinctively is my e-mail on my desk, and plops herself down in the chair opposite me. "What can I do for you, Virgie?"

"You can explain this letter is what you can do. And don't pretend you don't know what I mean, either."

This is Virgie's first book since Jack took over. I'm debating whether or not to let him take the rap. But no. That wouldn't be professional.

I clasp my hands on the desk in front of me. "Would you like to go over the letter point-by-point so we can discuss your concerns? As you know, these edits are meant to be a dialogue, not a command."

"I most certainly would not." Her voice shrills a little, and I can tell she needs a drink. And, believe me, if I weren't so dead-set against alcohol (because of my dad, you know), I'd offer her something to calm her down.

"Then I don't know what you want from me." My head is killing me. What did I do with the Midol I keep in the office for days like this?

"Young lady," she says.

Oh, good heavens. This is not going well. I can tell it's about to become an "I was writing before you were born" kind of talk.

"I started with this company before you graduated from college. I think I know when a character is fully developed."

"You mean Tallulah, the main character?" That's what's bothering her? I thought that was the mildest of Jack's suggestions. And, really, the most obviously correct of his observations.

"Who else?" She snatches up the letter. Lifts her glasses from where they hang around her neck from a gold chain—I know it's gold, because I bought it for her last year for Christmas. She slips on the glasses and looks at me over the top of them. "And I quote," she says (and you can imagine her tone). "'This character is inconsistent and her swings in emotion from paragraph to paragraph border on the ridiculous, even hilarious at times.'" She shoots me a look that says, "Well? What do you have to say for yourself?"

I pull out the manuscript. It's still at the top of the pile. Although I never dreamed it would happen this soon, I actually anticipated this little encounter with Virgie, so I sticky-tabbed several examples I thought might come up. (Ingenious on my part, as it turns out.)

Her face blanches as I start to read. By the time Tallulah has laughed, cried, flashed anger, and had her heart clench with compassion about ten times in two pages, I'm fighting hard not to laugh out loud.

Oh, who am I kidding? A giggle emerges.

The poor insulted prima donna lets out an outraged huff.

"I'm so sorry, Virgie," I say. And I might have gotten away with it, except then another giggle emerges, and another, until I'm wiping tears from my eyes and I'm absolutely about to—as Tabby would say—bust a gut.

I'm still reading, and laughing so hard I can't stop, when she jumps up, snatches the edit letter from my desk, and glares at me. "This isn't over," she hisses.

And oh boy, do I believe her. I sober up pretty fast.

Forty-five minutes later, I'm sitting in the back of a taxi, all traces of laughter gone. All I can do is cry. I don't believe it. I do *not* believe it. Mr. Kramer forced me to take a month of my built-up vacation time. All right. He isn't *technically* forcing me. Just strongly suggesting that if I can't keep from laughing in one of our top authors' faces, perhaps I'm working too hard.

Working too hard? Work is all I know. It's the only thing that makes me feel good about myself. Well, it used to, until Jack came along and made me feel insecure and incompetent. And he had already left for the day by the time Tony finished mollifying Virgie, walked her to the elevator, and then bulldozed into my office with his "suggestion."

"But what about my workload?" I asked, sounding whiny and pathetic even to my own ears.

"Fran can take over for you." Fran? Fran, who always tries to make me look stupid and inferior?

And to top it off, Fran was "conveniently" standing right outside the door that Tony forgot to close on his way in to ream me.

"Did you call me, Tony?" she asks, all innocent and professional.

"Oh, good, Fran, you're here." He smiles at her because she's the type to make him think she's the cream of the crop, and he's the type that is too absentminded about this sort of thing to know any better. Plus, well . . . I already mentioned the rumor about those two. "Dancy is taking some vacation time, and I'll need you to handle her pressing work. Do what you can, and see who's available to freelance the rest of her workload."

"Oh, you're finally taking a vacation?" Fran looks at me with a bright smile (for Tony's benefit, her voice is edged with concern). "It's about time. You work much too hard."

Tony nods his agreement. "My thoughts exactly."

And just like that, I'm out the door, and Fran has the edge on me. I'm not allowed back in the office for a month.

A month. What on earth am I going to do for a whole month?

I wipe my nose with the millionth tissue I've used since entering this dumb cab. Tears keep coming.

"You okay, lady?" the cabbie asks, with a furtive glance in the rearview mirror. He sounds annoyed, like he's sick of women crying in his car. As much as I'd like to open up to someone, I know I'm not going to get any sympathy from him.

"Let me off at the corner," I sniff. I mean, if the guy's not going to give me any sympathy, I'm not paying him an extra four bucks to go a measly quarter of a mile. I'd rather walk off the frustration anyway.

New York in the summer isn't exactly fresh. You can still smell things like garbage, gas, and ozone-layer-destroying emissions, for starters. But occasionally, when the atmosphere is just right, you can actually take a deep breath without bringing on a coughing fit. Those are the days I love, especially when the air is smooth in the aftermath of a cleansing rain, and holds the promise of more to come. Like now.

I slip into Nick's amid a rush-hour coffee run and, as usual, the line is backed up to the door. I actually notice some shoving going on. New Yorkers aren't exactly known for their politeness, but a twentysomething muscleman elbowing a grandmother out of the way just to get a cup of coffee and a muffin is wrong on so many levels, and out-of-bounds even for this city.

The thought crosses my mind that maybe I ought to leave before I get roped into helping, but you know, I guess I knew what was coming before I gave the cabbie the address. After all, it is five o'clock, and that's one of Nick's busiest times of day. So I admit to myself that I actually came to help out. I elbow my way through the crowd of more than one cussing patron and do what's becoming a habit. I slip an apron from the hook behind the kitchen door and slide it on over my head. Nick acknowledges my presence with barely a nod, but I can see by the way his face relaxes that he's glad to see me.

6

Valerie knew she shouldn't love the man who inadvertently caused her dismissal, but how could she not? John's arms felt too good. His kisses too sweet. Besides, he hadn't done it on purpose, had he?

Oh, how she missed long talks with her mom and her father's words of wisdom. The month that they'd been gone seemed like years. Perhaps a trip to Africa was just what she needed to get her mind off of her own problems. And perhaps she would find a way to help a child in the process.

—An excerpt from *Fifth Avenue Princess*
by Dancy Ames

try to convince myself that it is not the end of the world. But tell that to an overachieving rich girl with a controlling mother who is armed with unrealistic expectations for her daughter. Failure has never been an option. And a forced vacation, in our book, is like a thirty-day suspension. A punishment. In short—failure.

Ninety-nine percent effort might as well be zero, and second place means "loser" with a capital *L*. In light of this completely unfair and dysfunctional upbringing, is it any wonder that I derive no comfort from the thought that the sun'll come out tomorrow? I mean, I have my own Daddy

Warbucks and I'm still miserable. So take that, Little Orphan Annie, and get real.

Nick's brows scrunch together when I take him up on his offer of free food without any argument. I plop down with a white-chocolate mocha latte with double whipped cream and wait there sullenly until Nick sets a meatball sub in front of me. I swallow my first bite and swipe at my face.

"Look here, princess," he says. "It ain't that I don't appreciate the help, but you didn't do your best job today. Something's wrong. You wanna talk about it?"

Tears spring to my eyes, and I tell him what happened.

"So you get a break. Big deal! Everybody needs a vacation." He shrugs his big Italian shoulders. The ones everything obviously rolls off of.

"It's one thing to take a vacation because you have somewhere to go and someone to go with. But it's no fun to take a vacation because you laughed in someone's face and the boss is peeved."

"A vacation's a vacation," he says matter-of-factly. "It ain't like you got fired."

"Seriously, Nick. Do you understand that I'm actually upset about this? I love my job. I want to edit. I *need* to edit." I stop short of grabbing his shirt and saying, "Editing is my life." That would just be bordering on the obsessive.

"Geez, you are uptight. Maybe that boss of yours is right. Some time off'll likely do you some good. Maybe take a little trip."

That's when I really start to panic. "A trip?"

"Yeah. When was the last time you got outta this city?"

I open and close my mouth because I don't have an answer.

Nick gives me a know-it-all nod. "That's what I'm talkin' about."

"Oh, Nick. There's nowhere to go and no one to go with. My friends can't just pick up and take off right now. Besides, New York has everything I need. Seriously, it's a great town. There's no place I'd rather be than right here in the city."

Only I want to be working. I don't relax well. Why do people have to see that as a flaw? I think it's a sign of a good work ethic. And wouldn't you think Mr. Kramer would think the same? What more do they want than a dedicated, hardworking employee?

"Know what you need?"

I sigh. "Yeah, I need to edit."

"Besides that, girlie."

"What?" I say glumly, around a huge bite. Mother would be mortified if she could see me like this.

"You need to come over to old Nick's for some of my lasagna. My ma's recipe."

My mouth waters. "A cure for everything?" I'm feeling better already, just from the thought of it.

"You got it, princess. Bring them two friends of yours. Tomorrow. Seven sharp. *Capisce*?"

"I'll ask them."

He scowls as though I've thrown his offer back in his face in a most ungrateful manner.

"We'll be there."

I should go home right away. But Laini has a late class and Tabby's with David and his twins. The thought of going back to an empty apartment just depresses me. So I take the subway over to Dad's. I figure a girl needs her father at a time like this. I take the elevator up to the love shack and knock on the door, thinking only of the relief I will feel when I'm in my daddy's arms, crying on his shoulder as he consoles me. Why I thought that, I'll never know. He's never been Pa Ingalls before. But in my emotional state, I do what so many girls do and head to my dream father.

Reality hits as he opens the door and panic strikes his features. He slips out of the apartment, closing the door behind him. "Princess, what are you doing here?"

"Oh, Daddy," I say, throwing myself into his arms. "Mr. Kramer made me take four weeks off of work today. What am I going to do? I think Fran is trying to get me fired."

He gives me a quick pat on the back and pulls me away from him. "I'm sorry to hear that, honey, but I'm sort of in the middle of something right now. Can we talk about it later?"

I gape in disbelief, the betrayal slicing a thick chunk from my already raw and tattered heart. "Are you kidding me?"

"I'm sorry, baby. I just . . ." He clears his throat and shifts his gaze. Suspicion slips over my brain, and I'm starting to get just what his problem is. I recognize that look. It's sort of like a kid caught red-handed in the cookies and trying to convince his mom he doesn't have a thing to do with the missing treats.

"You have another woman in there!"

"No. It's not like that."

"Not like what?"

"I'm not cheating on your mother."

"So there is another woman in your apartment."

"Yes, but—"

"Are you kidding me?" Shoving past him, I grab the knob and twist. Locked.

Filled with indignation and desperately needing to release a little stress, I pound on the door. "I know you're in there. You'd better open this door."

"Dancy!" Dad hisses in my ear. "For the love of Pete. I live here. Don't cause a scene."

I glare at him and turn back to the door, where I start pounding again. "I said open up. I'm not leaving until you do!"

I hear the lock twist, and slowly the door opens. "Stuart, don't you think it's time she knew?"

My jaw drops. "Nanny Mary?"

Her eyes light with pleasure and guilt. "It's been seventeen years and you still remember me?"

"Of course, you were my fav—" My voice trails off as I realize something that would have been obvious to anyone else at first glance. This is why Nanny Mary left so abruptly without telling me good-bye. It was all about her and Dad.

"I don't believe it!" I practically shout. "I don't believe it. I just don't. Dad! What's wrong with you?"

"Wait. I'm telling you—it's not what you think."

"Tell that one to Mother. For the umpteenth time." I whip around and stomp down the hall.

"Wait," Nanny Mary calls after me.

"No thanks!" I send back over my shoulder. "Have a nice life. Actually, no. Have a terrible life. You deserve it. Both of you."

"Dancy!" They're nothing if not persistent. "This isn't what it looks like. Your dad was telling the truth."

"Yeah, right!" I stand outside of the elevator and push the button. Luckily it dings immediately and the doors open.

"You have a sixteen-year-old brother."

I freeze and stare at the elevator, unable to move. Wishing my legs would propel me forward, but they refuse. I watch wordlessly as the doors close without me inside. Slowly, I turn and face the guilty couple.

"What?"

Dad steps forward, his hands outstretched, palms up in a

plea. "Your mother knows about this. It was the real reason we split up for good."

"Our relationship was over a long time ago," Nanny Mary says. "Please believe me."

"Then what are you doing here?" Sarcasm drips from my trembling lips.

"Let's go inside, away from prying eyes," Dad suggests. As much as I want to take a page out of Nick's book of etiquette and suggest he take a long walk off a short pier, I need to hear about this crazy secret they've kept for all these years.

Nick's place is above the coffee shop, so the three of us—Tabby, Laini, and I—walk the few short blocks to dinner. Neither of them fussed at me for accepting an invitation for all of us without asking. I guess they figure I've had enough frustration in the last couple of days and don't want to add insult to injury.

"Wow, so you have another brother." Laini's voice breaks through our silence on this balmy summer evening. All around us, the night crowd comes to life, clubs fill up, horns honk, and dusk brings on streetlights and car lights. Call me crazy, but I love this time of night. And this is part of the reason I don't feel the need to leave the city. I love it. I really do. I'm sure the country is lovely too, but I love New York. It's my town. Have I said that before? Well, it is.

Over the last twenty-four hours, the girls and I have hashed and rehashed the fact that I now have another brother.

"And your mom knew about him all along?" Tabby asks.

I shrug, still trying to get that one through my head. "Apparently. I mean, she just decided I wasn't to be told. That Kale and I shouldn't have anything to do with our own flesh and blood."

"But your dad—"

"He's been involved with my little brother the whole time. Brandon knows him as Dad."

"Wow," Tabby says for the hundredth time.

"Yeah," I say.

"Are you going to get to meet him, now that the cat's out of the bag?" Tabby asks.

I cringe a little inside at the violent disdain I have for the suggestion. This whole thing is like a blow to the stomach. "I might not have any choice." I step aside as a group of teenagers barrels past without so much as a look in our direction.

"Kids," Laini says, shaking her head.

"Yes, and my brother's apparently just like those." We resume our walk. "Apparently Nanny Mary can't handle the little hoodlum anymore and wants my dad to take him for a while."

"Are you serious?" Tabby says. "Just like that?"

I nod. "Her mother is dying of cancer, and Nanny wants to live with her in New Jersey and take care of her minus the distraction of a juvenile delinquent."

Laini tucks her hand through my arm. "I guess you can't blame her for wanting to do that. It's sort of commendable. Don't you think so?"

I shrug. "Sure. I just don't see how my dad is going to handle this. He hasn't had much experience as a caregiver."

Laini adjusts the plate of freshly baked pull-apart dinner rolls she's carrying in her other hand. "Don't you think it's time he learned?"

I'd say so. But why does he have to learn this late-in-life lesson with a son I don't even know?

Nick is waiting at the door with a grin and a bottle of ginger ale when we arrive. "Right on time."

Tabby gives him a quick squeeze. "Thanks for the invite, Nick."

"That lasagna smells amazing." I sniff the air. "When do we eat?"

"It's coming right up, princess."

"Need some help?" Laini asks. I'm ashamed I didn't think to say that myself.

"No, no. You three are my guests. Nelda would have my head if I let you work."

We sit at the table while Nick bustles around in the kitchen. The table's set with plates, glasses, silverware, and salad. I realize all I've had to eat all day is a veggie fritter Laini made for me before she left the apartment. I slept all day. Literally got out of bed at one o'clock. Showered just in time for Laini and Tabby to get home and leave for Nick's.

By the time Nick gets everything on the table and sits at the head, I could eat just about anything.

Nick bows his head, and we follow suit. He thanks God for our presence and for the food, and asks for a blessing on his beautiful Nelda and "strength for Nita."

As soon as the prayer is over, he reaches for our plates, one at a time, and dishes up the lasagna. Between the salad, lasagna, and Laini's homemade rolls, my stomach fills up in no time and I enter my comfort zone. Warm and content. Maybe that's why I say what we've all been thinking, even though I know I'm opening myself up to Nick's barbs.

"Why don't you tell us where Nelda is?"

He scowls and looks like he's about to tell me off, then for no reason at all, he nods. "Okay. I guess I oughta let you three in on it. But"—he captures the three of us in a stern frown—"this is just between us."

"Scout's honor," Tabby says, giving the salute.

Nick's eyes tear up a little. I hold my breath, stunned at his sudden show of emotion. "Our daughter, Anita, is sick."

Silence permeates the room. I have no idea what to say, and I'm sure Laini and Tabby are struggling with their own lack of words.

"She ain't got a husband no more since he died a few years ago. Nita's got two kids in school and needs her mother's help while she goes through cancer treatments."

"Of course she does," Laini says, her voice filled with compassion. Poor Nick. I can't imagine how hard this is on the big guy.

I try to lighten the mood by focusing on what Nick loves: his coffee shop. "Hey, Nick, how's the search for an employee coming along?" I ask.

Nick shakes his head. "I got a kid starting tomorrow. He goes to college like your friend Laini here." He turns to her. "You seem like a real smart kid."

"From your lips to God's ears," comes Laini's rueful reply.

"I'll keep my fingers crossed that he'll work out for you." Somehow the conversation slips into another topic, and then another, and by nine o'clock, everyone is starting to yawn but me. We try to help clean up, but Nick's having none of it. "I didn't invite you here to work. I invited you to eat."

"It was truly delicious, Nick," Laini says as she walks to the door. "I'd love the recipe."

Nick shakes his head. "Sorry, sweetheart. Family secret. I can't give it out."

She smiles and reaches out to give him a hug. "I understand."

We say good night and head back to the apartment to decompress, as we always do at the end of the day.

Tabby plops onto the couch and flings her feet up on the coffee table. "Thank goodness my first scene isn't until after lunch tomorrow. I get to sleep in." She looks at Laini. "What time do you have class tomorrow?"

Laini sits down next to Tabby and crosses her arms over her chest. "I'm not going."

"What do you mean you're not going?" I ask. "If you have a class, you have to go." My work ethic demands it.

Her eyes fill with tears. I sit on her other side and slip my arm around her shoulders. "I can't do this," she moans.

Tabby takes Laini's hand and holds it tight. "Can't do what, honey?"

"Interior design. I'm just no good."

"We've talked all about this, Laini. You just have to—"

"I know, find my market." Laini looks from me to Tabby and back to me. "The thing is, I want to do it the regular way. I want to see what other people see. And if I can't, I don't want to do interior design. I like stripes with dots. I like lavender and orange. I think those colors together are nice."

"You only have two more weeks," Tabby says. "How about sticking it out and praying that God will show you what He wants you to do?"

I let Tabby take the lead on this topic of conversation. But then I remember something I read in Granny's Bible last night before bed. "I read something like that last night."

Tabby gives me a frown. "Read it where?"

"Where do you think? In the Bible."

A delighted smile lights her face, and there's no hiding the fact that Tabby's been hoping for this day. Praying for it, I'd venture to guess. "What was the scripture? Do you remember?"

"Hang on. It's marked in Granny's Bible."

I run into my room, carefully lift the book, and bring it back into the living room. "Okay, here it is. Proverbs three, verses five and six. And this was one my granny used to quote a lot. That's why I remembered it, probably."

"Read it, Dan," Tabby prompts gently.

I nod and direct my gaze to the written words. "Trust in the Lord with all thine heart; and lean not unto thine own understanding. In all thy ways acknowledge him, and he shall direct thy paths."

Somehow saying the words aloud causes them to mean more to me than just an encouragement for my friend. I wonder if God might direct my path, too.

We stay up discussing Laini's situation, weighing the pros and cons of her finishing the summer semester. By the time we go to bed an hour and a half later, I'm pretty sure Laini is at least strongly considering sticking out the last part of her semester.

Later, lying in bed, I stare at the ceiling and think about the possibility that God might be looking out for me. Or that He might be willing to take on the job if I'll let Him in on my life's decisions.

"What do You say?" I whisper to the ceiling. "I could use a little path-directing. Things are changing, and I'm out here on my own, floundering all alone. I wouldn't mind knowing someone is on my side. If You'd like the job, I suppose it's Yours."

Maybe not the most eloquent of prayers, but I think I might have cracked the ceiling. And if not, at least I feel better.

7

Valerie disembarked in Ghana, West Africa, after a long, bumpy flight. All she needed was a hot shower, a hot meal, and ten hours of sleep, and she'd feel human again. She got to the gate and fell into the waiting arms of her parents.

"Mom, you're as brown as an Indian!" she exclaimed. "I hardly recognize you."

Mom laughed. Her face showed signs of fatigue, but her pale green eyes radiated joy.

"Let's go find your luggage," Dad said. "We need to be back at the mission by dinnertime so we can serve the children who come."

Valerie trailed after these people she barely recognized, and suddenly she wondered what she had been missing all of her life.

—An excerpt from *Fifth Avenue Princess*
by Dancy Ames

My mother's face is white and strained as we sit in the living room during this little family powwow: Mother, Kale, and I sitting on the sofa, Nanny Mary and Brandon across from us on another sofa. Dad's sitting in a tan wing chair at the head of the room, nursing a rum and Coke as usual, and looking about as guilty as a puppy chewing on the strap of a Prada bag.

Even if I wanted to deny this new brother, there's no mistaking the family resemblance. Brandon looks like Dad and Kale. Square jaw, slightly large ears (that gave me quite a lot of "Dumbo" ammunition during sibling fights with Kale when we were kids), and a mouth like mine—full on the bottom, slightly thin on the top—a perpetual pout, which fits the current mood. He's leaning back, long legs sprawled in front of him, arms folded like he has better things to do and we're severely cramping his style.

I know how he feels. But I have to admit, my heart goes out to Mother the most. She never asked for this. And just as she's trying to get her life and marriage back on track, Dad's past comes back to haunt them. I look at her, standing by her man. Yes, I'm definitely feeling sorry for her while the other woman wrings her hands, even as she tries hard not to fidget. I have to say, I'm not feeling much sympathy for that one at all.

"Can we get on with it?" Brandon asks, breaking the silence with belligerence. "I have plans."

"Well, I just changed those plans, young man," Nanny Mary says. "And watch your attitude in your father's house."

In my head I know my dad is Brandon's dad, too, but hearing those words out loud in that context feels odd. Kale and I exchange looks, and I can see he's thinking pretty much the same thing.

"The purpose of this get-together is so you can meet your brother and sister," my dad tells his *other* kid. "You've been wanting this for years, and now you're acting this way?"

What? Wait a second. I stare at my dad, then back at Brandon. The kid's looking me in the eye, and I can tell he's reading my mind.

"Yeah, that's right," he says in a Nick-esque manner. Tough guy. "*My* mom doesn't believe in keeping secrets."

"How long has he known, Dad?" I ask, ignoring the kid's insinuation about my mother. The little twerp.

My dad looks a bit pale. "All of his life." He gulps down more of the contents of his glass. Nerves of steel.

Kale gives a short laugh and shoots from his seat next to me. "I'm out of here." He takes in the sight of our brother and extends his hand. "Welcome to the family, kid. Sorry it's so messed up."

Brandon's eyes light with something that makes me think he's been waiting a long time to meet his big brother.

"Okay, wait," I say. Kale turns to me. As a matter of fact, everyone does. "Here's the thing. Kale and I had our own issues with our parents' splitting up, but at least we didn't think we were being hidden away like something shameful."

"Listen, Dancy," my dad—our dad—says. "That's not what we did."

"Yeah, right," Brandon spouts, and who can blame him?

Mother, who up to now hasn't said a word, speaks up with a trembling voice. "Dancy is right." She turns to Brandon. "Please forgive me. I'm the one to blame. Y-your mother wanted you to know the children, but I—" She gathers a deep breath, unable to go on. My mother isn't well versed in the art of apology, so I have to hand it to her, she's definitely stepping up. I mean, sure she was wronged by my dad and the "other woman," but after all these years . . . Well, hopefully, we can just move forward.

"Brandon," I say, suddenly feeling the need to leave these three to their own mistakes. "How would you like to go out and get a pizza with your big sister?"

"And big brother," Kale chimes in. "Let's get to know each other. Gripe about our parents for a while. Exchange notes and figure out how Dad kept us from knowing about you. Masterful, Dad. Truly."

Dad refuses to play into Kale's baiting. His face is flushed, and I'm having a tough time staying mad at him.

"What do you say?" I ask Brandon.

He pulls on his eyebrow ring—a sure sign of nervousness. "Anything's better than being here."

He's got that right.

I toss a glance to Nanny Mary. "You don't mind, do you?" I ask, hoping the expression on my face warns her that she'd better not object.

"No, of course I don't mind."

"Let's go, sport," I say, restraining myself from ruffling the four spikes down the middle of his half-shaved head.

"Give me a break. I'm not six."

"I'll try to remember that," I say with a rueful smile.

"We'll take my car," Kale offers.

"Dancy," Nanny calls after me.

I can barely stand the sound of her voice. I gather a breath as I turn back to face her. "Yes?" I say, much more politely than I feel. Times like these are when my charm-school training really comes in handy.

"You'll see that he gets home safely?"

"I'm not a baby, Ma," Brandon gripes.

"Don't worry," I say drily. "We'll deliver him to your door safe and sound."

"Uh—actually," my dad says, "you'd better deliver him to my door. He's moving in with me for a while."

"How could I forget?" I say, sarcasm masking my spiking bewilderment. Why do I keep getting surprised here? I knew Nanny Mary wanted Dad to take on more of the responsibility with Brandon. I just didn't think it would be so soon.

"We were just getting around to talking about it." Dad swigs down the last of his drink and walks to the bar for another round. "You and Kale are both good ones to walk out in the middle of important moments. Now you're teaching your little brother to do it."

I can't help what I say next. "Just passing along a little family tradition. After all, we learned from the best, didn't we, Dad?"

"Dancy, please." Mom's voice sounds weary, and suddenly I feel ashamed.

"All right. I'm sorry. I'll get over it." I sling my arm across Brandon's shoulders, and of course he immediately shrugs me off. "Let's go, brothers."

"Hey, can I drive?" Brandon asks.

Kale looks like he might actually be considering it. But before I can raise my objections, he asks matter-of-factly, "Do you have your license?"

Brandon scowls. "Naw, but I can drive."

Kale rolls his eyes. "Nice try, kid."

"Whatever."

Three hours later, I slide into bed, full of pepperoni and cheese bread, thoughts swimming through my mind like a school of tuna. I've decided something: I like Brandon. He's smart, quick to the punch, rebellious, and in desperate need of some normalcy. We're all a little odd, I suppose. Coming from my family sort of makes that inevitable.

On the drive from my dad's place to my apartment, Kale and I agreed that we need to take the kid under our wing and try to make up for all the years he's missed. Heaven knows our dad is too wrapped up in his own life to even bother. I seriously doubt his apartment will be much more than a place for Brandon to sleep. It definitely will not be home.

My mind starts to settle around midnight, and I feel that fuzzy warmth of drifting into a cloud of sleep. Lazy, like a low hum . . .

Trust in the Lord with all thine heart; and lean not unto thine own understanding. In all thy ways acknowledge him, and he shall direct thy paths.

"We have a deal, right?" I whisper into the darkness just before surrendering to my fatigue.

I'm not sure if I didn't set the alarm, or if it didn't go off, or if I simply didn't hear it. But I jolt awake at seven thirty, half an hour after I promised Nick I'd be at the coffee shop. "I can't believe I'm going to be late when I promised Nick I'd help out today!" I say around a ravishing bite of warm, gooey home-made cinnamon roll.

"Here," Laini says, handing me a plate with a few more. "Give these to the big guy. Maybe he'll forgive you."

A quick smile shoots to my lips at Laini's naive belief that food solves whatever ails any man. She really should have been a mother in the fifties and raised a whole handful of adorable, chubby little kids.

I give her a quick squeeze. "Thanks, pal."

"Anytime."

I swig down a swallow of coffee, then hand Laini the cup. "Gotta go. Thank goodness I'm going to a coffee shop. I'll need it."

I breeze into Nick's a few minutes later, and thankfully, he's frazzled enough with the morning rush that he looks more relieved to see me than aggravated that I'm late. "Thought you changed your mind," he says in passing.

"Not a chance. Woke up late." I set down the plate of cinnamon rolls. "From Laini."

A scowl crunches his brow. "Put it in back. We ain't got room for nothin' up here that don't belong."

Am I really volunteering my vacation time (forced or not) so I can be abused by some mobster who is most likely using his shop as a front for illegal activity? I keep the comment to myself, but I can see this is going to be a long day.

By ten o'clock the morning crowd has thinned out, and Nick and I sit down to a cup of coffee and a cinnamon roll (compliments of Laini) and gear up for the lunch rush. Thankfully, Nick serves a limited menu, so we won't have too much confusion.

"This is pretty good," Nick says of the cinnamon roll. "You say Laini made this?"

"She's a culinary genius," I say. "I'm telling you, Nick, I think she could have her own TV show, like Rachael Ray."

"Ask her if she wants to send in a couple dozen of these for tomorrow morning, and we'll see if anyone'll buy 'em."

I stop and stare. "You mean you want to pay Laini for her baking?" My voice takes on a squeal as I get more excited with each word. "That's a perfect idea!"

"Tell her to make 'em as big as these and we can sell 'em for five bucks each. I'll give her three-fifty for each one I sell tomorrow, and we'll negotiate after that."

"Okay, I'll let her know."

At eleven o'clock sharp the door dings and the lunch rush begins. Nick and I are swamped for three hours. Finally, in the afternoon we sit, each with a bowl of chicken noodle soup. Nick pours me a glass of milk, which I happen to know is 2 percent.

"Oh, Nick, no thanks."

"Why not? It's that low-fat stuff."

"I know, but—" I haven't had 2 percent milk since the early nineties. It'd be like drinking cream. Mentally, I start calculating fat grams and calories.

"Drink it. It's good for your bones."

"Fine. Whatever." I swear, Nick's more like a dad than my own dad.

I lift the glass and down the contents in one tilt. Oh, that's so good! How on earth could I ever think skim milk tasted like regular milk? It's all a lie that weight-conscious (aka, obsessed) women have bought into so we don't feel deprived. But oh my. Fat tastes good!

"There, I drank it," I say to Nick. "Happy?"

"I'd be a lot happier if I thought you might show up tomorrow and help me again."

"I already planned on it." I grin and so does he.

"Anyone ever tell you you're a good kid?"

"Never." No, really. Never. Hmm.

He frowns and looks like he's about to say something, but just then the bell dings. From the corner of my eye, I spot a couple of long legs walking toward me. As I gaze upward, dread turns my stomach. "Hi, Jack," I say glumly, jealous that he's going to his job while I have to be on vacation. "What are you doing here?"

"Late lunch?" he replies, without the decency to look ashamed for his part in my forced vacation.

Nick grunts. "What'll ya have?"

Jack looks at my bowl. "I'll have what she's having." He sits across from me, taking the chair Nick vacates.

"I don't recall inviting you to join me," I say, wishing like anything that my heart wouldn't thump a million beats a second every time this man is in the vicinity.

"Come now, Dancy. Surely you're not going to hold a grudge for a little editorial interference? I find it difficult to believe you'd be so childish."

"Then you don't know me very well." I stick out my tongue to prove my point.

Rather than frown and walk away as I hope he will, he gives me an amused half-smile. Then, to my utter amazement, he snatches a napkin from the holder and leans forward. It takes only a second to register that he's coming toward me with that thing.

"What do you think you're doing?"

"Since we've just established that you are indeed nothing but a child, I assume you are waiting for me to wipe the milk from your upper lip. And about that edit—I never said you did a bad job. Everyone misses something occasionally. I was trying to help. Not interfere."

My jaw drops as he swipes the napkin gently over my alleged milk mustache. He winks. "There we go. All clean."

I'm dangerously close to bursting into tears. Rather than risk the humiliation, I push back my half-eaten bowl of soup and stand up. "See you, Jack."

Walking to the back, I grab my purse and make my way through the dining room without so much as a glance in Jack Quinn's direction. "See you Monday, Nick!"

"Be on time," he calls. Poor Nick. He's so used to being in control, he can be a real pain at times.

"I'm a volunteer, Nick. Don't forget it."

"Well, don't be too late, then. And you be careful out there, princess. Don't talk to no one unless you know 'em, and . . . well, don't get sick."

"Okay, Nick. See you."

A blast of August heat slaps my cheeks the second I step

outside, and sweat starts to bead around my hairline before I've walked a block.

In moments, I hear footsteps running behind me. Instinct drives me to slip my hand inside my purse and prepare for battle. After an unfortunate pepper-spray incident where I doused the cable guy, I've given it up, but I do carry a travel-size aerosol hairspray that they say will work just as well.

At the first touch of a hand on my arm, I pull the miniature can from my purse in a flash and aim. At Jack?

"Wait, for heaven's sake!" His hand goes up to protect his eyes, and I'm really glad I hesitated for a split second. He recovers from the near panic quickly and scowls. "Put that away, will you?"

"I thought you were eating lunch." I stuff the hairspray back inside my purse.

He holds up a to-go bag. "I confess, I didn't come in for lunch per se. I actually wanted to see how you're getting along."

"And you assumed I'd be helping at the coffee shop? Are you psychic and never told me?" I'm way too predictable. If I didn't love Nick's place so much, I'd find another place to hang out.

"I knew you were going to say that." Jack smirks.

"Funny." But I do sort of give in and crack a smile. Sometimes a girl just can't help it.

"Seriously, I had an early morning game of racquetball with Kale. He suggested you might be helping Nick, since you've nothing else to do."

I'm not sure I like the way Jack said I have "nothing else to do." I mean, how does he know? Maybe I have lots to do. Maybe my schedule is so full, I needed the time off just to get caught up.

But then, he hangs around with Kale. And my brother has a big mouth.

"Well, as you can see, I'm getting along just fine." I look at him askance. "My new colleague is a definite step up from *anyone* I've ever worked with before. And he yells at me on a regular basis."

"I suppose I deserve that. Well, I mean I don't, but I suppose in your mind I do, so that amounts to about the same thing. In your mind, that is." That's English bumbling if I've ever heard it. And it's actually strangely charming. Confusing, but endearing in a Hugh Grant sort of way.

Oh, could I just stop it with the fluctuating emotions? I'm worse than Tallulah in Virgie's manuscript. We stop at a light, and I jab the "walk" button.

"I'm afraid I didn't make myself very clear, did I?"

"I have no idea what you're talking about."

He chuckles. "Neither do I, to be perfectly honest."

"Well, then. I guess we have nothing more to say." I send him a tight smile as the "walk" symbol flashes. "I'll probably see you around in a month or so." I lift up a hand of farewell, hoping he'll take the hint.

"I suppose . . ."

And I hurry across the street, fighting to keep myself from looking over my shoulder to see if he's following.

8

Valerie's heart melted at the sight of all the children. Twice a day they lined up for their meal of oatmeal or beans. Valerie spooned food into their dishes. Their smiles of gratitude would brighten even the darkest heart. And somewhere in those grins and giggles, Valerie began to heal, until she wondered if maybe there was a purpose to her life after all.
—An excerpt from *Fifth Avenue Princess*
by Dancy Ames

The next day at Nick's floats into another hectic day of volunteer work, and by the end of the week I'm more tired than I've ever been in my entire life. Even worse than cheerleading camp. Amazing how the body runs down after twelve years—that's how long it's been since I *rah-rah-rah*'d for anyone.

I slip into a pair of pink crop sweats from Victoria's Secret and a short-sleeved T-shirt, pull my hair into a ponytail, and settle in to spend a quiet night working on my manuscript. Not that I think in a million years it could ever be published. But it's nice to let my creative juices flow.

Tabby's got a cast party to celebrate *Legacy of Life*'s twenty-fifth anniversary on the air. Laini went to support her, leaving me the freedom to stay home.

The only problem with Laini slipping out to a party is that she isn't home to cook. I suppose I'll have to order takeout. Actually, I should probably skip supper and go for a run. Since I've been helping Nick, I've graduated from really tight size 2 jeans to a full-blown, form-fitting size 4. My body won't fit into a 2, no matter how far I suck in and squeeze. It's just not going to happen. But I have to say, at least I'm never hungry anymore.

I'm just about to pick up the phone to call Charlie's Chinese Emporium when the buzzer goes off, informing me I have company. I jump and run to the door. "Who is it?"

"Two hungry men here to take you out for chili dogs at the bowling alley, little sister." Kale! He must have brought Jack with him, hence the two hungry men.

My heart picks up like I just ran two miles (which, in all honesty, I should have). "Hang on a sec, Kale."

I hate to admit this, but the first thing I do is sprint to the closest mirror to check out my appearance. Oh, brother. Smeary makeup and a really ugly ponytail. I yank out my ponytail and immediately crazy curls spring out all over the place. I spritz my hair and smoosh my curls back in place, then douse them with finishing spray until my hair looks, if not good, at least acceptable. The buzzer goes off again. Three buzzes in a row.

That's so annoying. I hate persistent buzzing, especially when he knows full well I'm on my way. "Okay," I mutter and buzz them in.

I open the door to the sight of Kale and . . . oh, it's not Jack. It's my two brothers. Brandon and Kale. My disappointment at Jack's absence is disconcerting, to say the least. All I can do is stare at my brothers, both of them standing in the hallway with grins on their faces. Even Brandon. Well, "grin" might be a slight exaggeration. But at least he's not sneering.

"This is a surprise. What are you guys doing?"

Kale pushes in without an invitation. "Where are those gorgeous friends of yours? We men need a little eye candy this evening."

"I'm telling Brynn," I say to Kale.

"Fine, tell her at the bowling alley. She's waiting for us there."

"Bowling?" I can't help but reveal my distaste for the game.

Brandon sneers. "Figures. She thinks she's too good for bowling." He spins around and heads for the door. "Come on, bro. Let's leave her here."

"Bro?" Since when did these two bond? I give Kale a questioning eyebrow-raise and he smiles. "Brandon went to church with me Sunday and Wednesday night. Now he's going to the church-sponsored bowling night."

Wow, Kale accomplished a lot in a week and a half. Where have I been?

"That's, um, great, Brandon." I give him a thumbs-up.

He rolls his eyes. "Let me guess. You don't bowl or go to church."

"Well, not regularly, but I've really been thinking I should start."

"You have?" Kale says in that mocking tone I know so well from childhood. "Church or bowling?" Kale's lips twitch, and I want to sock him.

"Church." I resist the urge to stick out my tongue like I did at Jack.

Brandon grunts. "Sure."

"I *have*!"

I've never felt more like an outsider. Except, of course, when my dad revealed that I've had a brother I didn't know about for the last sixteen years. Other than that . . . Brandon and Kale have formed a bond that has nothing to do with me. So if I have to bowl to break into that bond and feel loved, I suppose that's what I have to do.

"All right," I say with a nod. "Give me a few minutes to get dressed."

Brandon's eyebrows push together. "You are dressed."

Kale sits on the couch and pulls Brandon with him. He plops his size 12 Nikes onto the coffee table, grabs the remote, and looks at our little brother. "One thing you'll have to learn about our sister. She never goes anywhere without the perfect outfit. So just relax and watch some baseball."

"Oh, brother."

"Stop rolling your eyes. One of these days, you'll find a girl, and you'll be glad she takes a little time to make herself presentable."

Brandon snorts. "I already got 'em lined up to go out with me. Besides, who are you trying to be presentable for? Last I heard, you haven't had a date in a long time."

My face is hot as I step down the hall. I'm horrified at how aptly the kid has spoken. My life summed up in Anne Klein and Versace. He's right. Who am I trying to impress? I stare down at my pink crop pants and make a hasty decision. Rummaging through my shoes, I find matching pink flip-flops, grab my Prada bag, and stomp down the hall to my two brothers.

"Well? What are you two lazy men waiting for? Let's go bowl. I'm dying for a chili dog."

I have to smile at the bewilderment pasted on Kale's face. But once the shock is over, he does something I've rarely seen him do. He nods in approval. As though I've passed some sort of test.

Part of me appreciates it. The other part—the independent career woman—wants to tell him I don't happen to need his approval. But mostly, I bask in the glory of, for once, gaining a nod from my big brother.

"So, Brandon," I say as we settle into Kale's car. (Personally, I think he should park the thing and take public transportation or walk, like 90 percent of New Yorkers do, but with his schedule at the hospital and always being on call, he's determined to keep his car.) "How is school going?"

"It's summer," he grunts.

My face goes hot. Isn't that the icebreaker adults are supposed to use to get kids talking?

"Oh. Well, how's your summer going?"

He deadpans a look my way. "My mom split for Jersey and I'm living with a dad who doesn't want me."

"Give her a break, Brandon," Kale says in my defense, just as I'm about to tell him to let me out so I can walk back home. "She's trying to get to know you."

"Could have fooled me."

"Never mind," I say to Kale. "I didn't mean to upset you, Brandon. The questions were only meant to be conversation starters." I rack my brain. "So you like Kale's church, huh?"

He shrugs. "It's okay. For church."

Kale swings a sideways glance at me, and I read it loud and clear: "Leave the kid alone."

I settle into the seat and decide to just keep my mouth shut for the rest of the trip.

When we reach the bowling alley, Kale finds a place to park and we head inside. He grabs my arm and holds me back as Brandon saunters in like he owns the place.

"Don't take anything he says personally," Kale says. "He's had it tough, growing up without us."

I scowl. "I know that. Do you think I'm honestly so self-centered that I can't see the hurt behind his machismo?"

Kale's eyes scan my face. I'm almost afraid of what he might say. "Maybe you're growing up."

And that's all he says as he opens the door. I'm too stunned to even protest or demand to know what he means by that. Instead, like the weenie I am, I slither inside the bowling alley.

They're playing Christian music, there's no smoking, and I don't hear one swearword. It's almost like it's not a real bowling alley.

"The church rented out the bowling alley for the night," Kale informs me as though reading my thoughts. "There's Brynn. Let's go."

My brother's fiancée lights up like a Chinese lantern the second she sees us and she waves wildly. I'm drawn by her warmth, and it's hard to hold on to my grudge that she's getting my apartment just for marrying Kale. She's just too nice. It's a wonder Kale ever found a girl like this. But I do have to admit, he's changed a lot over the last couple of years. He's a regular offering-giving churchgoer.

And don't get me wrong, I'm not completely against church. As a matter of fact, as previously stated, I've been there a few times with Tabby this year.

I select a bowling ball, and my arm practically falls out of its socket. Sheesh. "These things are heavy."

Brandon laughs. "Haven't you ever bowled?"

"Not much."

"Oh, boy. This is going to be like taking candy from a baby. Want to bet on the game? I could use a little extra cash."

"Very funny."

As it turns out, as long as I do a two-handed "granny bowl" I don't do too badly. Do I win? Not by a long shot, but Kale, Brynn, Brandon, and I eat cheese fries and chili dogs, drink tons of Diet Pepsi, and laugh our heads off.

Finally I excuse myself and walk toward the ladies' room. Nearby laughter grips my attention, and I turn to see a group of teens having a water fight. I smile. They're going to get it in about three and a half seconds. I turn back just in time to slam into a rock-hard chest. Male hands steady me.

My instinct is to fight. "Hey, watch where you're go—," but I look up into Jack Quinn's gorgeous face, "—ing."

"Sorry," he says, his face inches from mine, his hands wrapped around my arms.

"Wh-what are you doing here?" Why can't I catch my breath?

"Church bowling night." He's looking at me like . . . I don't know . . . like no one's ever looked at me before. What's he saying? "I was going to invite you earlier. But you rather ran off before I could ask, didn't you?"

"Oh." He isn't turning me loose, and I don't care at the moment. Someone shoves against me from behind and presses me even closer to Jack. He draws a quick breath, his gaze flickering to my lips and back to my eyes.

"Hey, when did my best chum's little sister become such a lovely young woman?" he asks, a combination of British accent and huskiness nearly sending me through the floor.

He slips his arm around me just as I hear a woman's voice.

"There you are, Jack. Oh, look, you've found Dancy."

Wh-what? No!

I try to shake myself from my stupor, and slowly the fog begins to fade. Clarity is returning, and with it a touch of embarrassment at how quickly my resolve took a dive at the merest hint of attention from this man.

It's a good thing I'm being interrupted, right?

Jack looks like he's been hit by a truck. My cousin Sheri's eyes are twinkling with laughter. "Is this how you treat your dates, Jack? As soon as my back is turned, he hits on my cousin."

"No he didn't," I speak up. "He wasn't watching where he was going and slammed into me. He was just taking me to get some air so I could catch my breath." Am I talking too fast? I am, aren't I?

"That's mostly true," he says drily. "Only I believe I was the victim of the so-called slamming incident."

"No. I'm sure it was the other way around," I insist through gritted teeth.

"No, my dear Dancy," he says with that boyish grin, "I'm afraid you're completely mistaken."

Sheri gives what can only be interpreted as a befuddled little laugh. "Neither of you can remember how she ended up in your arms?" she asks Jack. "I'm not sure I like that at all. I'm going to have to insist upon the truth immediately. Or I might throw a hissy fit right here in the middle of the bowling alley."

"Well," Jack says, "if you insist."

My throat goes dry. Is he going to almost kiss and tell? I can hear it now, all about how I was desperate for a kiss and he was going to take me outside to talk some sense into me. I'm outraged. What do they teach those British guys these days? They used to be such gentlemen.

I suck in a breath, ready to refute anything he says as he turns to Sheri. "The truth of the matter is that your lovely cousin was completely distracted and had no idea I was standing there. She slammed right into me, and I had no choice but to steady her. That is how she ended up in my arms. Not an entirely unpleasant experience, I might add."

Well, that's better than "pathetic cry for affection," I suppose.

Sheri gives a laugh. "No harm done. Right?" She slips her beautifully manicured hand through his arm and looks down at me from her five-eleven frame. Then her gaze shifts to over my shoulder.

"Oh, there's Kale and Brynn. And, oh my goodness, that must be my new little cousin." She turns to Jack. "Shall we go get introduced?"

"By all means." He turns to me, his eyes revealing much more than I want to see. "I apologize for bumping into you."

I put on what I hope is a convincingly nonchalant look. "Like Sheri said, no harm done."

I watch them walk away, and I have to admit I just told a fat lie. There was most definitely harm done. I'm in desperate jeopardy of falling for my brother's best friend, my annoying superior at work. Why does Jack Quinn have to be the man of my dreams? And why does Sheri have to keep showing up and being so beautiful?

As it turns out, Sheri is a much better bowler than I am. Something I use to my full advantage. Especially when Jack decides to be my knight in shining armor.

"Let me show you," he says. His warm arms encircle me, and for the first time in my life I'm glad I'm an utter failure at something. Even with his help, my ball lands in the gutter.

I turn to him and shrug. "Thanks anyway."

For the life of me, I can't get the knack of this game. Bowling escapes my understanding on any level above using granny moves to get the ball from my hands, down the lane, and more often than not, directly into the gutter.

Brandon shakes his head and scowls. "You're hopeless. Seriously, there's no hope for you. Give up this game and go back to tennis or whatever you rich girls play."

"Oh, Dancy doesn't play anything at all," Sheri chimes in. I think she's still a little peeved that Jack is so close to me.

I've never seen this catlike side of my cousin before. Probably because I've never been competition before. "All she does is work."

She grabs her ball and gives me a smile. Why have I never noticed those venomous fangs before? She takes her steps, one-two-three, and releases the ball—into the gutter. "Oops," she says with a fake laugh. She turns her enormous blue eyes on Jack. "Maybe you should show me too?"

Jack looks like a deer caught in headlights.

I move back and take a seat next to Brynn. "Are you going to let her get away with that?" she whispers, as Jack's arms encircle Sheri.

Kale must have overheard because he leans in and says to Brynn, "What are you talking about? Jack doesn't think about Dancy like that. She barely had the braces off her teeth when they met. He thinks she's a spoiled little girl." And, horror of horrors, he reaches out and ruffles my hair. "Just like I do."

The statement rips through me, and I jerk my head away from his apelike hand.

In Jack's arms, Sheri gets a strike. She squeals and turns, throwing herself at him shamelessly. "See what a good teacher you are?" she asks over his shoulder as she presses against him.

Unable to bear the cliché of an idiotic male being manipulated by a beautiful woman, I shove to my feet. "I'm getting another chili dog."

"I'll tell Mother," Kale says with a snicker.

I stick out my tongue just as Jack and Sheri rejoin the conversation.

Jack chuckles. "She really is a spoiled child, isn't she?" he says to Kale.

Kale flashes a glance to Brynn in one of those "I told you so" looks.

"Where are you going, Dancy?" Sheri calls.

"She's getting a chili dog," Brandon butts in. "Hang on, I'm coming with you."

"Be a love and bring me back a Diet Coke, will you?" Sheri is relentless.

I wave over my shoulder.

"Why are you letting her squeeze you out like that?" Brandon demands as soon as we plant ourselves at the back of the lengthy line.

"I don't know what you're talking about."

"Come on. Every time Jack Quinn gets close to you, she's all over him."

I just learned something new about my little brother. Two things, really. He's extremely observant, and he's on my side. The latter revelation makes me smile.

"She is his date, Brandon."

He shakes his head. "Uh-uh."

"Yes." I distinctly remember Sheri asking him if this is the way he treats his dates.

"Sheri came alone. I saw her come in. Jack was on the other side of the bowling alley, talking to you." He laughs. "You should have seen the look on her face when she saw the two of you."

Like I said, very observant kid.

My heart lifts at the news. "So, are you having a good time?"

He shrugs and gives me a half-grin. "Better than staying at Dad's."

The way he says "Dad's" hits me hard. I wonder how long it's going to take for me to get used to someone else calling him that.

It's our turn at the counter. "What can I get for ya?" The gum-chewing teenybop girl is looking straight at Brandon, her eyes glowing. He preens but tries to pretend he barely sees her as he makes his order.

Amazing, the power of male-female attraction. I'm feeling a little of that myself tonight.

Back at the table, I set Sheri's diet soda on the table in front of her. She reaches for her purse, but I wave it away. "It's on me."

Ignoring me, she lifts out a fifty-dollar bill and slides it across the table. How much does she think sodas go for these days? "Don't be silly, Dancy. I couldn't possibly let you pay when you're not working right now. We were just talking about your suspension."

My glare includes everyone at the table. "It's not exactly a suspension. I'm on a four-week vacation." I give her a pointed look. "Paid. So I can afford the Diet Coke." I push the bill back across the table and grab my chili dog to show her the topic is closed.

Only she isn't very good at taking a hint. "I insist, really. Remember my promotion?"

The reminder hits me just as a glob of chili lands on my light pink tee. I think she orchestrated the whole thing just to humiliate me.

"That's great, Sheri," I say, standing with as much dignity as I can possibly muster. "Congratulations."

"Thank you, cousin." She pulls out a Tide stick and hands it to me.

I want to refuse, but of course, I don't.

"I'll be back," I mumble, completely defeated. My gaze sweeps the group and lands on Jack.

A little frown creases his brow as he stares back at me. I don't blame him. It's no wonder he still sees me as Kale's dumb little sister. At this moment, that's exactly how I feel.

9

How was it that John Quest showed up everywhere Valerie happened to be? It was one thing in Chicago, when their paths were likely to cross at an event or something job related, but there was no question in Valerie's mind as she stared across the pavilion where the children ate and there he was, standing tall and strong and staring straight back at her—he was following her. But how could she forgive him? If it weren't for him, she'd still be working in the field she loved.

He covered the distance between them in a few long strides, until they stood face-to-face. When he looked at her, she felt beautiful.

—An excerpt from *Fifth Avenue Princess*
by Dancy Ames

aini and Tabby make it home from the cast party twenty minutes after I get back. They bring cheesecake from Nick's, so we sit together at the table and rehash our evening. Tabby and David danced with the twins, and Laini got hit on by the new guy on the set, who has a recurring role as a tough guy who mugs Tabby's character, Felicia Fontaine.

"So? Are you going to go out with him?" I ask, glad to keep the attention off myself for the moment.

Laini shrugs. "I said we could have coffee sometime."

Tabby smiles. "Jeremy is really sweet. He's perfect for you."

"So," Laini says to me. "What did you do all evening? Get a lot of writing done?" I've sworn Tabby and Laini to secrecy about my novel, but they can't help asking about it.

I'm tempted to lie, but before I can form my thoughts into a good fib, I spill the whole thing. Everything from bowling to Jack Quinn saying I'm a "lovely young woman" to Sheri showing her claws to the glob of chili that didn't come out, even with the Tide stick.

Tabby lets out a low whistle. "You think you would have kissed him if Sheri hadn't interrupted?"

I frown and shake my head firmly. "I don't think so. We would have talked for a few minutes, and then he would have reminded himself that I'm a subordinate at work." Glumly, I spoon cheesecake into my mouth. "I don't want to talk about him anymore."

My friends stare at me for a second.

"What?" I say. "I mean it. Let's talk about something else."

"Okay, then we'll talk about me," Laini says, enthusiasm lilting her voice. "Guess what?"

"You got a good grade in one of your classes?"

She rolls her eyes. "Don't I wish? This is even better. Wait'll you hear this."

"Tell us!" I toss a napkin at her.

She deflects it easily with a bubble of laughter. "The cinnamon rolls went over so well the other day that Nick wants me to bake two dozen every day next week. If they sell, he wants to make it a permanent arrangement."

A genuine smile splits my face. "Laini, that's fabulous. The last two days we've sold out in an hour, so two dozen are going to sell easily. Congratulations."

She sighs. "It makes me feel good to be contributing some-thing."

Poor Laini. Her self-esteem has really taken a beating lately, between getting laid off at the accounting firm and doing so poorly in interior design school. Baking has become cathartic for her. I'm glad she's going to be able to profit from it. And it won't hurt to have the apartment smelling of yummy baked treats all the time, either.

"I have an announcement too," Tabby speaks up.

"Finally set a wedding date?" I ask sardonically, slipping an-other forkful of sweet cheesecake into my mouth. I really *must* go running tomorrow. No excuses!

"Yes!" Tabby bounces in her chair like a giggly teen.

Laini and I gasp. I was just kidding. With their busy sched-ules, I was beginning to doubt Tabby was ever actually going to become David's wife.

"When?"

"The Saturday after Christmas." She grins. "Think you can make it? I have a couple of bridesmaid spots open." Her sister, of course, will be matron of honor.

"I wouldn't miss it for anything, Tab," Laini says, sniffling like this is the first she's heard that Tabby's getting married. The girl's been engaged for months.

"A Christmas wedding!" I say, jubilant at my friend's happiness.

"Technically, after Christmas. We didn't want to take any chances on our family and friends not being able to make it. But we're still going with Christmas colors."

Laini gives a groan. "Are you kidding me? Red?" Laini's freckled skin and red hair don't mix well with red clothes.

We turn to her, and silence reigns supreme for a second as we consider the implication. I give a mock gasp. "Tabs! We aren't wearing Mrs. Claus costumes, are we?"

"Don't give me any ideas. You know we actresses can't bear it if anyone looks prettier than we do. And you will most certainly be the two most gorgeous women present." She turns to me. "Dancy, with that dark hair and dark skin, in a red shimmering gown."

Laini groans again.

"And you, my friend," Tabby says with a tender smile, "will be just as beautiful in a gown of deep green. Shelly is going to wear green as well, and the flower girl—my sweet Jenn, of course—will wear red to match you, Dan." She takes a nervous breath and looks at us for approval. "Well?"

"Perfect," Laini utters. "I would have worn the red for you, but thank God you're going to put me in green."

I have always sworn I'll never do the bridesmaid thing. But for Tabby I'll make an exception, and for Laini too, I suppose, when the time comes.

Even the most independent of girls can't help but get caught up in romance when her best friend is planning the wedding of her dreams. We talk late into the night, dreaming and hoping and imagining what sort of day it will be when the first of the three of us walks down the aisle. Three different bride magazines rotate between us as we ooh and ahh over decorations, flowers, and of course, gowns.

I slip into bed, floating on a cloud, dreaming of another wedding. One where I get to be the one in white. I'm not telling who the groom is. Seriously, my lips are sealed.

I manage to stay awake long enough for the preacher to say, "You may now kiss the bride . . ."

Nick has hired two employees, so I'm off the hook as far as working at the coffee shop on a regular basis. I still find myself gravitating toward Nick's for coffee every day, though. I just can't stand to be alone in that apartment with nothing to do. So during extremely busy times, I still hop up to bus a table every now and then.

Today they seem to have everything under control, so I pull out Granny's Bible. Somewhere around Leviticus I gave up on my ironclad rule of never reading a book out of sequence. I doubt even the most devout of believers could read that book without falling asleep. I have to say, I'm fascinated with the romantic portions of the Bible, though. Isaac and Rebekah, Jacob and Rachel, Ruth and Boaz, Hosea and Gomer. The Bible is an amazingly romantic book.

Every time Nick passes by to refill my coffee cup, he gives me a proud nod and a smile. Finally, after the rush is over, he drops a plate with a chicken salad wrap on the table in front of me. "Eat up, princess."

"I didn't order this, Nick."

"I know, but you gotta eat. And besides, I still owe you a lot."

I smile. "Thanks, Nick. I'll take the wrap, but you know you don't owe me a thing. I was glad to do it."

The chair across from me scrapes along the floor as Nick pulls it out and sits. "I notice you been reading the Bible."

"My granny left it to me when she died." I take a bite of my glorious chicken salad wrap. Mayo and onion burst into my mouth, and I'm in heaven. "This is so good, Nick. You're the best."

"Don't change the subject. I want to talk about this new Bible-reading phase."

"Okay. Sorry." I gulp down a mouthful of 2 percent milk.

"Does this mean you believe in Jesus?"

I stop at the way he phrased the question. There's never

been any question of belief. "It's always been more of a trust issue than a belief issue for me, Nick."

"Trust? How can you do anything but trust God? He's so big and powerful."

"I know, but I need to know why He doesn't always use His power for everyone. It's almost like He plays favorites."

"What do you mean?"

"Well, you know how Kale got the condo?" Why can't I just let that go?

Nick leans forward, resting his massive forearms on the table. "Yeah, I remember."

"It feels like my parents favored him over me by giving him the condo just because he's getting married first."

"What's that got to do with God playing favorites?" Nick turns toward the kitchen. "'Ey, you two stop playing around and finish cleaning up."

"Sorry, Mr. Pantalone."

He shakes his head when he turns back to me. "Kids. Both of 'em put together can't measure up to you."

I can't help but laugh. I've suddenly risen on Nick's list of employees. "Be patient. They'll get better."

"Can't get any worse, that's for sure." But his face splits with a smile. "Now, back to what we were saying."

I could kick myself for bringing up the issue of trust versus belief in God. "It's really not worth discussing, Nick. Really, I don't want to bore you."

"Don't try to skirt around this, princess," he says with a stern frown. "You brought it up, so let's get it out and talk it over. If there's one thing I can't let slide by, it's anyone calling God a liar."

My eyes go wide. "Nick! I never did that."

"You said you didn't trust Him. That's the same as saying He isn't trustworthy."

"Okay, let's suppose I *am* saying that." I lean back and cross one leg over the other, swinging my foot a little to bolster my courage. "Okay, I used to pray that my dad would pay attention to me."

"What's that got to do with God's promises?"

I shrug. "I don't know. I guess I just felt like if I asked God for help, He might help my dad love me a little."

"Your dad loves you, princess."

I give a short laugh. "How do you know that?"

Nick gives me such a long and serious stare that I'm about to look away when he says, "You want to know how I know your dad loves you?"

Silently, I nod.

"Because, princess, any man would be proud to have a daughter like you. He can't help but love you."

My jaw goes slack. Nick winks and looks like he's about to say something more when a crash from the kitchen turns his smile into a scowl. "What happened? These kids are going to kill me."

"Thanks, Nick."

He waves away my thanks and hauls himself back to the kitchen.

I'm still basking in the glow of Nick's praise when my cell phone vibrates against my hip and nearly scares me out of my skin. I look down and recognize the number for Lane Publishing. My heart lifts, because it's the first time in almost three weeks I've seen that number. "This is Dancy," I say.

"Hi, Dancy. It's Crystal." Jack's assistant.

"Hi, Crys, is everything all right?"

"Jack asked me to call and schedule an appointment with you."

"What about?"

"I really don't have a clue. You know how Jack is."

"All right. When does he want me to come in?"

"Uh, actually, he'd like to meet for dinner. Are you available this evening?"

"Like a date?" Oh, darn. Of course not like a date. Jack has dinner meetings all the time. "Scratch that. I don't know why I even said it. I know better."

Crystal laughs. "Don't worry about it. I understand."

I give an inward groan. And I feel I must defend myself. "Truly, Crys. I was just going to say there's no way I'm meeting him for a date. Then I realized he meant a dinner appointment. Believe me," I say in a way-too-desperate tone, "Jack Quinn is definitely not my type."

"Sure he's not. Because perhaps you're not breathing."

I can see there will be no convincing her that I'm not panting for her boss, so I simply try to recover as much dignity as I can under the circumstances. "Where would Jack like to meet for dinner tonight?"

"He said Morton's Steakhouse on Fifth Avenue. Do you need directions?"

"No, we've been there before." It's a favorite of Jack's. "What time?"

"Looks like reservations are for eight. Will that work?"

"He was pretty sure I'd say yes, wasn't he?"

"I doubt he's too familiar with women saying no."

She's probably right about that.

I glance at my watch. I have exactly five hours to go home, scour my closet for something to wear, shower, shave my legs, and hop on the subway for my evening with Jack.

"Hey, Nick," I say after hanging up. "I have to go."

"Remember what I said, princess."

What he said? Oh, right. My dad loves me. "Thank you." I slip Granny's Bible into my Louis Vuitton handbag and leave listening to Nick hollering at his new help. My lips curve into a smile. I can imagine how those poor kids feel.

My curiosity is almost overwhelming as I stand in front of the closet thirty minutes later, trying to find something suitable that Jack hasn't seen me wear a hundred times. "Stop it!" I say out loud. "This is Jack Quinn we're talking about, and this is not a date. It's business."

Refusing to allow myself one more second's thought about it, I reach in and grab a nice, appropriate Ralph Lauren suit. It's black and businesslike. Resisting the temptation to wear a lacy camisole under the jacket, I choose a simple white silk blouse instead. I will not have it said that I tried to flirt with Jack by dressing up for our date—I mean, business dinner.

I finish dressing way too early to leave and have to fight the urge to binge on last night's leftovers. By the time Tabby wanders through the door at five thirty, I've been working on my book for a good thirty minutes.

I glance up from my laptop. "You're home early."

"Yep. I'm staying home tonight. The twins have been out late every night this week and are very cranky. David is going to keep them in and put them to bed early. Besides, I need to go over lines for a new story line they've concocted." She gives me a twinkle-eyed smile. "I get to play my evil twin for the next few months."

"I didn't know Felicia Fontaine had a twin."

Tabby waggles her eyebrows and slips off her shoes at the door. "She does now."

I laugh. You gotta love the soaps. They kill people off, bring them back to life, give birth to babies, and three years later, when the story line dictates, age them to teenagers. They can do anything, and soap fans blink and accept. Try that with a book series and readers howl.

Tabby gives me a once-over. "Where are you going?"

"I have a business dinner later." I can't bring myself to tell her who I'm meeting. The omission sort of hangs out there in the silence until Tabby has had enough.

"Are you being evasive on purpose, or do you genuinely think my curiosity gene has suddenly mutated into a to-each-his-own gene?"

I give a resigned sigh. "Jack Quinn's assistant called to set up a dinner appointment."

"For Jack?"

"Who else?"

Tabby frowns and takes a seat next to me. "What do you think he wants?"

My stomach flips at the question. It's the same one that has been swirling around in my head for hours, so it isn't as though it's something new. But hearing the words voiced this close to the time when I'll find out fills me with butterflies. "I honestly don't know."

"Not even an idea?" she presses.

I'm afraid to address my suspicions, but Tabby isn't going to go away, so I give voice to my hopes. "Jimmy applied for the senior editor position at Stark Publishing."

"Isn't that the exact same position he already has? Why would he leave without advancement?"

"Stark is more about nonfiction, which is Jimmy's first love, and we're scaling back on nonfiction."

"And you think they might want you for his job?"

I shrug one shoulder, afraid to say it out loud for fear of jinxing the whole thing.

Tabby smiles and pats my knee. "No one deserves that spot

more than you. That's for sure." She glances at the computer. "Writing?"

I nod, suddenly feeling timid. I close the computer screen.

"All right. I can take a hint," Tabby says. "But I'd better get to play the heroine when someone buys the movie rights."

"Yeah, sure. I'm never even going to send it anywhere."

She rolls her eyes and stands. "What a waste of a perfectly good book."

"For all you know, it stinks."

"No it doesn't."

My suspicious nature rears at the confidence in her tone. "Have you been reading it, too?"

"Of course not! And don't accuse Laini of anything. I know she read part of it, but that was innocent and you know it."

"I know. I'm sorry. I guess I'm just nervous about this dinner tonight."

"Relax. You have more talent in your little finger than anyone I know. Even if this dinner doesn't turn out the way you hope it will, you're still an editor at a publishing company you love and you're writing a fabulous book."

I open my mouth to remind her that it might stink when she holds up her hand to shush me. "The reason I know it's wonderful is because you know a good book when you see one. You know good writing, and you couldn't possibly produce a manuscript that isn't something a publisher would die to contract. And don't argue."

How does she do that? With a few short sentences she makes me feel like the smartest, most accomplished person on earth. Oh, now I know. . . . She's an actress.

"You're paid to sound sincere."

Tabby rolls her eyes. "You're hopeless. I'm going to go shower. If you're gone when I get out, I'll see you later to rehash. I wonder if Laini's coming home to cook, or if I have to fend for myself." She grins. "I guess if we didn't love her so much, we could be accused of using her, couldn't we?"

I watch her leave, then turn my attention back to my computer, but words elude me. So much for my amazing talent. I close the laptop screen and glance over at Granny's Bible instead. I don't pick it up; still, the one quote I know by heart comes to mind: "Trust in the Lord. . . ."

Trust. Weird, I never put my admission to Nick about trust together with this scripture. I can't help but wonder if this is a coincidence, or if God truly is interested in my life after all. Something to explore, for sure. Later.

It's still light out at six forty-five when I step onto the sidewalk and start the two-block walk to the subway station. I notice a black car at the curb but don't think much about it. After all, there aren't too many thugs sitting around in black town cars in broad daylight. Well, maybe there are, but I don't ever notice them. But as I walk, the car follows. My heartbeat starts to pick up speed. Slowly, I reach into my bag and wrap my fingers around the travel-size can of hairspray. I poise myself for defense in the event of an attack.

"Dancy, whatever are you doing?"

Jack?

I whip around to find him seated in the backseat of the car, his window rolled down as he stares up at me with bewilderment washing over his features.

I stop. "I was headed to the subway to meet you for dinner."

"Didn't Crystal mention I'd be arriving around seven o'clock to fetch you?"

To fetch me? Am I a stick and he's a dog? Oh, well. That's not a line of thought I need to follow. Just answer the question. "No, she said you wanted to meet for dinner to discuss business."

Irritation flashes in his eyes, but only briefly. He steps out of the car and moves aside for me to slide in. "I'm terribly sorry for the misunderstanding."

"Don't be. I'm sure Crystal assumed we'd meet at the restaurant, since this is not a date."

"I suppose."

We engage in small talk for the first half of the trip. How's your mum and dad? Did you have coffee at Nick's today? And so on. Finally, I can stand the suspense no longer.

"It's going to be another fifteen or twenty minutes in this traffic," I say. "Would you prefer to go ahead and discuss whatever's on your mind?"

He gives me a half-smile. "I never discuss business on an empty stomach."

I roll my eyes. "Okay, then. I guess we'll wait until after you've had a few bites of filet mignon. Then we can talk business."

"We will discuss business after we've had our dessert and are enjoying a cup of coffee."

I give a huff and cross my legs. "Why have a business dinner if you don't want to actually discuss business over dinner?"

"That's a valid question. I'm not sure I have an answer." He leans in a little, and I catch the subtle scent of Polo cologne against clean-shaven skin. I fight the urge to shiver as a heady sensation washes over me. "Perhaps," he says, "I was hoping you might consider this a date."

Oh, be still my beating heart. I know he's not a bit serious, and I can't let him think I'm naive enough not to understand that he's just being facetious. "I rarely accept dates from men who ask me through their assistants."

"Interesting." He grins. "I'll have to remember to call you myself next time."

I give him a wry smile. "Yes, do that."

His eyebrows go up, but the car pulls to a stop in front of our restaurant. The driver opens my door and I slide out. Jack follows me, his warm palm heating up the small of my back, not to mention making me a little weak in the knees as we enter the restaurant.

Dinner is more small talk, and I realize I know virtually nothing about Jack's life. Kale rarely discusses Jack beyond the casual passing comment. "Where exactly are you from in England, Jack?"

"London. My parents own a little pub. Prince William even ate there a few times."

I give him an impressed smile. "Exciting."

"My nieces were all aswoon."

"Nieces? I didn't know you had any."

He pulls a billfold from his coat pocket and proudly displays school pictures of two cute teens—one with braces, one slightly older. "Pretty."

"Yes. They know it, too. Get their looks from my sister." He flips the picture to the next one. "That's Lizzie. She's two years younger than I am."

"Beauty must run in your family," I muse absently.

"I'll take that as a compliment."

My eyes go wide, and I jerk my head up as I realize I just told Jack I think he's beautiful. I can only imagine. But there is no trace of teasing in his eyes. He is, however, scrutinizing me intently.

His gaze makes me uncomfortable. "What?"

"Forgive me for staring. But beauty also runs in your family."

Pleasure swells my chest, and I take in a deep breath.

"Thanks, Jack. That's nice of you." Then a thought strikes me. What if he's including Sheri in the mix?

The waiter arrives with our salads just in time to save me from making a complete idiot of myself, which I inevitably would have done.

One thing I have to say about Jack: he's skilled in small talk and in making a person feel good about herself. I guess that's why I'm caught off guard as the waiter brings our coffee, clears our dinner and dessert plates, and Jack folds his hands on the table.

"I suppose it's time to get down to business now."

The way he says it fills me with dread.

Wretched man! Wretched, wretched man! And he calls himself a gentleman. All that suave, sophisticated British charm. Nothing but a ploy to lull Americans into a false sense of security. We let our defenses down, and whammo! He lands the big punch.

I have to warn my brother. His best friend is nothing more than a wolf in sheep's clothing, ready to pounce when least expected. I couldn't care less about severance packages. I don't need the money. This is about me finally doing something for myself. Something I can feel good about. Something I thought I was good at, until Jack Quinn came along and destroyed my self-esteem, and now my career.

10

Fool, Valerie chided herself. *You're nothing but a fool.* Tears streamed down her face. Tears of anger, humiliation, heartbreak. How could she have ever thought John Quest loved her? She let down her guard and he used her vulnerability against her.

And now she was left with nothing . . . absolutely nothing.

—An excerpt from *Fifth Avenue Princess*
by Dancy Ames

take the subway. Preferable by far to sharing a car with Benedict Arnold. When I get home, Brandon is sitting on the step. "Hey, what are you doing here?"

"I got into an argument with Dad. Can I stay here tonight? Kale's at the hospital."

"Why didn't you ring the buzzer? Tabby's home. Probably Laini, too, by now."

"They said you weren't here."

"They didn't ask you to come in?"

"Yeah, I just didn't want them asking questions and acting weird. I said I wasn't staying."

I unlock the door. "Well, let's go in. I'll have to call Dad, but I'm sure you can spend the night on the couch."

Truthfully, I'm relieved to have something else to focus my mind on.

I open the door just wide enough to stick my head in before I walk in with a teenage boy. "Everyone decent? My little brother's here."

"We're in the kitchen."

The apartment smells like chocolate. I grin at Brandon. "Smells like Laini's been baking. This is your lucky night."

We head into the kitchen, and sure enough, a wonderful-looking chocolate cake is sitting in the middle of the table with a chunk missing. "Girls, this is Brandon. My little brother."

"Younger brother," he corrects.

Tabby and Laini grin at him. "Nice to meet you, Brandon," Tabby says.

Laini stands. "Sit down. I'll bring some more plates and forks."

"This looks good," I say. "But I'd better pass. Jack forced me to share a chocolate mousse and I'm stuffed."

"How was dinner?" Tabby asks.

"Hang on. I need to call my dad about Brandon. And I'm going to change my clothes."

"Go ahead," Laini says. "We'll get to know Brandon."

I put in a quick call to Dad and find out he's more than happy to get Brandon out of his hair. They had quite an argument about Brandon moving to Florida with them. Brandon says no. Apparently Mary is glad to have him out of her hair, too. According to Dad, she's turned the poor boy over to him, claiming she's raised him for sixteen years and now it's Dad's turn.

My heart goes out to Brandon as I slip into a comfortable pair of white yoga pants and a pink T-shirt. When I enter the kitchen, he looks up with eyes full of questions.

"Dad says you can hang out here tonight."

His face reveals his relief. "Good, because I wasn't going back there."

"Do you want to talk about it now, or wait?"

"Maybe I don't have anything to say about it."

Laini and Tabby exchange glances and pull the stretch-and-yawn routine. "Boy, am I tired," Laini says.

Tabby stands and rinses her plate, then slides it into the dishwasher. "I have lines to learn."

"Good night, guys."

Tabby nods. "We'll talk tomorrow, Brandon."

Laini gives him a smile. "I'll fix breakfast."

"G'night," he says around a large bite of cake.

When they're gone, I focus on him. "Okay. Dad says he wants you to go to Florida with him and my mom. Why don't you want to move to paradise?"

He gives a short laugh into his milk glass, swallows a drink, then sets it on the table. I cringe as he wipes his mouth with the back of his hand. "I already live in paradise."

I can't argue with him there. And I'm gratified to find a kindred spirit who shares my blood. Mother, Dad, and Kale are all dying to leave New York. Of course Kale's stuck here, but he'd rather be on a farm somewhere. It's just beyond comprehension.

"You have my sympathy. But you could always come back after you graduate."

"Don't worry, I will. For sure. Only, I'm supposed to start at Juilliard's precollege program next month."

"What? Brandon, that's incredible. What do you play?"

"Piano." He shrugs, and I see pain in his face. "But it doesn't matter. If Mom doesn't want me living with her anymore, and Dad's gone to Florida, I'm sunk."

"Wait. Dad and your mother know you were accepted to Juilliard, and they aren't doing everything in their power to let you go?" I shouldn't have blurted that out. But quite frankly, I'm livid. It's an amazing feat to be accepted into the prestigious school for drama, music, and dance. And to be accepted and then not allowed to attend, even in the precollege program, is unacceptable.

"Brandon, I understand how upset you are." I sit there, wishing I had anything to offer my brother that might help his pain. Then I remember the Bible verse. "Listen. You've been going to church with Kale, right?"

Brandon nods. "Gives me something to do."

"Well, I don't go to church, but I've been reading my granny's old Bible, and I have a verse that might help. Hang on a sec."

I go to my room and lift the Bible from my nightstand, where I put it earlier, before my dinner with Jack (that I do not want to think about).

Brandon is downing the last of his milk when I return.

I open the Bible to Proverbs even though I know the passage by heart. It just seems like it will pack more of a punch if I read it.

"You ready?" I ask.

He shrugs. "I guess."

"Trust in the Lord with all thine heart; and lean not unto thine own understanding. In all thy ways acknowledge him, and he shall direct thy paths."

When I finish, I look up. Brandon is staring at me with a blank expression, and I know he either wasn't listening at all or doesn't get it.

"It's saying that if you trust God to lead you and don't try to figure things out by yourself, He'll direct you in the way you're supposed to go."

I'm not positive, but I think I see a little bit of a nod.

"All right, kid," I say. "Let's get the couch made up for you."

I get him all set up, then make my way down the hall to Tabby and Laini's room. Light shines out from underneath the door, so I give a little tap. "Can I come in?" I open the door a crack.

"Yes," Laini says, waving me inside. She's lying down with a book. "Is Brandon all tucked in?"

I can't help but grin. "Well, I didn't tuck him in, but he's settled in for the night. Thanks, you guys, for letting him sleep over." I quickly relay the conversation with Dad and Brandon.

"Wow," Tabby says. "I can't imagine a parent not sacrificing almost anything so a child could attend that school. Even the precollege program. It would only be for one year, right? Maybe your folks will put off the move if you explain how important this is for his future."

"I'm going to Dad's tomorrow night. Maybe I can explain it in such a way that he'll really get it." But I'm not holding my breath.

Tabby is sitting up in bed with pages on her lap. "Okay, Dan. We're dying to know about your dinner with Jack."

I flop down at the end of her bed. "Don't ask. You aren't going to believe it." I pause. "They've decided that, instead of scaling back on nonfiction, they're going to scale back on fiction instead. Not much, but enough so that my job is gone." My voice breaks at the admission. I thought a four-week vacation was horrible. But looking into my future without Lane Publishing is dismal, to say the least.

Laini sits up on her bed. "Dancy, I'm so sorry."

"That Jack guy actually took you out to dinner to let you know you're being fired?" Tabby's voice is filled with outrage.

I shrug. "At least I got dinner out of it."

Laini pulls her legs in to sit cross-legged. "That's good! You're accentuating the positive. I can think of another bright side."

Tabby groans and tosses a throw pillow at her. "Bright side?"

"Yes! Now Dancy can finish her book." She looks at me. "It's not like you need the money. Take some time off. You always work way too hard anyway."

"I've been off almost three weeks! I'm going crazy."

"There are all kinds of opportunities for you in the city, Dancy," Tabby says. "You'll find another job soon."

"Or you could finish your book."

"Maybe I will." Dejected, I stand. "'Night, guys."

As I lie in bed and stare at the ceiling, I can't help but ask, "Is this what trusting You gets me?"

When I step into my dad's condo the next night, I'm shocked by the changes my mother has already made. There is not one trace of animal prints anywhere that I can see. Not even in his office, where he takes me after Brandon stalks off to his room.

My dad gives a vehement shake of his head while I try to explain how horrible it would be for him to deny Brandon the opportunity to go to Juilliard. "Princess, my hands are tied. I've already sold my practice here, and I start at a clinic in Destin in February. It's too late to change it now. Brandon will have a lot of opportunities. And there's no reason to believe he won't be accepted to the college program for the following year. He's a gifted musician."

Is that a hint of pride I hear in my dad's voice? Maybe I can work with that. "Dad, do you honestly want to put this between you and Brandon? Think about it. For all intents and purposes, his mother is abandoning him. And now you're going to deny him this amazing, once-in-a-lifetime opportunity? There must be a way."

"I don't see it, princess. If I did, I'd let him stay. Precollege students don't live on campus. They have to stay with a parent or guardian and live in the city. Those are the rules. Believe me, I've already looked into it. I don't want to disappoint him either."

It amazes me that he doesn't want to disappoint, yet he always seems to do just that. He didn't want to disappoint Mother, yet he couldn't—or wouldn't—stop cheating on her. He didn't want to disappoint Kale, and yet a plastic-surgeon convention in Hawaii took precedence over Kale's graduation from medical school. Oh, and he didn't want to disappoint me either. But never once in all of my growing-up years did he come to a game I cheered at, a pageant I competed in, or any important moment in my life. Mother says he wasn't even there at my birth. Too busy playing in a very important golf tournament, so she says. I'm guessing "golf" is code for "another woman."

Nick's words come back to my mind. "Any man would be proud to have a daughter like you."

A short laugh escapes me, and Dad's brow creases. "You okay?"

"Yeah, Dad." I grab my purse from a wingback chair. "I have to go home. Tomorrow I have to redo my résumé and start sending it out."

"You looking for a new job?"

"Yeah." For some reason I can't keep a smile from my lips. "I got fired. Imagine that."

"What happened? What did you do?"

"Not a thing. Blame it on downsizing." I sling my purse over my shoulder. "Spend some time with Brandon, Dad. He needs you right now. Disappointment is hard to take when you're a kid."

When I step out of his office, I'm greeted by the unmistakable sound of Jack's British accent. Dread hits me full in the stomach. He's standing in the foyer, chatting with Kale and Mother.

"What are you doing here?" I blurt out.

"Dancy!" Mother says, her tone tight with admonishment.

"It's quite all right, Mrs. Ames." He stares at me, not smiling, but watching. Waiting, I suppose, to see if I'm going to make a scene. Which I most certainly am not.

"Jack has graciously agreed to help Kale move some furniture into storage before the movers bring the furniture from my apartment tomorrow."

For a minute I forget about Jack's betrayal and face my mother. "You're already turning the apartment over to Brynn and Kale?"

"Really, darling," Mother says. "I told you I was going to, so Brynn can decorate to her taste before the wedding."

I can feel Jack's eyes on me, and it's disconcerting, to say the least. "That's right, I forgot. Well, I guess I'll leave you all to your furniture moving."

"Shall I call you a cab?"

I shake my head. "I'll take the subway." I give Jack a pointed look. "I'm trying to save money."

Jack stares at me, his former stoic look giving way to a frown. "Do you honestly think you should take the Tube alone this time of night?"

"It's barely seven. I think I'll be okay."

"Really, Dancy. Jack is right. Call a taxi."

"Everyone rides the subway, Mother," Kale says. "She'll live through it, I'm sure. It's not even dark."

"Thank you, Kale." I guess I could take a cab. Now I'm just being stubborn. "Mother, Jack, I appreciate your concern. The subway will be fine." I kiss my mother on the cheek.

"You're as stubborn as your father." She shakes her head but doesn't dwell on it. "I'll talk to you in a day or two." Never one to stay with a single topic for long, she immediately turns to Kale. "Let me show you where to start."

"I'll be right with you, Kale," Jack says. Instead of following my mother, he follows me to the door. "Dancy, wait. Please."

"What?" I say, not very nicely now that Mother has left the room.

"If you insist upon taking the Tube, at least allow me to escort you to the station."

My heart does a little dance inside my chest as he touches my elbow just like a real live gentleman.

"It's not necessary, Jack."

"Perhaps you could simply humor me, then."

I can see he's going to be stubborn. I give a little wave. "Fine, do whatever you want."

"Wonderful." His chest rings. Well, no. Not his chest, obviously. "Blast," he mutters, reaching into his jacket pocket. He gives it a quick glance. "I need to take this. Pardon me for just a moment, won't you?"

He speaks softly, but I can't help overhearing. "Sheri. I was just about to call you. I'm afraid something's come up and I won't be able to meet you for coffee later after all. You will forgive me, I hope."

Sheri? As in my model-beautiful cousin with the legs that won't quit? My heart drops into my stomach.

"I changed my mind," I whisper. "I don't need an escort. See you, Jack." I slip through the door, hoping he won't follow. But of course he does.

"Wonderful," he says into the phone. "I'll be looking forward to it. Good-bye." He slips his cell back into his pocket. "I'm dreadfully sorry about that."

"Don't be. I couldn't care less."

"Listen, Dancy. I've been thinking about you all day. I'm so sorry I was forced to be the one to break the news to you. Tell me, how are you getting along today?"

Hot tears spring to my eyes. "I'm getting along splendidly," I say in a really poor British accent. There's no point in pretending the tears aren't there. He's seen them, and to deny them would just be idiotic and immature. So I go in a different direction—sarcasm. "I woke up yesterday on vacation"—I put air quotes around "vacation"—"and today I woke up jobless. How else would I be getting along, if not splendidly?"

He fishes a handkerchief from his pocket (who still does that?) and gently wipes my tears. Something about the gesture makes me want to cry all the more. So I do.

And suddenly he wraps his arms about me—in a brotherish way, of course. "I do wish things had worked out differently, my dear. I know it was an abominable thing for me to do. But I was simply given no choice. Tony insisted."

I jerk back and stare into his face. "What do you expect me to say to that? 'Oh, I see. It really wasn't your fault at all'?"

His gaze darkens, and he stuffs the hanky into my hand. "I don't expect a thing from you. But you seem so distraught, I thought it might help to know I had no control over the incident."

The incident. I can't believe he has the audacity to minimize the upending of my entire life to something as trivial as an "incident." I give a short laugh but don't even bother to address the comment.

"Why are you walking so fast?" Jack asks, scurrying to keep up.

Anger tends to kick my steps into high gear, and now is no exception. I've picked up the pace so much, I'm practically jogging.

"I don't want to miss the top of the hour. No sense waiting an extra ten minutes if I don't have to."

"All right then."

I stop at the top of the steps and eye him. "I loved my job, Jack. It was the only real thing in my life besides my two best friends."

"Wait, Dancy."

I turn back to him, hip out, hand resting there as I stare at him with all the attitude I can muster. "What?"

His face reddens, and he clears his throat. "It's just that I hope—well, I was wondering really—when you've seen reason and realize—"

"Look, what's with the Hugh Grant routine? Just say whatever it is you're trying to say, will you? I have a train to catch."

"I was wondering . . ." He holds my gaze and I'm starting to think . . . no! He's not even thinking . . . "Well, I was hoping really," he says, "that you might have dinner with me."

Is he kidding? "I don't think so. Bye, Jack," I toss over my shoulder, just before getting lost in the crowd of commuters. I mean, really. How can he even ask? The last time he took me to dinner, he fired me. I shudder to think what he might come up with for an encore. Dinner! I am so sure!

I repeat the entire conversation once I get home to my friends. "And then he had the nerve to ask me out!"

"That's the most horrible thing I've heard in ages," Laini sympathizes, her voice so sincere that I have to fight to keep from bursting into tears.

"I hope you told him off," Tabby says.

"No. I just sort of ran away." I drop my face into my palms. "I'm pathetic."

"No you aren't." Laini gives my shoulders a squeeze. "Have you eaten anything?"

"Not since breakfast," I mumble pathetically, in that whiny voice that comes out sometimes when I'm feeling particularly sorry for myself.

"You must be starving!"

My stomach reacts to her suggestion with a rumble.

"You're right. I'm starving. Did I miss dinner?"

"I just pulled some bread bowls out of the oven. I'm going to fill them with chili."

Chili in the middle of summer? The thought makes me hot all over again.

"Don't worry," Laini says, as though reading my thoughts. "We have the air-conditioning on really cold. I'm testing the recipe for Nick's fall and winter menu. You and Tabby get to be my guinea pigs."

"I can think of worse things to be."

"All right," Tabby says, hopping up from the couch. "Tomorrow we'll worry about joblessness and Jack Quinn. But tonight, we feast!"

And feast we do. With the apartment air turned to subzero temperatures, we revel in the winter meal that conjures up images of falling snow and the lighting of the tree at Rockefeller Center.

Satiated, I sit back with a smile, feeling good for the first time all day. "Laini, that was amazing."

My redheaded friend smiles and crunches her freckled nose. "Think Nick'll go for it?"

"He'd be nuts not to."

"What about school, Laini?" Tabby asks, her brow puckered into a frown. "Your new semester starts in a week, and you barely passed the summer semester as it was. How are you going to have time for more cooking and keeping up with your schoolwork?"

Laini shrugs. "I'll cook during my time off. I'll only be doing the cinnamon rolls and these bread bowls, if Nick likes them. That won't take too much time."

Who does she think she's trying to kid? Bread dough takes forever to make, and she'll be making dough for cinnamon rolls *and* bread bowls?

I shake my head. "What is Nick thinking?"

Her face relaxes into an expression of serenity. "He's so lovable. I just couldn't say no when he asked if I could add something to his winter lunch menu."

"When did Nick ask you, by the way?" I'm surprised I didn't get wind of that. And I'm a little insulted to be kept out of the loop.

Laini beams. "He called me this morning."

Tabby's still wearing the same frown. "But, Laini, what about study time? You can't go to school, make bread bowls, *and* cook two dozen cinnamon rolls every day."

"Three dozen, starting the Monday after Labor Day. That's when all the moms with kids going back to school will start meeting for breakfast at Nick's again."

Tabby can't seem to let it go, and I'm starting to see her point. I can't help but jump on the bandwagon. "Laini, I know you enjoy baking. But since you're already struggling with interior design, maybe you shouldn't bake three dozen cinnamon rolls per day."

"Yeah," Tabby pipes in. "Plus, the bread bowls are going to be a huge hit, and Nick's going to have you baking more and more. You won't have time to do all that cooking and keep up with studying, too. You'll burn out. Not to mention flunk out."

Laini turns on us in un-Laini-like fashion. She stands and begins to pace, and I know we're about to get what for. "You two—just—" Her hands wave in the air as she tries to formulate the proper words to tell us where to hang ourselves. "I can make my own life decisions," she finally expels. "I mean it! I don't need you two acting like my mom. So from now on just—"

"Mind our own business?" I ask, suddenly aware that we're doing to Laini the thing we both despise in our own mothers: telling her how to live her life.

"Butt out?" Tabby interjects.

"Yes," she squeaks, and wilts back into the chair.

"We're sorry, Laini," Tabby says.

See, in friendship, it's all about support. Really. I mean, it's okay to play devil's advocate with your sisters or long-lost cousins, but friends—especially best friends—come along so rarely that when you get the opportunity to make your support count, you should. Tough love has its place. But not here.

Our ready apology takes the thunder from Laini's eyes, and tears begin to flow. "It's just . . . I don't know . . . Mom's putting on the pressure, and Mr. Ace called." She gives a shuddering sigh. "He wants me to come back to work for them."

I frown. "Come back to where? I thought the accounting firm went bankrupt."

A shrug lifts her slender shoulders. "Ian Ace gave the money back—or, well, most of it."

Tabby's eyes widen. "You don't see that every day."

"His mom came up from Florida and laid into him, from what I understand."

"Nothing like a mother's guilt."

"You said it."

The three of us observe a moment of silence for adult children everywhere who are still controlled by their mothers. Of course, in Ian's instance, it turned out to be a good thing, but you have to admit that's rare.

"I guess I should consider Mr. Ace's offer," Laini says, breaking the silence between us. "He even offered me a ten percent raise."

I want to say, "Yes, consider it! Go back to what you're good at." But I can't, because I know, in her heart of hearts, that's not what she wants to hear.

"Why would you consider going back to a job you didn't like?" Tabby asks. Tabby is suddenly extremely matter-of-fact, not to mention somewhat uppity about this. And I'm this close to reminding her of her last job before *Legacy of Life* called her back to her Emmy-nominated role. But I don't have the chance, because Laini's feeling just feisty enough to stand up for herself.

"This from the girl who dressed up in an itchy bunny suit and got into an argument with a child about the gender of Peter Rabbit."

It's true. And Tabby's red face attests to the fact that she concedes the point. She nods. "True. You're right. Do what you have to do to get by while you pursue your dream. Can you work for Ace Accounting and still keep up at school?"

Laini rolls her eyes like she considers the question to be completely rhetorical. Which it probably is, anyway. She's not keeping up with her classes as it is, and all she's been doing so far is going to school and baking cinnamon rolls. Poor Laini.

"What can we do to help?" I ask in a sudden rush of generosity.

Laini's mouth lifts into a twinkly grin. "Eat up. I need references for Nick."

Tabby opens her mouth like she's going to say something. I send her a silent but firm shake of my head, and she gets the message to drop it.

As though we never veered, I slip a bite between my teeth and wander back to the original topic—and yes, I'm speaking with my mouth full, which is gross, but completely okay when you're with your two best friends, as long as there are no children, men, or mothers around the table. "Nick's going to love these, Laini. Who knows, you might start making enough money at baking that you don't need to be an accountant or an interior designer."

Laini purses her lips into a scowl. It's not always about making enough money, is it?

"That's not the point, Dance," Tabby says. "She has to do what she loves. Her passion is interior design."

Oh blast, here we go again.

11

Valerie closed her eyes, listening to the sounds
of the city outside her window. She hadn't been
out of the apartment in a week, and her friends
were beginning to wonder if she had fallen off the
face of the earth. Maybe she was hiding, but what
was there to leave the apartment for? All she had
ever known was advertising. And working at M&J
Advertising had always been her dream. What was
a person supposed to do when her dreams were
crushed? What more was there to live for?

—An excerpt from *Fifth Avenue Princess*
by Dancy Ames

I take my laptop and a notebook and head to Nick's the next
morning around nine, leaving Laini to her cooking. It's cathartic for her, so I figure I have no right to tell her to stop
cooking and concentrate on her real career. Besides, she only
has a few more days of freedom before the grind of classes
begins again.

When I get to Nick's, there's a new guy behind the counter
and no Nick. "Hi. I'll have a green tea," I say. The guy has jet
black hair, brown eyes, and a dark complexion. If I were looking
for a man to break my heart, I'd almost bet he could do it—if
someone else hadn't already taken on the role. But I refuse to
discuss that. "Where's Nick?" I ask as he turns to get my tea.

"In the back." He swings his gaze around. "You know my uncle Nick?"

"Oh, you're family." Well, that explains the gorgeous Italian looks.

As if on cue, the kitchen door swings open and Nick appears.

"'Ey, princess. I was just talking about you."

Oh no. Don't tell me he's going to try to set me up with his nephew. Not that he's not great-looking, but I'm not in the market (or the mood) today. I brace myself for what is bound to be an awkward moment.

"This is the girl I was tellin' you about, Joe."

Oh, groan. I wonder if he told him I have a good personality.

"The uppity girl who gave up her time to help you out?" Joe flashes a million-dollar smile that almost makes me forget he called me uppity.

"Nick!" I say with mock hurt. "What do you mean, 'uppity'?"

Nick sends Joe a fierce scowl. "Next time, don't repeat everything you hear." He turns back to me. "Joe here is taking over the business. He's going to be my manager so I don't have to be here no more. What do you think about that?"

My heart sinks at the news. Nick can't leave. I need him. I feel the tremor in my voice and swallow hard trying to disguise my fear of change. "I have no idea what to say, Nick."

"I'm retiring. My Nelda needs me to help her with our girl and those kids. I'm ready to get out of the city and enjoy my retirement."

I can't begrudge him a chance to be with the woman he loves. "Wow, Nick. I can't believe you're leaving. When?"

"As soon as Joe can run things on his own."

"My degree in restaurant management should help some, if Uncle Nick will let me use my education."

"Education." Nick snorts. "Books can't teach you how to run

a place like this. I been running it for forty years with only an eighth-grade education."

"And just look at what you've done. It's a great place." Joe smiles.

Nick's chest puffs out. "That's right."

"But think how much better you might have done with some knowledge of running a business in today's market."

"Well, he's just been named one of Manhattan's best-kept secrets. Business is booming," I say.

"Not like it could with a little adjustment here and there," Joe says with a cocky grin. I have to say, he's starting to lose a little of his charm.

I can't help but frown. "Are you planning to make changes?"

"Only if Uncle Nick approves."

"You gotta learn the ropes that already exist first. Then we'll talk about new stuff."

"Hey, Nick, what did you do with the other two new workers?" I ask. *Eat them alive?*

Nick grunts and jerks his thumb toward the door. "They were a couple of idiots. Didn't last a day, either one of 'em."

"Are you looking for someone else, or is Joe here it?"

"Why?" Nick peers closely at me. "You interested in a job? Just say the word and it's yours."

A smile tips my lips. He has no idea how close I might be to taking him up on that offer. I shake my head. "My little brother could probably use an after-school job."

"He got any sense?"

I shrug. "A little. About as much as any sixteen-year-old boy, I guess."

"Bring him in and I'll talk to him. If he has enough sense to make a cup of coffee and clean off a table, I'll give him a try."

"I'll tell him. Thanks, Nick."

I settle into a booth in the corner to work on my manuscript. I barely even look up for two full hours as Valerie plots her revenge on John Quest. My imagination runs rampant. I know the decision to fire her wasn't all John's fault. But he was certainly part of the process. He could have fought for her. Couldn't he? He could have. I know he could.

After a couple of hours, Nick comes over to my table and takes a seat across from me without even asking if I'd like company. But that's Nick's way. "So, you still reading your Bible?"

Ready to take a break, I close my computer and look up at him. "Some."

"That's real good, princess. The best way to find God is through His Word. So you're on the right track."

I give a short laugh. "What I really need to find is a job."

His eyebrows push together into a bushy frown. "What do you mean?"

I give him the *Reader's Digest* version of Jack's so-called business dinner.

"Hmm." And that's all he says as he leans back in his chair and folds his arms across his chest.

"What do you mean by 'hmm'?" Does he not notice that I'm jobless and without purpose in my life?

"Well, maybe I don't mean anything by it. Maybe I'm just thinkin'."

"All right." I give a little sigh. "I didn't mean to sound huffy." Tears flicker in my eyes. "I just really thought, after I started reading the Bible and praying, that God was going to make a difference for me."

Nick gives me a long look, long enough that I start to squirm under his scrutiny. "You got it all wrong, princess. You don't seek God to find happiness. You seek God to find *Him*. Whatever comes along with that is icing on the cake."

"But what about Proverbs three, verses five and six?" I quote them. "I've been trusting Him. And look what happened!"

"So you got fired."

That's exactly the point I'm trying to make, but it seems like Nick is being deliberately thickheaded about it. "Yes, and don't you think I shouldn't have, under the circumstances?"

"What does trusting God to direct your life have to do with getting fired? For all you know, God wanted you to get fired."

My jaw drops. I can't even fathom that possibility. "Why would He?"

A shrug lifts his massive shoulder. "I don't know, princess. I ain't God, am I?"

12

Valerie mustered up all of her confidence and walked into Harrison & Sons Advertising. This interview had been hard-won, and she refused to take even the smallest chance that she would leave without the coveted job. Her résumé was extensive. She knew that, so there was absolutely nothing for her to feel nervous about.

Only, she'd been working for M&J since she graduated from college. How could she ever fit in at another company? Still, she squared her shoulders and stepped from the heat of the city into the coolness of the ten-story building.

—An excerpt from *Fifth Avenue Princess*
by Dancy Ames

H oney," Dad says, "we need to ask a favor."

I should have known my parents wouldn't just invite me to dinner for no reason. They've been buttering me up for the last two hours during dinner, so I should have expected this. But did they have to wait until I'm about to leave to spring this on me?

"Can you stay with your brother next week while your mother and I go look at property in Florida?"

I stare at my dad like he's lost his mind, which in all honesty, I'm afraid he has.

"What? Dad, I don't think that's a very good idea."

Mother adds her two cents' worth. "Really, Dancy. It isn't as though you have anything else to do these days. Would it really hurt you to do this one thing for your father and me?"

I give a stubborn lift of my chin. "Quite possibly."

Dad shoots me a glare. "I can't leave him alone. And you know if he doesn't have someone to keep him in line, he'll end up getting into trouble."

"What about Nanny Mary?" I've got to stop calling her "nanny," don't I? "I mean, she is his mother. What's wrong with her keeping him for a week?"

"I told you, she's been staying with her mother in Jersey. The woman has cancer. Listen, if there was any other way, I'd take it. But we need your help. Mary can't leave her mother's side. Apparently the cancer is terminal. Besides, she says she needs a break from Brandon for a while, remember? Are you going to make your little brother feel unwanted by you, too?"

Guilt is the tactic of the truly controlling. Dad must have learned this from my mother. It's working. Still, I give one last-ditch effort to get out of it. "Did you even bother to ask Kale?"

Mom plants her hands on her hips and gives me her stern look accompanied by a huff. "Dancy, your father promised if there were any other choice, he wouldn't be imposing. Can't you be gracious? It's only for a week."

A lot can happen in a week. Creation, for instance. "I'll ask Tabby and Laini if he can stay on the couch, but I'm not staying at your place."

"Thank you, honey."

"Wait, what about Kale? Did you ask him?" Because, come to think of it, Dad never actually answered me about whether he asked Kale or not. And it won't hurt for my brother to share some of the load.

Dad's face goes a little red, and he averts his gaze. "Well . . ."

Uh-huh. Just what I thought. "Okay, I'll see what I can do, but I'm going to ask Kale to split the responsibility some. Do you have a problem with that?"

Mom gasps. "With your brother's schedule at the hospital?"

Why does she always have to act like I'm imposing when they're the ones—

"Caroline," Dad says firmly. He must have picked up on my attitude—I was just about to tell them to forget it. "If Dancy thinks she needs to share the responsibility, she's more than welcome to talk to Kale. He'll probably have a day or two to spare."

I know when I'm being patronized. Still, it's nice to have Dad take my side, so I relish it for the two seconds it lasts. He turns to Mother and holds out his arm, leading her toward the back of the condo. "Shall we go, my love? There's coffee awaiting us on the terrace."

She beams up at him. "How lovely."

And I suppose it is. Lovely, that is. For them.

I flounder through the rest of the week until Sunday arrives. I honestly thought I might attend church, but chickened out at the last second. After all, I do need to prepare for Brandon's arrival tonight, don't I? Dad feels so guilty about shirking his responsibility that he surprised us with a new sofa bed. By midnight the thing arrived on our doorstep and the delivery guys took the old one away. Don't ask me how Dad managed it that late, but after all, this is the city that never sleeps. The girls are beside themselves with excitement because it's a La-Z-Boy and came with a matching overstuffed recliner. The fabric is a grayish green. (Laini sees only gray, and we don't have the heart to tell her it's more green.)

After Tabby leaves for church and Laini heads for her mother's house as she does most Sundays, I enjoy a cup of coffee alone on the new couch and read the Sunday paper. By ten, I snatch up my dirty laundry and head downstairs to the building's laundry room just as my cell phone rings.

I look at the caller ID and sigh. *Sheri.*

I'm not sure this is such a good idea, but I decide to answer anyway. "Hello, Sheri."

"Dancy! I'm so glad I caught you." She always sounds genuinely happy to talk to me. I really can't figure her out. But she is family, and I choose to give her the benefit of the doubt.

"I'll come straight to the point because I know how you hate to talk on the phone."

No. I just hate to talk on the phone to *you.* But of course I'll keep that to myself.

"I'm giving a dinner party at the club tomorrow night, and one of the couples backed out on me last minute. The table is all set for ten, so I need another girl and guy. Would you mind pinch-hitting for me—and bringing Brandon?"

I'm an afterthought. How can my cousin not realize how insulting that is? The least she could have done was pretend I was on the guest list to begin with. "I don't know, Sheri."

"Listen, I would have invited you in the first place, but Mrs. Bartell saw me writing out my guest list. She finagled a spot for Floyd. I know how you feel about him, so I crossed off your name rather than forcing you to endure him."

That was sort of sweet, right? And that alone makes me suspicious. After all, she's never been sweet before. "That's thoughtful. Thanks."

"But now that Brandon's going to be with you, you can bring him along as your escort and I'll seat you next to him."

I don't happen to enjoy this camaraderie with Sheri. It's unnatural, unwanted, and uncomfortable.

"So you'll come? If I promise to seat Floyd at the other end of the table?"

"I don't know." The last thing I want to do is go to this party. I don't want to be around Jack, and I don't want to watch Sheri try to sink her claws into him. I'd rather stay home and read a book.

"How about if I promise to seat myself next to Floyd?"

Hmm. That might be fun to watch.

"Oh, all right. But I swear, if he starts slobbering on me, I'm leaving."

"I promise. Listen, be at the club around seven thirty. Coat and tie for Brandon."

"Yes, Sheri. I'll make sure he's dressed appropriately."

"Can you do something about his piercings and Mohawk spikes?"

I laugh, because I wouldn't even if I could. This is going to be too much fun. "I don't know. I'll ask him if he can tone it down some."

"Every bit will help, I suppose."

I'm about to hang up when she says, "Oh, I forgot to tell you. The party is for Jack."

"Jack?" She's known him for less than a month and she's throwing him a dinner party at the club?

"It's his birthday. But I'm sure you knew that."

"Why would I?"

A long silent pause. "I don't know, I just assumed—"

"That I'd know my former boss's birthday?" I know I'm defensive. If I hadn't already agreed to go, I would certainly back out.

"I just meant since he's a close friend of the family, being your brother's best friend."

"My relationship with Jack was strictly professional, and now that I'm no longer working at Lane Publishing, it's nothing."

"Well, you'll still come to the party, won't you?" She pauses again. "For Brandon. Don't you think it would be good for him? After all, if he's going to be part of our family, he needs a little refinement."

"He needs a lot of refinement, but I'm not sure a dinner party is the best place to start."

"You said you'd come."

"I know. I'll be there."

"Thank you, cousin dear. You're a real lifesaver." She hesitates a second, so I suppose she's trying to figure out a way to hang up.

"I have to go, Sheri."

"All right then." Just as I suspected, she sounds relieved. "I'll see you tomorrow night."

13

The woman's nails were bloodred, long, and firmly wrapped around John Quest's arm. Valerie fought her jealousy as she stared at the couple across the room, sitting in a cozy booth side by side.

Why had she come back to the restaurant where she'd first dined with John? She'd been crazy enough to think this was their special place. Well, apparently it was special, all right. He came here with all of his dates. Anger boiled her blood. First he'd taken her job away, and now he was breaking her heart. How much more did he expect her to endure?

—An excerpt from *Fifth Avenue Princess* by Dancy Ames

Laini is in heaven with Brandon gobbling up her food like she's the best thing since . . . well, sliced bread. Last night she had brownies waiting for him and practically hovered like Mrs. Cleaver, filling his milk glass and waiting on him hand and foot. And this morning she's gone all out for breakfast: bacon, eggs, biscuits and gravy, and little plates with an assortment of berries and a dollop of whipped cream.

"I swear, Laini," Tabby says, stumbling sleepily into the kitchen. She heads straight to the coffeepot. "What time did you wake up? Two?"

Laini grins. "Four thirty, but I couldn't sleep anyway."

Brandon's hair is sticking up—and not on purpose. It's that bedhead that, I guess, is sort of cute. Gives him a look of innocence. Something about that disheveled look brings out the maternal instinct in me. "So, how'd you sleep, Brandon?" I ask, sipping my coffee and reaching for a biscuit.

He shrugs. "Okay. The new-couch smell stinks, though. I thought I was going to hurl."

"Well, you won't have to sleep on the couch for long," Laini soothes. "Here—have some orange juice."

"Thanks," he grunts.

She's fawning all over him. My goodness, Laini needs to get married and have some babies to take care of. I've never seen anyone become domestic and love it the way she has.

Okay, back to reality. "So, Brandon," I say, "you remembered to bring a jacket, right?"

He stares at me like I'm from Mars.

"You have a jacket for the dinner party, right?"

He nods. "Dad bought it for my concert next week."

"What concert?" No one told me. But I'm relieved he's got the jacket.

"I'm playing in Central Park with honors orchestra. It's for Jerry's Kids."

Laini beams as though he's her own child. "Brandon, that's tremendous. What night are you playing?"

He glows right back at her. "Tuesday. You think you could come?"

"Are you kidding? Of course we're coming. Right, Dancy?"

"If my little brother is playing in the park, I'll be there."

Brandon is grinning so broadly, I almost cry. Hasn't anyone ever paid attention to this remarkable teenager?

I swallow hard and change the subject before I make a scene

and embarrass us both with my tears. "Okay, Brandon. Did you bring it?"

"What?" he mumbles around an enormous bite of eggs.

"Your jacket. Focus on me for a second, will you? I feel like I'm talking to myself."

He looks up at me and frowns. "Yeah, I brought it. You told me to."

Tabby snickers and Laini fights to keep from laughing. I can tell. "What do you think is so funny?"

"Nothing at all." Tabby crams the last of her bacon in her mouth and downs the coffee in her mug. "I have to run. Early makeup call. They're making me up as Francesca today."

"Francesca?" I ask.

"Felicia's evil twin."

"Oh yeah. When does that story line start?"

"In a couple of weeks."

I never watched soaps until Tabby started on *Legacy of Life*. But she's got me hooked. When I can't watch, I TiVo. And that's nonnegotiable.

"I'm headed to Nick's with three dozen cinnamon rolls," Laini says. She looks straight at Brandon. "I could use some muscle. Want to help?"

His eyes light up. "Sure. Let me go fix my hair first." He gobbles down the last morsels of food on his plate and washes them down with orange juice. "Be right back."

Laini grabs his dishes and heads to the dishwasher. "What a great kid."

I shrug. "I agree. I was led to believe he was quite the handful. He's definitely his own strong personality, but he's not a thug by any means."

"Do you want to go to Nick's, too? I thought I'd have some coffee before class."

"Yeah. I told Nick that Brandon might want an after-school job." I drain my coffee cup and walk to the sink with my breakfast dishes. "I need to introduce the two of them."

"Have you said anything to Brandon?"

"Not yet. I need to before we go, though, so he can decide if he wants to—"

"Decide if I want to what?"

Brandon has returned with all four spikes sticking straight up as, I suppose, they were meant to do. Every piercing is in place, and his nails are effectively painted black. He looks put together. Literally. Sort of like Frankenstein.

"The guy who owns the coffee shop is looking for some part-time help. I thought you might be interested."

"You think I need a job?"

"I just thought you might want one."

"I'll think about it."

He seems a little put out. "Hey, Brandon. You don't have to. It's no big deal. No one will be mad at you if you decide you don't want to get an after-school job." I send him a wink. "It's not like Dad can't afford to support you. And a small country in Africa."

That brings a smirk to his mouth, and I know we've connected. "I've been wanting to get one, but it's hard to find a respectable job with this kind of look."

"I see your point."

Laini finishes loading the dishes and adds soap. "Nick's not like that, Brandon." She pushes the button and the water begins to swirl. "He won't judge you by your outward appearance."

I'm not sure where she gets her confidence, but she seems very sure.

"I have to practice my music, so I can't work long hours."

"He's only open until six o'clock through the week, eight on Saturday, and he's closed on Sunday."

Brandon gives a nod. "Okay, then. Maybe it'll work out."

I think I see a spark of interest. A real spark.

Laini goes straight to the kitchen to drop off the rolls when we get to Nick's. The line is ridiculous. I feel like I'm waiting for a roller-coaster ride at Disney World. Brandon and I happen to be in line behind the same stringy-haired girl from a couple of weeks ago. "Hey, there," I say, tapping her shoulder to get her attention. "Remember me?"

Her face goes red, but she nods.

"I'm Dancy Ames."

"Emily Lewis." In her hand is a copy of *Wake Me with a Kiss*, Cate Able's latest book.

I grin. "Hey, don't you love her?"

A spark flashes in her eyes. "My favorite contemporary author."

"Me too! Don't you wish she'd write one every year, at least?"

"Definitely! Or do interviews, or something. There's not one picture of her on the Internet. And I heard she never, ever makes personal appearances. Not even book signings."

"Well, it just so happens I know a few things about her."

Her eyes go wide. "You do? How?"

"I used to be an editor at her publishing house."

Her face takes on a look of awe. "Really?"

I smile and nod. "Scout's honor."

"What's she like?"

"She only has dealings with Mr. Kramer, the guy in charge of the whole company."

"I wonder why."

I shrug. "I really don't know."

"What do you know about her?"

"She's English. And single. And she makes a ton of money. But that's about all anyone knows, except for Mr. Kramer, the publisher."

"I felt sure she was English. I love British authors."

It's finally Emily's turn at the counter. Joe is standing there patiently. Much better disposition than Nick's, that's for sure.

"Is that Nick?" Brandon asks.

I shake my head. "That's his nephew, Joe."

Just then, Laini and Nick come out of the kitchen. "'Ey, Joe. This is Laini—the girl who bakes the rolls for me. Laini, my nephew, Joe Pantalone."

Joe glances at Laini. "Nice to meet you." He turns back, and I see a spark. I turn my gaze to Laini, whose face is beet red. Methinks there's been a moment here.

"Hey, Nick," I say. "This is my little brother, Brandon, I told you about."

Nick gives him a once-over without changing his expression. "That hair of yours a rebellion?"

"No, sir," Brandon says. "Just a look."

"You got manners. I like that."

"Thank you, sir." Okay, now he might be putting it on a little thick, the charmer.

"What'll you two have?" Joe asks.

I order green tea, and Brandon gets a mocha latte plus one of Laini's cinnamon rolls.

"Let me help my nephew knock out this rush and I'll be over to talk to you, Brandon."

Brandon nods, and we head over to the dining room to find a seat in the crowded coffee shop. Emily waves at us. "You're welcome to sit here," she says shyly. "It was the only table available. I hate to take up a four-top all by myself."

"My friend with the red hair should be right over. Is that okay?"

"Sure. I don't mind."

Laini returns in no time, carrying a cup with whipped cream piled on. Her eyes are shining and her face and neck are splotchy red. Some people blush prettily. Laini isn't one of them. "Isn't he gorgeous?"

"Who? Nick?" I tease.

Brandon snorts.

"Yeah, right. Nick." Laini rolls her eyes. "Joe said he'll definitely want to keep up with the rolls and would be happy to sample anything else I have in mind that would be appropriate for the type of menu they have, including the bread bowls."

"That's great, Laini."

Within ten minutes, Nick joins us. He focuses his attention on Brandon. "You want to come back to my office for a little talk?"

If it were me, and I didn't know Nick, I'd be scared. But Brandon doesn't look the slightest bit intimidated. "Yes, sir."

The two of them get up, and Brandon even has the presence of mind to take his latte with him.

"Don't look now," Laini says. "Benedict Arnold at two o'clock."

I frown and turn to the counter. "Who?"

"Two o'clock," she says. "Not ten."

Emily giggles. I turn a little red and twist the other way so I can look at the door where I suppose "two o'clock" is supposed to be. Jack is standing there. He catches my eye, nods, and heads across the room.

"Shoot, he's coming over."

"Who is it?" Emily hisses.

"My boss who fired me." I frown. "Don't be taken in by the accent."

"Don't worry, I won't."

"Good morning, ladies."

Emily gives a little gasp. "G-good morning." She actually found her voice. I don't believe it.

"I don't believe we've met," Jack says. He holds out his hand. She takes it, and I swear she's about to faint. "Jack Quinn."

Emily's eyes are wide and she gulps. I've heard of speechless. But I've never actually seen it.

I heave a sigh. Won't be taken in, huh? "Jack, Emily. Emily, Jack."

Jack flashes that smile, and she's completely worthless. "If you'll excuse me," he says. "I'll go order my breakfast."

"We have an extra place, if you'd like to sit with us," Emily says.

"That's Brandon's seat," I remind her. Not very subtle. But then, neither was he when he said I was fired.

Jack's lips twitch into a smirk. "Why, thank you, Emily. That's very kind of you. I'm sure we can find another chair to borrow, if you don't mind my company."

"Not at all!"

"Smashing." He winks at me, and I'm tempted to grind the three-inch heel of my Manolo Blahnik into the upper of his leather shoe. Let him see how smashing that is. "I'll just be a minute, then."

Emily watches in awe as he walks away.

"Why didn't he ask if *I* mind his company?" I grump.

Her eyes grow wide. "Do you?"

"He fired her, Emily." Laini states the obvious.

Emily gasps and covers her mouth. "Oh my gosh. You said that. I'm so sorry. I told you I love British authors. I'm even more of a sucker for an English accent."

"Obviously."

"Should I go tell him he can't sit here after all?" Her eyes plead with me to say no.

"No." My mother's voice in my head would haunt me for the rest of my life. "I can endure his presence for a few minutes, I guess."

"Dancy," Laini says. "I hate to leave you, but I have a ten o'clock class. This is my first final and I can't be late." She gulps down her latte just as Joe, followed by Jack, appears. *Oh, Laini,* I think. She has whipped cream on her nose as she smiles up at Joe.

He winks at her, reaches forward, and thumbs it away. "A little whipped cream," he says. Emily sighs. I have to admit it is a bit romantic. But Laini is horrified.

She shoots to her feet. "Thank you, Mr. Pantalone. I have to go."

"I'll walk you to the door," Joe says.

"Well, fancy that," Jack says, taking the seat Laini vacated, which happens to be the one directly in front of me. "Now there are just the right number of chairs, even when Brandon returns."

"Yes, fancy that," Emily says with just the smallest hint of a British accent.

Jack utterly charms Emily, and I think the girl has forgotten I exist. By the time Brandon returns, she's pretty much told her life story. A daughter of hippie parents, she helps them in their health food store and goes to college.

"Hi, Jack," Brandon says as he sits down next to me. "You made it."

I frown and turn to Brandon.

Apparently Jack notices the look and recognizes it for what it is. "You didn't know I was joining you?"

I shake my head. Jack scowls at Brandon.

"Sorry, dude," Brandon says with a sheepish grin. "I got to smelling those cinnamon rolls and forgot to tell her."

"Tell me what?"

"Jack called your cell phone while you were in the can getting ready. I told him to meet us here."

Does he have to call it "the can"? I feel my face go hot. Still, I recover enough to turn my attention to Jack. "Do you need something?"

"I called to ask if you'd be interested in a freelance project."

"You fire me and then ask me to freelance?" Is he serious? "I haven't done one edit in the months you've been at the company that you haven't butted in on. What makes you think I'd be a good freelance editor?"

He scrutinizes me. "Perhaps you're right." He stands. "I apologize for interrupting your breakfast."

Without another word, he whips around and heads to the door. Bewildered at the abrupt departure, I have to resist the urge to turn around and watch him leave. Emily doesn't resist. She gives a sigh when the bell dings, and I know he's left. "He turned around before he left," she says. "I think he wanted you to be looking."

I sip my tea. "Well, he was disappointed then, wasn't he?" I turn my attention to Brandon. "Did Nick hire you?"

A grin tips his lips, and I know the answer. "I start at five tonight."

"Brandon! You can't start tonight. What about Sheri's dinner?"

"I already committed to Nick."

"All right. Nick closes at six, so you could—"

He shakes his head. "After we close I have to clean. Mop floors and stuff. Nick said don't expect to get off until after eight thirty."

Sheri's going to kill me. Emily shifts and takes a drink of her green tea. And I get an idea. "Emily, how would you like to go to dinner at the country club tonight?"

Her eyes go wide. "I couldn't!"

"It's being thrown in Jack's honor," I say, tossing out the bait that I know she won't be able to resist.

I'd like to say I hate the country club and all it stands for, but I really don't. I grew up well-off, so it's always been a part of my life. Heaven forbid Mother isn't a member, you know? It boasts several swimming pools, a full gym, two elegant restaurants . . . everything my mother could possibly want in a club.

I can see Emily trying hard not to look impressed. She's wearing a hippie dress that her mother probably sewed her-self—in 1969.

I guess we're the last ones to arrive, because the table is filled except for two places. Floyd stands, intercepting my trek to the other side of the table. His face glows with pride as he looks at me as though he owns me. Okay, I haven't seen him in two weeks, and of the twenty-five calls he's made to my number in that time, I've answered two and returned one. Why does he think he has a right to step out and take my hands? "You look beautiful," he whispers before landing a cold kiss on my cheek.

"Uh, thanks," I say. "You—uh—look great, too, Floyd." And I mean it. He does. The boy knows how to dress. But that's not the point. If knowing how to dress was my only criterion for a husband, he'd fit the bill fine and dandy. But a personality is a must. Not to mention that any man I fall for must have a spine and something resembling the intelligence to recognize when a woman isn't interested.

"Dancy." Sheri stands. Her eyes widen with horror as she takes in Emily's presence. "Who's this?"

"I tried to call," I say. "Brandon had to work."

Her lips form a wax smile. "I see."

Emily's face is red, and I realize she is picking up on Sheri's coolness. "I-I'm sorry," she says. "I should go."

"Go? I'd be so hurt." We turn at the sound of Jack Quinn's voice. He looks down at her, takes her hand, and presses it to his lips. "This little soirée is being thrown in my honor, you know. It's my birthday."

Sheri quickly recovers her manners. "Well, of course she must stay. I'm Sheri, Dancy's cousin. And you are . . . ?"

Emily's gaze never leaves Jack's face as she answers. "Emily. Nice to meet you, Sheri."

"Let's sit, shall we?" Sheri says. "Hors d'oeuvres are about to be served. Here, Emily, have my seat next to Floyd." She turns to me. "Dancy, have you seen that divine new painting in the foyer? I've been dying to show you."

"Excuse me," Jack says.

I'm grateful for his kindness to my new friend, and I reach out and take his hand. "Happy birthday, Jack," I say, hoping my gratitude shows in my eyes, and perhaps makes up for my coldness earlier when he was trying to send some work my way.

He stares down at me and slowly lifts my hand, and I think he's going to kiss it like he did Emily's. Instead, he hugs it to his chest. I catch my breath as he leans forward and presses warm, soft lips to my cheek. "Thank you for coming," he whispers.

"Shall we go see that painting now?" Sheri asks, her tone so taut I think her vocal cords might snap any second.

She ushers me out of the room and whips me around with the strength—and manners—of Mike Tyson. "What on earth do you think you're doing, bringing that nightmare of a girl to my party?"

"I told you, Brandon had to work. He just started his job today and couldn't take off. And the whole point of you asking me to the dinner in the first place was so the numbers were even."

"Couldn't you have found another man so the ratio fit?"

"No I couldn't, as a matter of fact. I don't have any male friends."

She stops and stares. "I guess I should have known that. All right. I forgive you, for now. But if she does anything to embarrass me in front of my guests, I'm holding you personally responsible."

With that she stomps back into the room, her stilettos clacking on the marble floor.

I stand still for a second. Why didn't she seem surprised when I said I had no male friends? I think I feel insulted.

14

John Quest stood in front of her, his blue eyes piercing her until she couldn't stand it any longer. "What do you want, John?"

"I need you back," he said softly.

Valerie's pounding heart nearly burst from her chest. "It's too late. I've found another job."

If only he would ask, she'd leave the competitor and run back to M&J Advertising in a split second. He reached forward and took her hand.

"I'm not talking about the job." Pulling her close, he leaned forward, and she knew he was about to kiss her. "I need *you*."

—An excerpt from *Fifth Avenue Princess*
by Dancy Ames

Sheri's taken a spot next to Jack. And the other seat is on his opposite side. It turns out I'll be sitting between Jack and Brynn. Sheri will monopolize Jack, and Kale will be absorbed with Brynn. Sheri has to have known that. I suppose solitude is my payback for upsetting the balance of Sheri's party.

As I walk around the table to my seat, Jack stands and smiles, holding my chair out, as one would expect a British gentleman to do.

"Thanks," I murmur. I take my seat and pull my napkin

from the silver ring, shifting a little as I slip the cloth into my lap.

"Old Floyd was right, you know," Jack says once he's sitting again. "You do look beautiful."

I take a sip, then realize Jack's waiting for a response. "Thanks. You look good, too."

I feel like such an idiot to even say something like that to a guy like Jack. I mean, of course he looks good. He always does. I'm sure he doesn't need to hear it.

"Excuse me, Dancy," Sheri says, leaning closer to Jack than necessary. "I need to steal the birthday boy for a few minutes."

"No problem," I murmur and take a sip of water.

Brynn leans toward me as Sheri demands Jack's attention. "Are you going to let her get away with that?" Didn't we have this same conversation at the bowling alley a few weeks ago?

I smile at my soon-to-be sister-in-law. She knows nothing about me if she thinks I can just yank a man back from anyone, let alone from my beautiful cousin. "I couldn't care less if Jack would rather chat with Sheri."

It's not exactly the truth, but maybe a little white lie is called for. Maybe?

"Trust me, he wouldn't."

I appreciate her support, but I refuse to get into a tug-of-war with Sheri over a man who wouldn't stand up for me when I needed him most. Plus, I know that he had to have helped Mr. Kramer decide whom to get rid of. It would have come down to Fran or me, so why did they choose me? I know why Mr. Kramer would want to keep Fran around, but Jack could have fought for me. And he didn't. Instead, he agreed with the decision and then broke the news to me over a steak dinner. I'll never eat another filet mignon as long as I live.

Dinner is served, and I eat in silence and solitude. Kale and

Brynn are caught up in some sort of heated conversation, and, of course, Sheri will not give up one second of Jack's attention— not that I care—so I might as well be home watching *The Biggest Loser.* Which would be ironic, since that's exactly what I am.

I'm feeling sorry for myself and imagining a scene for my book where Valerie is the life of the party, when I reach for my water glass. In a twist of what can only be regarded as fate, Jack actually breaks free from the bonds of Sheri's control and turns to me.

"Are you having a good time?"

I've always startled easily, and this is no exception. Instead of grasping the glass, I knock into it and down it goes. Ice water rushes out onto the linen tablecloth in all directions.

I give a little screech and yank my napkin off my lap, shooting to my feet and trying to do damage control. At the same time, Jack scoots his chair back and tries to get up in an effort to avoid the sudden rush of water heading toward his lap. But in doing so, he knocks against me or I knock against him and—oh, yes, cliché of all clichés—I land squarely in his lap, with the water pouring off the tablecloth and soaking into my little black Anne Klein dress.

Kale is laughing so hard, I think he might hyperventilate. Even Brynn, whom I thought I could count on to be on my side, is nearly choking with laughter.

Then I realize that just about everyone is laughing. Everyone, that is, except for me, Floyd (who looks like he might challenge Jack to a duel), Sheri, and Jack, who is waiting patiently for me to get off his lap. I suppose I should be grateful he didn't just shove me off.

"I'm so sorry," I say, stumbling away from him.

"It's okay." His voice is smooth, and there's not even a hint of his usual mockery. Which is probably good, because one untoward look and I know I'd burst into the tears threatening just beneath the surface of my calm exterior.

I look around the table, and it's all I can do to muster enough dignity to calmly excuse myself from the room.

Late August evenings in New York can go either way, if you want to know the truth. It can be rainy and cool, or summer-warm with a slight breeze. Or, like tonight, cool but clear. I can't go back into that dining room, so I sit on the patio outside. I'm pretty much alone out here, with the exception of a waiter who keeps asking me if I need anything. All I want is to be left alone to nurse my humiliation. If not for Emily, I would have left for home immediately. But to do so would mean having to walk back through the room with everyone's eyes on me to tell her we're leaving. That would be worse than just toughing it out and waiting for her to find me.

Only, she doesn't. I've been out here for about thirty minutes when I hear movement behind me. I assume, of course, that the waiter is coming back to ask me if he can *please* get me something to drink, at least, and I turn expectantly, ready to give in and order coffee just to make him feel better. But it's Jack's face that greets me.

I stiffen and prepare to be mocked, now that he's over the surprise of my landing in his lap. Instead he sits in the love seat next to me. "May I?" he asks, although he already has.

"Sure."

"Sitting out here to dry your dress off?"

Rather than explain that I simply can't bear the humiliation of going back into the dining room, I nod. It's so much better than the cowardly truth. "It's almost dry."

"We're having cake in a few minutes. Thought you might want to watch me blow out the candles."

I can't help a self-deprecating grin. "Aren't you afraid I might set something on fire?"

"You're pretty good with water. We'll just pour you another glass."

"Shut up!" I bat him lightly on the arm.

He chuckles. "You know, it wasn't so bad, having you on my lap."

"Poor Sheri nearly had a heart attack. I suppose she thinks I ruined your birthday party."

"Well, yes, she isn't pleased. But it had more to do with appearances than the company."

"And I'm sure it appeared as though I was throwing myself at you." I sigh. "I bet you get that a lot."

"You flatter me." His response makes me realize how that sounded. But there's no way to recover from a comment like that. So I don't even bother. Besides, he's sort of staring into my eyes, and my breath is so shallow I think it might have stopped a few seconds ago.

"There's something I feel I must tell you."

He loves me? Can't bear to be without me? All the times I've imagined this scenario, I've made him beg. But at this instant all those power-trip daydreams flee, and I'm not sure I know my own name.

"Dancy." Oh, that's it.

"Hmm?" I ask lazily, my eyes drawn as though by their own volition to his sensuous mouth. My mind conjures up the image of him leaning in closer and closer, and my eyes sort of start to droop like they do just before—

"I hired Sheri today."

What? "What does Sheri have to do with this?"

"Um . . . I'm not sure what you mean."

Snap out of it, idiot. He's not moving in for a kiss. "Hired her for what?"

"Sweetheart," he says slowly. I'd relish the endearment if not for two things. First of all, I've heard Simon Cowell say exactly the same word, in exactly the same tone of voice, when speaking to Ryan Seacrest. Not exactly a term of undying love. And second, by the hesitation in his tone, I have a feeling I already know what position Sheri will be taking at Lane. "Editor."

My entire world upends with the utterance of two little words. *Sweetheart. Editor.* Words that might have been insignificant and passed unnoticed in any other context. But the wretched truth is that Jack Quinn not only fired me, but he hired my cousin to take over my job at Lane Publishing. Well, not my job, really. I knew they'd be hiring someone of my rank to work on nonfiction. But still, did it have to be her?

I know I must compose myself. Never mind that a few seconds ago, I was ready to pucker up and make him forget that Sheri ever existed. In my fantasy scenario I was going to upend his entire world with a kiss to end all kisses.

He's looking at me kind of funny, and his dark, normally sturdy brow is creased with a little worried pucker. In his eyes I see a question forming. And I know I'd better speak up before he comes to the wrong conclusion.

Okay, think. Think. Think. How do I get myself out of this with grace? I sit up straight, humiliated to discover I've been leaning in way too close to him. But there's no time to dwell on that little stupidity on my part. It's time for damage control. "That's—wow, um—fantastic. Sheri's a fantastic editor. She'll be a fantastic addition to your staff." I swallow hard. He hasn't responded, and I must do something to fill the silence. I clear my throat. "So, you hired Sheri. That's really—" I take a deep breath.

"Fantastic?" he supplies.

"Yes. Fantastic. I just thought . . ." No. Do not even consider mentioning that he said they were doing away with the position.

"Thought what?"

"Well, I thought she was getting promoted at Sharp. Why jump ship to take a demotion?"

"You'd have to ask her that question, to be honest."

I'm just about to sink through the cobblestoned patio floor when I hear a string of obscenities that everyone knows we just don't use at the country club.

Alarm shoots to Jack's eyes. "Is that Brandon?"

"Who else?" I jump up and head for the door leading into the lobby. Sure enough, there's my little brother, dressed in a nice suit, being physically escorted toward the door by two tuxedoed thugs. "Hey!" I holler as defensiveness shoots through me. "What do you two think you're doing?"

"We're sorry, Miss Ames. We caught this punk wandering around the clubhouse. We'll take care of it."

"That's my sister, you—" (More profanity—not repeating it.)

"Brandon, calm down," I say, stepping forward. "I'll handle this."

Shawn, the night shift head of security, frowns. "You know this kid?"

"As a matter of fact, I do."

"You do?"

"Yes, he's my little brother."

The security guard peers closer with a skeptical look on his face. "I've been working here for ten years and never saw a little brother before, Miss Ames. Are you sure you're not just taking up for this kid so he doesn't get into trouble?"

"Fellows," Jack says, stepping to my side. "I assure you, Miss Ames isn't exaggerating her relationship with this young man. He is, in fact, her younger brother."

Shawn's face goes red.

"Would you be so kind as to turn the lad loose, gentlemen?" Jack continues.

Shawn nods at the other guard, and they drop their death grip on Brandon's arms. He jerks away like it was his own doing and straightens his clothes.

"Please keep him with you. His unorthodox appearance scared Mrs. Hamilton."

That explains a few things. Mrs. Hamilton is a dowager who comes from old money and whose father actually built the country club, so she's got a lot of influence. But my family pays our dues. We have all the benefits of any other club member, regardless of Mohawk spikes or piercings. I mean, he is dressed appropriately, isn't he?

"Listen, Shawn," I say, ready to defend my younger brother to the death. "None of the other young people are asked to stay with their folks. He has every right to join a dinner party to which he was invited without being harassed by the country club *staff*." I stress *staff*. And I'm sorry to do so, but he's snubbing my brother, so maybe I'll snub him right back.

"Yes, I suppose I see your point, Miss Ames. I apologize for the misunderstanding."

"It's no problem. You didn't know. But please pass the word along that my brother has the right to be here."

"Yes, Miss Ames, I'll do that."

"And I think you owe him an apology."

Okay, I'm sort of inflated with power right now, so that was probably a bit much. I hold my breath, half expecting him to tell me where to get off.

Instead, he turns to Brandon. "I apologize for any embarrassment I caused you, Mr. Ames."

"It's Mr. Cunningham," he replies with a sneer.

Shawn's look of suspicion returns. And now I'm forced to explain. Why can't Brandon just let well enough alone? "He's my half brother."

"Half brother, huh?" Shawn nods. "Have a good evening."

"I was just about to knock that guy's head off," Brandon says.

"Sure you were. What are you doing here?"

"I got off work a little sooner than I thought, so I changed and came over. I didn't think you should take the subway alone after dark."

"You were looking out for me?" My eyes are getting misty.

Brandon slings his arm around my shoulders. "Well, I couldn't have my sister getting mugged, could I?"

I throw my arms around him. "What are you hungry for? My treat. Anything you want."

He sends me a grin. "How about pizza?"

What else would a teenager want?

"Don't the two of you want to stay for cake? I'm told it's red velvet." Jack grins, and his voice has a lilt to it. He knows how much I love red velvet cake. But then, not enough to go back into that room. "Brandon hasn't had his supper yet. He doesn't need to eat dessert first."

The mirth leaves his eyes, and he nods, suddenly sobered. "Oh, right."

"I'll go see about Emily and be right back," I say.

I steel myself as I walk into the dining room. Emily is deep in conversation with Floyd and doesn't see me standing there. I'm forced to tap her on the shoulder. She turns, eyes bright. "Hi! Isn't this a great party?"

"Terrific," I say. "My little brother showed up and I need to get him home. Are you ready?"

Her expression drops faster than a ride at Six Flags. "Oh, I suppose so."

"I could take her home."

Emily and I both turn our attention to Floyd. Emily beams. "How sweet. That would be wonderful."

"I know a little coffee shop just around the corner that stays open all night, if you'd like to join me after we leave here."

I think, after all these years, I'm finally free of Floyd.

"Thanks, Floyd," I say. "Emily, I'll see you at Nick's, I'm sure."

Neither seems to hear me. I can't help but smile as I leave the dining room.

"What's so funny?" Brandon asks. He's still chatting with Jack in the foyer.

"Oh, nothing. Emily is staying. Floyd will drive her home."

"Do I detect a love connection?"

"From your lips to God's ears."

Laughter rumbles in his chest.

"'Night, Jack."

"Good night," he says, opening the door for us. "Oh, and Dancy—"

"Yes?"

"If you reconsider the freelance job, give me a call."

"I will. Thanks."

During the cab ride home, Brandon gives me a nod. "That was pretty cool, how you stood up to that wannabe cop. Calling me your brother and all that."

"Well, you are my brother."

"Yeah, I know." He pauses and then turns to look out the window. "I still thought it was cool, the way you did it."

And, just like that, I know I'm going to do everything in my power to convince my dad and his mom that Brandon needs to stay in New York and attend the precollege program at Juilliard. He just has to.

I'm sorry when the next weekend comes—truly sorry that Brandon will go back to our dad's apartment on Sunday afternoon. I guess that's why I agree to go to church with Brandon, Kale, and Brynn. Kale arrives to pick us up at nine o'clock. I have Granny's Bible, and I look the part. As I walk into the church, my knees are shaking a little. The music begins, and I glance at Brandon—spiked hair, piercings, yet a look of reverence on his face, arms raised. I can't help but remember the kid from Friday night who cussed out the guard at the country club. I suppose Rome wasn't built in a day, though, was it?

Tears shoot to my eyes. My hands are curled around Granny's Bible, and I truly look like every other churchgoer. Only, maybe that's not true. These churchgoers look—different. Like I said, it's not something I can put my finger on. Rather, it's how they worship. Their hands are raised, some have tears streaming down their faces, and many are kneeling as the music plays with soft reverence.

And then it strikes me. These people *know* God. I wonder . . . could I know Him, too?

After the service, Brandon drags me around the church as only a teenager can, wanting to introduce me to every person who has been kind to him since he started attending. I'd venture to say that's most of the church, because my smile is starting to feel pasted on.

As we reach the back of the church, the pasted smile freezes at the sight of Jack Quinn standing in the foyer, apparently waiting for us to reach him. His smile is obviously genuine, so I try my best to relax. "Hi, Jack," I say with as much nonchalance as I can possibly muster.

Brandon looks beyond Jack to a group of teens and adults at the door. "Be right back." And he's gone before I can form a reply.

Jack is staring down at me. I gather my courage and smile.

"It's good to see you, Dancy." He takes in my appearance with an appreciative light in his eyes, until he observes my hat. His smile falters only a split second, and if I hadn't been watching so closely, I probably would have missed it.

"You look lovely," he says.

If we weren't in church, I'd whack him ever so lightly on the arm. Instead I purse my lips just a second. "Stop it. I can tell you hate the hat."

His eyes widen. Then his lips curve into a boyish grin. "I didn't realize I was that transparent."

"Like an open book," I shoot back.

He gives a throaty chuckle that raises goose bumps on my arms. "Or perhaps you know me too well."

"Could be," I say flippantly. "Is that a blessing or a curse?"

"I suppose that remains to be seen, doesn't it?"

I don't have a chance to respond as Brandon rejoins us. Next to him, a thirtyish woman in dressy shorts and flip-flops stands smiling so pleasantly that I can't help but respond in kind. "Hi, I'm Anna," she says. "My husband and I are the youth pastors here."

I shake her hand. "It's wonderful to meet you," I say.

"Same here. We've known Kale and Brynn for a while. Then Brandon, now you. Looks like we'll be getting the whole family here before long."

I hate to disappoint her, but I don't think I should be duplicitous. "Well, I'm just visiting."

Confusion slides across her face. "Oh, but I thought—"

"What?"

Brandon shuffles his feet and stares down at the floor. What on earth did he tell her?

"I told them you were coming to our church now and wouldn't mind chaperoning the back-to-school pizza blast on Friday night. Sorry, guess I was wrong."

Jack makes a noise, and I have a feeling he's fighting to keep from laughing at my predicament.

Anna reaches forward and presses her hand to my arm. "It's okay, Dancy. We'll find someone else."

"How badly do you need the help?"

She shrugs and gives me a sheepish smile. "One of our usual chaperones just had a baby, and one had to leave town suddenly. Church policy states that we have to have one chaperone per twenty-five kids, and we have two hundred kids signed up. We're two chaperones short. But I couldn't impose, not if you don't feel comfortable doing it."

"Nonsense," Jack butts in. "Dancy loves teenagers. She'd be perfect." He gives me such an innocent smile that, unless a girl really knew him well, she would be completely fooled. But I'm not.

"Jack's right," I say. His eyebrows go up. "I'm happy to do it"—I slide my gaze to his—"if he will."

All eyes turn to Jack, who grins. "I'd be delighted."

I narrow my gaze and look at him. I have a sneaky suspicion I might have just been set up.

I wait outside with Brynn and Jack for Kale to fetch the car. He'll be driving Brandon back to Dad's since it's in the opposite direction. I've decided to take the subway home. It's not far. Besides, I'm still upset with my dad for not being concerned about Brandon's chance to go to Juilliard.

"I had fun this week. I'm glad you came over."

He nods. "Thanks for putting up with me."

"I didn't just put up with you. You're my brother."

"Dad can't cook like your friend Laini."

"No one can," I say, sympathetic to his plight. It gets tiresome ordering out every night, which is what Dad does.

Kale pulls up in his SUV.

Brynn turns her glance to me. She gives me a quick hug and slips into the car.

I can't help but laugh as they drive away and Brandon waves at me through the moonroof.

"That's nice."

I turn to find Jack staring at me. I'm not sure what he means, but I'm smart enough to recognize approval in a person's voice.

"What's nice?"

He grins down at me. "The sound of your laughter. It's nice."

Oh, that. My heart takes a flying leap. I avert my gaze. "Thank you."

"You don't know how to accept a compliment. Do you know that?"

"I said thank you. What more do you want? Lifelong devotion? A kiss?"

He leans a little closer. "Lifelong devotion sounds nice, although I don't think we're quite ready for that step. But I wouldn't turn down the kiss, if you're offering."

My cheeks warm. I deserve it. I fell right into that one, didn't I? Or did I set it up to begin with? Either way, the man's just a little too smug for his own good. "In your dreams, Hugh Grant."

"Now, no reason to be insulting after I've just complimented you on your beautiful laugh."

"Being compared to Hugh Grant isn't exactly an insult."

"I was referring to your comment about only being allowed to kiss you in my dreams."

If I thought he was even a little serious, he wouldn't have to wait for his dreams. But we both know Jack is teasing, as he's been doing to me since I was sixteen. "Well, anyway, you insulted me first by saying I can't take a compliment."

"No insult intended, my dear." He takes my hand. And his hand is warm and wonderful and soft, like you'd expect from an editor's hands, and oh, my stomach jumps and my legs go weak. He brings our clasped hands to his chest, and I can feel the steady, strong beat of his heart. "I only meant," he says softly, "that you aren't complimented enough."

"H-how do you know that?" Standing this close to Jack, I can't think clearly enough to keep up my end of our exchange.

"It's obvious by the way you have difficulty accepting them graciously."

He touches his fingertip to my nose, like he's an older cousin or an uncle or something. Whichever, it's not flattering, and I feel stupid for getting all worked up. Never mind that he's holding my hand against his chest in clear uncousinly form. Feeling confused, I lift my chin.

I have to end this ridiculous moment before I lose my heart to this man who has no more than a brotherly interest in me. I pull my hand from his, and for once I don't make a spectacle of myself. "Actually, Jack," I say with an air of confidence. "*Everyone* tells me what a great laugh I have. What you interpreted as being uncomfortable is merely nonchalance about compliments like that, since they happen so often."

There. Let him be the one to feel silly this time.

He chuckles. "Well, then. Apparently I stand corrected." We have walked to the corner, where I'll descend the steps and catch the next subway. It'll take a full hour and twelve minutes to get home.

"I have my car," he says suddenly, as though reading my hesitation. "How about if I give you a lift? I'm going in that direction."

That actually sounds like a great idea. "Are you sure you don't mind? I'd really be grateful."

A smile splits his face. "I'd be delighted."

So Jack drives me home from church in a little Mazda Miata. The top is down and the weather is perfect. Even my hair refrains from blowing in my face. Jack slides in a CD, and I recognize a couple of the songs from worship this morning. I settle in, relax, and enjoy the ride.

15

It wasn't often that Valerie had to admit she was wrong, but in this instance, she knew she had no choice. How could she have thought M&J Advertising was the best place to work in her field? After a month at Harrison and Sons, she felt at home in a way she'd never felt before. The atmosphere was much more relaxed, something that would have caused her stress before. Ben Harrison was an easygoing widower with three children and kind eyes. He, along with his father, George, and his brother, Kenny, owned and operated the family-friendly office. A sense of integrity and morality seemed to float through the place, and Valerie had never felt so at home.

—An excerpt from *Fifth Avenue Princess*
by Dancy Ames

Tuesday evening, Brynn and Kale have a party—a painting party—at their empty soon-to-be home. It's one of those spur-of-the-moment things that came up that afternoon while we listened to Brandon's little orchestra playing in Central Park. He played violin. Apparently, he's quite the musical genius. Along with violin, he plays the piano, and pretty much any stringed instrument you put in front of him—including electric guitar, which doesn't thrill my dad when Brandon "practices."

Anyway, Brynn was planning to paint today, but Kale said, "Why don't we make a party of it? If you guys will come help, we'll spring for pizza." And that's how we got roped into it.

This goes against everything my mother stands for, and she seemed confused when Brynn told her we were painting tonight. "Darling, we'll just give you the number of the painter we use," Mother said. "And don't worry—we'll cover the cost for you and Kale."

"It's not that we can't afford it, Mrs. Ames," Brynn said. "That's just the way we do things at our house. Why waste thousands of dollars when we can do it ourselves?"

I love that philosophy. But it's completely opposite of Mother's, which is, "Never do anything yourself that you can have done for you, no matter the cost."

I suspect this might be the first of many disagreements between them. But Mother is too civil and Brynn is too respectful for it to get out of hand. It will definitely be fun to watch Brynn stand her ground. The blessing for Brynn is that Mother is moving to Florida, so she will very rarely have to deal with the disapproval.

Brynn has chosen tasteful, neutral colors. We set out to work: Brandon, Kale, Brynn, Sheri (her reason for coming is highly suspect since she isn't doing much painting), Jack, and me.

This is the first time I've seen Jack in jeans since he was in college, and even then he mostly wore slacks. Preparing to be the professional, I suppose. But now . . . let's just say he's looking pretty good, wearing a pair of ripped-at-the-thigh jeans with a T-shirt. Over the tee, he's wearing a long-sleeved striped shirt with the sleeves rolled midway up his forearms.

He looks . . . manly. And to my embarrassment, he keeps catching me staring at him.

I have been given the job of working around the bottom of the wall with an edging brush. I'm sitting cross-legged and working with meticulous precision so I won't mess up.

I'm having a little trouble dealing with Sheri's presence. We haven't spoken since Jack told me about hiring her. And I'm still curious about her reason for taking a position lower than the one she already held. Plus, she had bragged about getting a promotion at Sharp.

I get my chance after about two hours of steady work. We're painting on the same wall, I around the edges, Sheri with the roller behind me.

"So," I say, hoping I sound nonchalant. "Jack says you're working at Lane Publishing now."

She stops in her tracks and stares down at me. "You don't hate me, do you?"

I shrug. "No. I'm just surprised. I thought you were pretty much a company girl at Sharp Publishing. What happened?"

She squats next to me, balancing her roller on the floor so that the paint will drip back into the pan. "Do I have your word of honor that you will not say any of this to anyone?"

I nod. "Of course."

"I'm dating Kevin Martin."

My eyes go wide. "The associate publisher at Sharp? I thought you were interested in Jack."

"Jack?" A laugh bubbles to her lips and she nods in understanding. "I have to stop being such a flirt, don't I? Kevin says if I don't, he's going to hire a P.I. to follow me around. But, you know, he doesn't have anything to worry about. I've loved Kevin for five years, and he finally noticed me. There's no way I'd take a chance on ruining it."

"Wow, it sounds really serious."

She nods her lovely head. "It is. As a matter of fact—" She reaches around her neck and produces a huge diamond ring looped through a silver chain.

"Sheri—congratulations," I say, surprised at how much I mean it. "I'm so happy for you."

"Are you?" She looks intently into my eyes. "I thought you might hate me for taking over your job at Lane."

"You'll be working on nonfiction. That was never my strong suit, so you really didn't take it over."

"Well, I could talk to Kevin for you. I'm sure he'd be happy to have you at Sharp. He's been wanting to build our fiction department." She gives a little giggle. "I mean *their* fiction department."

I smile. "I actually already have an interview with Kevin in two weeks, on the seventeenth."

"Well, I'm going to tell him he has no choice but to hire you."

I can't help but warm to the way she's taking up my cause, but I place a restraining hand on her arm. "Let me handle it my way."

"You always were the independent one." She winks. "But if he asks my opinion, I'll tell him what I think."

As I turn back to the wall, my favorite proverb runs through my head. Maybe God is directing my path after all.

During the past month, I've been plodding along on my book, enjoying the creative process. Tabby and David are off somewhere with the twins, doing family stuff. Laini is baking, and I have decided to finish this story. By and large, it's not bad. With a little revision and thirty-five thousand new words, it might actually be something I can be proud of. Not that I'd ever try to get it published.

But what if I did? What if I, Dancy Ames, actually had a book published? I wonder if Jack would look at it when it's finished. No. That would be awkward. Good grief. No.

Besides, right now I need food, and Laini's baking is calling to me. I set aside my laptop, stand, and stretch. Laini turns and smiles when I walk in. "I wondered how long it would take you to decide you're hungry."

This is something new. I frown and point to the rack of bread mounds cooling on the counter. "What are those?"

"Okay." She hands me one on a plate. "Taste this and tell me what you think. It's something I'm trying out for Nick and Joe."

I bite into delectable homemade bread baked around turkey and Swiss cheese. It's warm and comforting and delicious. "Oh my gosh, Laini. This is the best thing I've ever tasted." I say that every time, but she knows what I mean.

"You think?" Her face glows, and I might add that it's getting a little round. I think we've all put on about ten pounds over the past three months. Laini's feeding us too well. I thought she'd settle down after she finished her semester, but with more time on her hands until her next classes begin, she's cooking more than ever. She'd better end this phase soon, or we'll all be signing up for Jenny Craig.

"It's fantastic. Nick's going to love it."

The house phone rings, and I pick it up just as Laini says, "Don't answer it!"

Too late. I give her a shrug of apology.

"Hello?" the male voice on the other end of the line says. "May I speak with Laini Sullivan, please?"

Laini rolls her eyes and holds out her hand for the cordless. "Hello? Oh, hi, Mr. Ace. Yes, I have been giving your offer some thought. I just don't see how I have time to fit in anything else right now."

I have to wonder how Laini can give up a job she's great at, where she's obviously being pursued. I'd love to ask her again, but when she hangs up the phone, she gives me a look that clearly says not to even bring it up. So I don't. That's the kind of friend I am.

Besides, Tabby picks this time to breeze in, bringing with her her fiancé, David, and his too-adorable-for-reality twins. Which, I suppose, is why they're child actors.

"Hey, you guys. What's up?" Tabby says.

Laini smiles at the kids. "Trying a new recipe."

"Looks good. Smells good." David hovers over the stove looking a little like he's the wolf staring down Little Red Riding Hood. Laini is, of course, thrilled with the interest. "Take one. Or two. Or however many you want."

Tabby grabs some plates. "Now aren't you glad we didn't stop for lunch? Do you want to help the kids wash their hands before we sit down?"

David dutifully ushers Jenn and Jeffy down the hall.

"What are these, Laini?" Tabby asks. "Homemade Hot Pockets?"

"Yep," I pipe in, unable to resist grabbing a second one myself. I mean, they're not really that big, so—I don't know—, maybe not *that* many calories. I'll run an extra mile later.

"How was the exhibition?" The kids are ice-skaters and have one exhibition per month. Every few months, they compete.

"Jenn fell during her spin. She was not happy."

"Darn," I say. "Next week is their last on *Legacy of Life*, isn't it?"

Tabby nods. The thing is, David never wanted his kids involved in acting. But his wife, who died of cancer, signed a contract, and he had to let them work it out. But he has no intention of re-signing, and that is just fine with the kids, who really just want to be kids.

They hop (don't kids always hop?) into the kitchen and find a seat at the table. Jeffy looks dubiously at the hot stuffed sandwich in front of him. "What is it?" he whispers loudly to Jenn.

"I don't know," she whispers back. They each cut a glance to Tabby, who laughs.

"Just try it. It's a warm sandwich."

With a sigh, they each take a tentative bite. I hold my laughter at the look of horror that lights each set of big blue eyes.

Laini giggles. "For Pete's sake, guys. They look like they're about to cry. Let me fix them a peanut butter and jelly sandwich."

The kids push their plates away and nod fervently, trying with valor to swallow the bites in their mouths.

"So, how are the wedding plans coming along?" I ask.

David and Tabby give each other a look.

"What?" I ask, as sudden fear sweeps through me. If anything happens between David and Tabby, I swear . . .

"Well, the thing is—" Tabby begins.

David puts his hand over hers and takes over. "We're going to have to put the wedding off for a little while."

"Oh, no!" Laini expels. "Why?"

"Neither of our parents are available to keep the twins during the Christmas holiday so we can go on the honeymoon."

Tabby's lip quivers a little. "I told him we can get married when we planned and wait for our honeymoon. I honestly don't mind putting off the Bahamas. The marriage is the important thing, right?"

She looks at Laini and me for support, but we don't have a chance to respond.

David shakes his head. "I don't want to start our marriage off like that." His eyes dart to the kids, and I think we all get the point. He doesn't want to start sleeping with his new wife when his kids are in the next room. He wants to devote his attention to getting to know Tabby intimately when they can be alone.

"I think that's sweet," I breathe.

Tabby scowls. "Well, sure it's sweet. But don't you think it's unnecessary? Especially when I want to get married as we planned."

Her unspoken, "And if you say no, I'll kill you," silences me. I avert my gaze and keep my mouth shut, because I'm not going to say I agree with her when I don't.

I can feel her hostility. Her blue eyes bore into me like she'll kill me if I don't immediately reverse my opinion. But I won't. However, I might have another solution.

"Why can't I keep the twins while you're gone on your honeymoon?"

"You?" Tabby sounds scared. And I must say, I'm a little insulted.

The kids let out a "Yay!" which makes my heart soar and brings a grin to my lips.

"Wait a minute," Tabby interjects into the fray. "I don't know if that's a good idea. Dancy doesn't have any experience with kids."

I do, too! "Hey, have you forgotten that I kept my little brother while my folks were away? And besides, you didn't either, until Jenn and Jeffy came along. Remember the job you got fired from because you started an argument with a six-year-old?"

"Okay, listen, honey," Tabby says, as if she's talking to the twins. "First of all, the little girl was a tyrant. *So* different story."

David snickers, then shuts up fast as Tabby spears him with a glare. He covers well with a cough.

"Second of all," Tabby continues, "Brandon is a teenager. So you didn't take care of him. You gave him a place to eat, crash, and take a shower. You've never taken care of children. They have to be fed, bathed, taken to school and to ice-skating and all those things. How are you going to do that and still work?"

"She can take them to day care," David interjects, ignoring Tabby's frown. "Besides, the week after Christmas, there is no ice-skating or school. So two less things she'd have to worry about."

"But this apartment—" Tabby says.

"We have the pullout couch," Laini reminds her, taking up the cause.

I grin.

Tabby opens her mouth and then sits back in the chair, letting her jaw relax. "Well, if you're sure."

"We are," Laini says decisively. She glances at the kids. "We'll have a swell time, won't we?"

They nod as they tear into their yummy peanut butter and jelly sandwiches. I look at Laini as she eyes those two kids. I hear the unmistakable sound of her biological clock alarm going off. Or is it mine?

16

Ben Harrison stood over Valerie's desk, the scent of his aftershave swirling through her senses until she had trouble concentrating on the account in front of her. She was in no way ready to consider a relationship with someone new. Not after the heartache of John Quest. Not that Ben acted even remotely interested in her. But the only things that seemed to interest Ben were named Amelia, Eric, and Donnie. His children were his life. Valerie had known only one man who put his family first, and that was her own dad. And in the presence of a father like Ben, her biological clock began to *tick-tock, tick-tock*. Ben turned and glanced at her, and in his eyes, Valerie saw the first spark of hope.

—An excerpt from *Fifth Avenue Princess*
by Dancy Ames

breathe in the smell of new carpet as I walk through the newly renovated offices of Sharp Publishing. The atmosphere seems friendly enough. I see smiles and flirting going on, typical for this kind of office. Overflowing bookshelves line the spaces between departments, and office doors are open. One even has a bicycle parked in front of a desk. For some reason, that impresses me. Mr. Kramer wouldn't put up with it, that I know.

Kevin's office is large and plush, with an oak-finished desk and a chair that probably set the company back a couple thousand dollars. He flashes a million-dollar grin and motions to the chair across from him. On his desk is a photo of him and Sheri, arm in arm in someone's front yard.

"So you're Sheri's cousin." He looks me over like he's trying to find a resemblance. His eyes stay on certain parts of my anatomy, and I fight the urge to cross my arms over my chest.

"We don't look much alike," I mumble, feeling like I should apologize.

"You're both beautiful . . . where it counts." My face goes hot. Surely I am misunderstanding his comments. Surely.

"So, you worked for Lane Publishing for . . ." He looks over the document in front of him, suddenly all business. I relax, hoping I indeed misunderstood his intentions.

"Ten years," I supply.

"Impressive staying power." His eyebrows go up and his lips twitch a little, and I wonder if he's making a sexual innuendo. I decide to give him the benefit of the doubt.

"I loved it." I try to remain professional. But discussing Lane Publishing feels personal, as though I lost a part of my family by leaving the company.

"Why did you leave?"

Is this a trick question? I feel sure Sheri has told him every detail. "I was let go because they want to focus more on nonfiction, and my strength is fiction. That's why they hired Sheri."

"I see."

I swallow as tense silence fills the air between us. I don't know if I should speak, so I don't. I read in Granny's Bible the other night, "Even a fool when he holdeth his peace is counted wise: and he that shutteth his lips is esteemed a man of understanding." Personally, I'd rather be considered quiet and smart than be a loud idiot.

"Your résumé looks good. I've been in contact with Lane Publishing, and they tell me the same thing you did. That you were a good employee. Faithful and loyal. That's exactly what we're looking for here at Sharp Publishing. You do know this is a senior editor position, right?"

My heart jumps into my throat for a second. "Yes, I do know that."

We talk about what the job entails, the starting salary, and a start date. The interview ends precisely thirty minutes after it began, and Kevin stands. I follow his lead. "I'll be calling you soon to let you know our decision."

I paste a smile on my face. "I'll look forward to hearing from you."

"Dancy," he says as I walk to the door.

I turn. "Yes?"

"One question."

I stop and wait.

"Sheri mentioned to me that you're writing a book. Is your passion to be an editor or a writer?"

I stare, speechless. How did Sheri know I'm writing a book? I know my roommates would cut off their own arms before betraying my confidence.

Now that it's out there, I have no choice but to answer the question. "Two months ago, I would have said editing, hands down. But I've been focusing on writing since then, and quite frankly, I love it. I love my book and I love the writing process."

He nods.

"However, I also miss my job as an editor. Can't I love both?"

He stares at me for a second, and I have a feeling I've completely blown this interview. "Can you divide your focus between the two, or will one suffer in favor of the other?"

"I'm not sure how one could suffer in favor of the other. My writing is a matter of the heart. I do it in my spare time because it makes me happy. Editing is what I do as a job, and I enjoy that too. One has nothing to do with the other. I don't think I should have to give up writing in order to edit or the other way around, any more than a chef should give up eating to be a good cook or vice versa."

I hold my breath as he scrutinizes me for a few seconds. I have no idea what might be going on in his head. Finally he gives me a nod.

"We'll be in touch."

Nothing in me thinks that's good news. Defeated, I leave the Sharp building and walk for a while. My steps take me past Lane Publishing. I truly didn't mean to go there, but somehow I find myself climbing the steps and entering my former place of employment.

I haven't been here in six weeks—since I cleaned out my office. I get smiles, hellos, and good-to-see-yous. I stop at Crystal's desk. "Is he in?" I ask Jack's assistant.

"He is. Let me see if he can meet with you."

She picks up the phone. "Dancy Ames is here to see you." She pauses. "But she doesn't have an appointment. Okay, Jack."

She sets down the receiver and looks up at me. "This is a first. He said to go on in."

"Thanks, Crys."

Jack opens the door just as I reach for it. The action throws me off balance. I stumble and catch myself from falling face-first onto the floor. Predictably, Jack reaches out and grasps me. "Easy does it," he says.

"I'm okay," I say abruptly, aware that we are most likely the focus of plenty of stares. I clear my throat and smooth my jacket as he turns me loose.

"Come in," he says, stepping out of the way for me to enter. He closes his door and motions to the couch against the wall. "Would you like something to drink?"

Normally I'd say no, but I find that my throat is parched. "Water?"

He nods and opens the door. "Crystal. Could you bring Dancy a bottle of water?"

He sits down next to me on the sofa. His large body looks out of place as he tries to find a comfortable position. "What brings you here?"

Before I can answer, Crystal taps on the door and enters with my bottle of water. She frowns when she sees us on the couch. I suppose she expected us to sit at the desk. Quite frankly, so did I.

"Thank you, Crystal. Please close the door on your way out," Jack says pointedly.

I take up the conversation where it left off at Crystal's interruption. "I'm not sure why I'm here."

"How did your interview with Kevin go?"

Is my life an open book? "You knew about that?"

"Kale." He grinned. "Then Sheri."

I roll my eyes. "We're too closely connected."

"You think?" His eyes twinkle. "I've been thinking lately that perhaps we're not close enough."

Breathe, Dancy. Breathe.

"What do you mean?"

He leans in. "Surely you know exactly what I mean."

"Y-you fired me."

"Are you going to forgive me? I had no choice."

"Why didn't you fight for me?" Tears burn my eyes and throat. Oh, why do I always cry?

"You were no longer right for the position."

"How do you know?" Anger flashes through me. "You didn't even give me a chance to acquire nonfiction, did you? I read quite a bit of nonfiction, as a matter of fact."

"It's done, Dancy." His jaw twitches as he clenches his teeth together. A telltale sign of irritation. "Surely you didn't come all this way to talk about something that can't be changed at this point."

I hop up from his couch. "Forget why I came."

I grab the water from the table and slam out of his office. "Thanks for the water, Crys."

"You're welcome," she says meekly.

It isn't until I reach the street that I realize something horrible.

"Dancy! Wait."

Humiliation rips through me as I turn toward Jack. I don't even have to ask why he followed me. He hands me my purse. "Thank you."

"You're welcome." He stuffs his hands in his pockets and stares at me. "Are we ever going to move past this? It seems like we start to, and then you bring it back."

"I don't know, Jack. I try. But I need someone to fight for me, and you just let me go."

He steps forward, hands still in his pockets. "Is this about work? Or is it personal?"

His presence is so overwhelming as his eyes pierce me. I stumble back to escape the intensity.

"I have to go, Jack."

Thankfully, a cab stops as soon as I raise my arm. I slide inside and slam the door. Unable to help myself, I turn to look out the window. Jack is still standing on the sidewalk. He lifts his hand in a farewell. I press my palm to the window and watch him until he fades into the distance.

After a month of nail-biting, I finally get a call from Kevin at Sharp Publishing, offering me the job as senior editor. It's the middle of the day and there's no one to share my news with, so I pack up my laptop and walk down to Nick's. Joe is behind the counter.

"Hi, doll," he says. "What can I get you?"

"Green tea would be lovely." Then I notice a sign with a picture of a pumpkin latte. "Since when did you start serving those?"

"It's for the fall." He grins. "My idea. Try one. On the house."

"Who are you giving drinks to on the house?" Nick barrels through the kitchen door, a frown firmly in place until he sees me. Then he smiles. "'Ey, princess. I thought you fell off the face of the earth. Fix her that latte and don't take a penny," he commands Joe.

Joe grins and sends me a wink.

Nick comes from behind the counter and slips his massive arm around my shoulder as he leads me to a table. "You want I should fix you a meatball sub?"

I shake my head. "I'm having the latte. I'd better save the rest of my calories. I have news."

"You gettin' married finally?"

Nick! He douses my enthusiasm without even trying.

"No. I'm not getting married. I got a new job." I grin. "A better position with more money."

"'Ey! This is a celebration!"

"You know, you're right. Do you have any of Laini's stuffed sandwiches left?"

Joe delivers my latte and overhears my question. "Are you kidding? We sold two dozen between eleven and twelve thirty and had at least two dozen more orders. People weren't too happy when I told them we were sold out."

"Laini's going to be so excited."

"What's she doin', wastin' her time goin' to school when she can sell her food like this?"

"Well, this isn't a business, Nick. It's just a way for her to burn off stress. If she can make a little money on the side, so much the better."

Sort of like my writing. I'm an editor first. But if I can sell my book and make a little bit on the side, so much the better.

The door dings and I look up. Emily enters, wearing her typical bell-bottoms and peasant blouse. She has a crocheted bag slung over her shoulder and heads straight for me. "Hi, Dancy." She gives me a hug and takes the seat next to me since Nick's sitting on the other side of the table. She seems to be less terrified of him now, but not completely comfortable.

"What can I get you, Emily?" Joe asks.

She orders a chai tea.

Nick hauls himself up. "I'll let you two girls chat." He clasps my shoulder as he walks by. "I'm real happy for you, princess."

"Thank you, Nick."

Emily stares. "Happy about what?"

"I got a new job."

Her face lights up. "Congratulations."

I can't hold back my crazy grin. "Thanks."

"I have news, too," Emily says. Her grin is about as crazy as mine.

"Spill it."

"I'm dating someone."

"Floyd?"

A blush creeps across her face. She nods. "He said the two of you have sort of been a fixture at dinner parties and family get-togethers since you were kids, but it never went anywhere. Is that true?"

"Very." I smile. "Believe me, I couldn't be happier for the two of you."

I can't help but wonder what she sees in him. I also can't help but wonder what Mrs. Bartell will say about the possibility of a hippie tainting the blue blood of her family line.

My first day at Sharp Publishing dawns crisp and sunny, as late autumn is bound to be in Manhattan. It's Halloween, so the subway ride is interesting, to say the least. Costumes abound on folks from two years old to fifty-two. Once I arrive downtown, I walk the crowded streets, past Lane Publishing and beyond, to the steps leading to my new life.

Senior Editor. Senior Editor. Dancy Ames, Senior Editor. I can't keep the stupid grin from splitting my face. I smile in the elevator and no one smiles back, but even those sour faces can't dampen my happiness. I've been thanking God every second, it seems, for directing my steps.

I get to the tenth floor and say hello to the assistants and editors who occupy cubicles instead of offices.

Gloria, my assistant, is right outside my office. I can see her from my desk if I leave the blinds open. Which I won't, for now. I need my privacy as I learn the ropes at my new company.

On my desk are a basket of flowers and a bouquet of roses.

I look at the card on the basket first. It's from Tabby and Laini, congratulating me on my new position.

My hand shakes a little as I lift the card from the roses. I can't believe I'm hoping they're from Jack. But I am. My heart plummets as I read: "Welcome to Sharp Publishing. I look forward to working closely with you. Kevin."

Well, that was sort of nice, I suppose. Roses, though?

Of course, it's because I'm his fiancée's cousin. I set the cards aside and walk to the window. An office with a view. Granted it's a view of other buildings and busy traffic. But still I have a view. I feel like Melanie Griffith at the end of *Working Girl*.

Gloria taps on my door almost immediately. I smile a welcome, and she seems relieved. Was Sheri that hard to work for? "Kevin has a couple of meetings this morning, but he asked that you join him for lunch. He'll send a car to pick you up at noon."

"Okay. That sounds good. Thanks."

She motions to a pile of manuscripts on the floor. "Those are proposals that are still under consideration. She points to another pile. "Those have been rejected but no one has gotten around to sharing that information with the agents."

I toss a wry smile. "I suppose that's my first order of business?"

She grins. "Something like that."

"Thank you, Gloria."

"Can I get you anything?"

I shake my head. "Nothing I can think of."

She closes the door as she leaves, and I plant my hands on my hips. Where do I start?

At noon, I slide into a town car to find Kevin in the backseat waiting for me. "Hi, gorgeous," he says immediately. He leans over and gives me a kiss on the cheek. I'm taken aback by the gesture, and I suppose it shows because he holds up his palm. "Don't worry, just a little welcome kiss between soon-to-be cousins."

"Sheri and I aren't that close, normally," I say.

"That's not what she says."

Oh.

The restaurant is dim, and we're escorted to an even dimmer corner booth where Kevin sits close enough to press his thigh against mine. I scoot and he stays. Whew!

Three margaritas (for him) later, and he's all hands. But not blatantly. He sort of reaches over me to get the salt and happens to brush my hand. He goes for his wallet in his back pocket and "accidentally" presses against me. I'm telling you, this guy is a lecher. I wonder how on earth Sheri doesn't know this.

I breathe a sigh of relief when lunch is over. But then comes the car ride back to the office.

Kevin presses his hand to my knee. "So, tell me," he says, slurring his words slightly. "How is your first day going?"

I take his hand and move it.

He offers me a sheepish grin that I in no way believe. "Oops, my bad."

"My day is going just fine, Kevin."

He makes small talk for the rest of the trip. I nearly kiss the ground when we reach the office.

By the time I get to my office and close the door, I'm fighting tears, because I have no idea what I'm going to do. I cannot work for a man who makes passes at me! I just won't. It's not worth it.

The next day goes off without incident. By Friday I'm feeling pretty confident that Kevin got the message. I'm back into the groove of office life. My inherited piles of proposals are diminishing, and I'm looking forward to Brynn and Kale's engagement party on Saturday. When I get to work Friday, I'm surprised to find I already have a bunch of unopened e-mails. Three are instructional, which I appreciate. One is from Kevin, and one is from Jack.

I read the one from Kevin first.

Dancy,
Please come to my office.
Kevin

I wiggle the mouse, running the arrow over Jack's e-mail without actually clicking it open. Finally, my curiosity gets the better of me.

Dancy,
I trust you've had a successful first week. You are a much better editor than you know. Be confident and stay true to your convictions. If you need me for any reason, don't hesitate to contact me.
Sincerely,
Jack Quinn
Senior Editor
Lane Publishing

I click reply just as my instant message pops up.

KMartin: Did you receive my e-mail?
DAmes: Hello, Kevin. I was just about to head down there.
KMartin: Good. I'm looking forward to it.

Jack's reply will have to wait. I leave it where it is and stand. Gloria jumps when I open the door. "Do you need something, Miss Ames?"

"Call me Dancy, Gloria. And, no. Mr. Martin wants to see me in his office."

"I bet he does," she mumbles, just loudly enough to be heard.

"Excuse me?"

She gives me a guilty glance. "Nothing."

I head to Kevin's office, aware that all eyes are on me as I walk. I've never felt more self-conscious. Well, not since my beauty-pageant days, anyway. His door is closed, and I glance at his assistant. "Kevin asked to see me."

"Yes, Miss Ames. He told me to have you go on in."

I smile at the busty, blond Pamela Anderson wannabe and give the door a tap. "Thank you." I know he said for me to go on in, but something about a closed door begs a knock.

"Come in."

I twist the knob and push open the door. His face lights up when he sees me. He stands and walks around the desk, meeting me at the door and closing it behind me. "Come sit on the couch." His hand is on my back, right where my bra strap connects. I'm not crazy about the way his hand is caressing me.

He sits next to me, and I immediately smell alcohol on his breath.

His face flushes with pleasure. "You have the prettiest hair," he says. He reaches forward and wraps a finger around one of my curls. "I usually prefer blonds, but these dark curls could drive a man crazy."

Every muscle in my body begins to shake. I shoot to my feet, standing on wobbly legs. Has this guy never heard of sexual harassment? I wonder if I should call Nick and tell him to bring his buddies over to give Kevin a good talking-to. Or something more than a talk.

"What do you want, Kevin? Remember, you asked me to come to your office?"

"Come on," he coaxes. "Sit down and talk to me for a while."

"Mr. Martin . . ."

"Kevin." His voice has taken on a silky, slithery tone, and I know he'll be making his move soon. It's time to bolt. "Kevin. I have work to do, so if you don't have anything to discuss, I'm going back to my office."

He takes my hand and tugs, causing me to lose my footing and stumble back to the couch. "Don't be a party pooper. Do you want a drink to relax?"

Is this guy kidding? A drink? I could sue his behind off! Why hasn't anyone done just that by now, if this is his MO? "Back off, bud!" Am I seriously fighting off an octopus wearing Armani? This is crazy.

"Sheri didn't mention you were such a prude."

"Maybe Sheri didn't know I was." I frown. "Or maybe she didn't imagine her fiancé would be making passes at other women in the office."

He chuckles. "I'm sure she didn't, although I made plenty of passes at her. Come on," he says, leaning in so close I can smell the coffee mixed with alcohol on his breath. Ugh, I may never drink coffee again. "It's all in the family."

Anger shoots through me, driving away my fear. I press my palms against his chest and give him a shove.

"What the—"

I shoot to my feet while he's off guard and stomp to the door, fists clenched. "Never touch me again, Kevin. Or I'll punch your lights out."

Trying to compose myself, I pause a second by the door before swallowing hard, twisting the knob, and leaving his office.

My gaze stays steady in front of me as I scurry back to my office. I close the door behind me and click the lock. I can't bear the thought of facing anyone. Guilt assails me. Did I mislead Kevin into thinking I wanted him to make a pass at me?

Tears pool in my eyes as I sit at my desk. My instant-message alarm sounds, and instinctively I know who is trying to get my attention.

KMartin: I apologize for the misunderstanding. It will never happen again.

I stare at the screen. I bet you do, buddy. That sounds like the cry of a man who knows he's in a position to get sued for sexual harassment, not to mention having his fiancée informed of his womanizing.

An odd mix of relief and anger threads through me, until I'm not sure which emotion is stronger. One thing is for sure: I'm not answering his instant message. Let him apologize. I'm not answering.

I see Jack's message behind the instant-message screen and click reply.

Jack,
Thanks for the note. Are you still interested in giving me a freelance job?
Dancy Ames
Senior Editor
Sharp Publishing

I stare at my in-box and wait, hoping he will write me back quickly. Jack doesn't disappoint.

Dancy,
What's wrong?
Jack

Tears stream down my face. I can't believe I'm even telling him this.

Jack,
This is between us only. Kevin hit on me—first Monday and then again just a minute ago. He apologized, but I don't want to work for a man like that.
Dancy

A minute later, my cell phone rings and I know it's Jack.

"Are you all right?" he asks as soon as I answer.

I heave a sigh. "Just disappointed and feeling like an idiot."

"Don't. You've nothing to feel idiotic about. Shall I come and punch this Kevin fellow in the nose for you? I'd be happy to defend your honor."

I can't help but laugh. "No." I groan. "What should I do, Jack?"

"Gather your things and leave immediately. You can e-mail your resignation from your home computer."

"Should I really do that?" I glance at my clock. "I've been here less than a full week. That has to be some kind of record."

"Probably." He pauses. "I have some time this morning. Would you like to go to breakfast?"

I open my mouth to refuse when he says, "I'll bring an agreement for you to do freelance work for us. And we can discuss the terms. What do you say?"

I can't help but feel disappointed. The man I had hoped to work with wanted something more. And the man I want something more with can only keep his mind on work. What an awful day.

17

Valerie waited impatiently at the airport for her parents to deplane. It had been six months since they left for Africa. Six months that seemed like six years as far as she was concerned. This furlough would only be for two weeks, but she planned to make the most of every minute.

Her heart lifted at the sight of them. She ran, desperate to fall into her daddy's open arms and pour out her heartbreak over John, her confusion over Ben.

But when she reached her parents, she stopped short and stared. Daddy looked weak, ill really. "Mom?" she asked. "What's wrong with Daddy?"

"Honey, we didn't want to tell you."

"What? What is it?"

"Let's wait until we get home," Dad said.

"No." Tears streamed down Valerie's face. "I need to know."

Mom took her hands. The three stood in the middle of the terminal while travelers buzzed around them. "Your dad was diagnosed with lung cancer right before we decided to go to Africa."

"What?" Valerie felt the betrayal to her bones. "Why didn't you tell me?"

"We've always wanted to go. To feed the hungry. Dad wanted the chance to do that before he died."

"You're not going back, are you?"

Dad shook his head. "This was a one-way trip for me."

A sob caught in Valerie's throat.

"Shh," her dad said, caressing her hair with his gentle hand. "Don't cry for me, honey. I'm about to take another one-way trip. The one I've been waiting for all my life."

—An excerpt from *Fifth Avenue Princess*
by Dancy Ames

Tears are flowing freely by the time Jack meets me halfway between Sharp and Lane.

"May I?" he asks, holding out his arms.

I nod and he gathers me close into warm, strong arms. People swarm past us, but I don't care. I feel safe, and right now that's all that matters to me.

When my tears are spent, Jack pulls out a handkerchief and dabs my eyes for me. Then he puts the cloth to my nose and I laugh. "I'll blow my own nose, thank you very much."

"Good. Your sense of humor is still intact. You may blow."

"I can't believe I quit my job less than an hour into my fifth day. What is that going to say about me in this business?"

"You're not going to have to worry about that. If you want to launch a freelance business, I can guarantee you will be in high demand."

I laugh. "You're just trying to cheer me up."

He shakes his head. "Not at all."

We find an outdoor café and sit. Jack pulls out a sheet of paper and hands it to me.

Nondisclosure? "What is this?"

"You need to sign it before you can see the manuscript we'd like you to edit."

I quickly read it over. It says only that I will not disclose the contents of the manuscript or discuss the author with anyone outside of approved personnel. I shrug. "Who's the author? President Bush?"

He grins. "Hardly."

I scrawl my name on the dotted line and hand the pen back to Jack. "All right, secret-agent man. Let's see this manuscript."

He pulls out a padded yellow envelope with a manuscript inside. I take it and reach in. "Wait until later," he says. "Let's have our coffee and breakfast."

I frown. "What? After all that? There's no way I can wait until after breakfast. My curiosity won't let me."

He gives me a half-smile. "I'd forgotten you're still a child."

I stick out my tongue as I pull the four-hundred-page manuscript from the envelope. I gasp as I read the title and the name of the author.

My Heart Weeps No More by Cate Able.

"Are you kidding me?" I look up at Jack. "Jack! Are you kidding me?"

"I wouldn't make you sign a nondisclosure form for a joke, would I?"

"Cate Able is my favorite author." I'm aware that I'm gushing. But I never thought I'd be given the chance to edit the reclusive author.

"Is that so?"

"Oh, come on. Everyone knows that."

He sends me his boyish Hugh Grant grin along with a wink, and I realize this is more than an editing job. This is a huge favor. A gift.

I'm in such awe, even I can hear it in my voice. "Does this mean I get to meet her?"

"We'll see. For now, just work on the manuscript. And, Dancy," he says, his tone suddenly serious, "you must give this manuscript a one-hundred-percent effort. Ms. Able is not like Virginia Tyne. She will not throw a fit and get you sent on vacation if you give honest feedback."

"Are you sure about that? Cate Able can likely call her own shots."

"I give you my word that if you give all you have on this edit and do what I know you can do, Ms. Able will be most pleased."

"Jack, I just have to know one thing."

"Yes?"

"Why on earth would you ask me to edit for Lane Publishing's biggest author?"

"I'm not sure I understand the question."

A short laugh erupts from my throat. "Face it, when I worked for you, you critiqued my edits, then made me face the cranky authors—so much so that I was forced on vacation and then eventually fired."

His eyes flash alarm. "You think I was critiquing your edits? Dancy, I read your edits because they fascinated me. I enjoyed your insights. And yes, I added my two cents' worth, but not as a criticism. You were perfectly free to discard my thoughts."

"Well, I mean, I agreed with most of them," I admit. "Still, I felt like you were undermining me."

"Then why didn't you come to me, silly woman?" His eyes are kind and a little confused. "I would have certainly apologized."

"And getting fired?" Fresh anger washes over me. "Why didn't you fight for me?"

"You keep saying that," he says. "What makes you think I didn't?"

Rays of hope finally break through my cloudy day as he continues. "I don't decide the direction of our program. Your heart is clearly in fiction. We are expanding in nonfiction, and there was no way Kramer would have fired Fran. You know that without me expounding upon the reason."

He's right. "So I was just the sacrificial lamb."

"Something like that." He waves away the waitress as she starts to give him a refill. "So, if I've answered all of your questions satisfactorily, may I please have your answer?"

"You know I can't pass this up."

"Lovely!"

Clasping my hands together, I can feel myself practically beaming. "I just can't believe this! Wait until I tell Laini and Tabby."

He expels an exasperated breath. "Dancy, darling. Do I need to explain what nondisclosure means?"

I stare. "Oh, Jack. I can't edit Cate Able and not tell my friends. They live with me. They know everything. We don't keep those sorts of secrets." I slip the manuscript back inside the envelope. Swallowing hard, I push it back across the table. "I'd better not take the job, Jack. I can't keep from telling Tabby and Laini. It's just not possible."

He gives me a little scowl and pushes the envelope back to me. "Take it. But do not tell anyone else. Is that clear? And you mustn't reveal the contents before publication. Not even to your girlfriends."

"That's no problem. They don't care for her books."

"Why not? Don't they read?"

"Oh, sure. Laini reads romance, and Tabby reads *Soap Opera Digest* and the Bible."

"Now that's a combination." Jack laughs.

I smile. "So I get to keep the job?"

He nods. "You do. I can't help but admire your honesty. Many people in your position would have broken the agreement without being honest about it. You were willing to give it up because you know you can't keep a secret from your two chums. I respect that."

"Thanks, Jack." My heart lifts at his smile. "I needed those kind words."

Later, I stand on the subway, holding the pole with one hand and clinging to the treasured manuscript with the other. Just when I should be crawling home, defeated and depressed, I actually have to say this might be the best day of my entire life.

Kale and Brynn's engagement party is huge, formal, and about as pretentious as an Academy Awards after-party. Mother and Dad reserved the entire club, and Brynn's folks flew in from Oklahoma.

My mother is showing off. That's all there is to it. And there's no reason to. Brynn's parents are kind, simple folks. Salt of the earth. Farmers. And even dressed appropriately. Secretly, I think my mother hoped Brynn's mother would need her advice on what to wear. But she wasn't given the satisfaction. The woman is dressed beautifully in an understated black dress that, unless I miss my guess (and I rarely do where little black dresses are concerned), is Gucci.

Really, was it necessary to commission a five-foot ice sculpture of two swans, their heads pressed together so their necks form a heart? Has Mother never heard of subtlety?

The foyer is set at a freezing-cold temperature to keep the ice from melting too quickly. No one's sticking around to enjoy that particular decoration anyway, though, so it just seems like a waste of money. But Mother likes it, so I guess if that's the goal, it was worth it.

The core of the party is taking place in the huge dining hall. Twelve round tables that host six guests each are placed strategically so that there is plenty of room for dancing. There's a bar, but I won't go there. Besides, Dad is imbibing enough for the whole family.

The band is playing a wonderful combination of new and old love songs, from Dean Martin to Clay Aiken.

I'm at the table of second importance. First, of course, being the parents of the bride- and groom-to-be, and the lucky couple themselves.

At my table, Mom has placed Floyd (she knows all about his new girlfriend, Emily, so I'm a little upset that she won't give up), Jack, Sheri, Brandon, and Brynn's younger sister, Carol, who speaks with a sweet midwestern accent and has Brandon rethinking the spikes. I can tell because he keeps touching them. I want to tell him he's just bringing more attention to the fact that his hair sticks straight up in several pointy arrows aimed at the ceiling, but I don't want to embarrass him. Maybe if we have a minute alone later. . . .

Sheri is stunning in a gown of shimmering navy blue set against a spray-on tan. Not much—just enough to give her skin the glow that is so often missing in the winter. She looks more than stunning, actually. She looks regal.

I feel completely pale in comparison in my champagne-colored gown. And I was feeling so confident before I set eyes on my elegant cousin. Even the men look stunning in their tuxes. And of course, Jack, predictably, outshines every man in the room.

I haven't actually seen Jack since he handed over the coveted manuscript a few days ago. But he's just as handsome as ever, and I'm trying not to stare.

Floyd won't stop talking about Emily, and as happy as I am for them, if I have to hear one more thing about how refreshing it is to date someone who isn't an absolute clone of every other woman in the country, I'm going to stuff a dinner roll in his mouth.

"So my mother says I should do it, but I'm still waffling," Floyd is saying. "What do you think?"

What do I think? What do I think about what? I stare into Floyd's hopeful eyes and realize that I've only been listening to about every third word he's said.

Think. The words I remember. Time off, cost, rest. Vacation? Is he asking my opinion about where he should go? He's a broker, so he could go anywhere he chooses. France, Italy, Ireland, Greece, Hawaii. Anywhere, really. Even London. And speaking of the British, my gaze lands on Jack. We have some world travelers at the table . . . two, anyway. Jack and Sheri. Floyd's vacation would be interesting conversation for an entire table, I'd say. Time to draw Jack into my world.

"Well, Floyd." I take a sip of my water. "What do *you* think?"

He frowns. "I'm not sure. I'm waffling."

Oh, that's right. He did just say that, didn't he?

"Well, let's get Sheri and Jack's opinions, shall we?"

"I suppose it wouldn't hurt to get the added input."

I clear my throat. "Hey, guys," I say. "Floyd has a real dilemma and would like your opinions. Do you have a minute?"

Sheri and Jack turn. Sheri looks at Floyd and smiles. I haven't had the guts or the heart to tell her about Kevin. I'm not sure she would believe me if I did. "Of course. What's the problem, Floyd?"

"Well, it's a little embarrassing," he says, his face glowing a bit.

Embarrassing? What is there to be embarrassed about? Working for a brokerage firm in Manhattan is stressful. A nice vacation is well deserved. Unless I'm wrong and vacation isn't what he was talking about in the first place. But really, what else could it be? I clear my throat and take another sip of water.

"It's nothing, really," he says. "I just . . . I'm considering having my ears tucked."

I practically spit water across the table. We're not talking about vacation? Lord, have mercy. Brandon looks at him like he's from Mars. "What's that?" I sputter.

And all eyes are drawn to Floyd's ears, which I have to admit do stick out, but he's not exactly Dumbo.

And now he's all embarrassed and the air over the table has suddenly become extremely tense. It's all my fault. I forced Floyd to bring it up out of my desperate need to get Jack's attention. I'm a horrible, horrible person. But, I mean, if I had known he was talking about his big ears, I never would have suggested a group discussion.

"What does Emily suggest?" Sheri asks. It seems the whole world knows about Emily.

His ears go bright red. "She says they're perfect."

"Then I wouldn't change a thing, Floyd," Sheri says softly. "Your ears are just the way God made them."

His face brightens and I'm struck by Sheri's kindness. "You think?" he says.

"Definitely."

Floyd seems genuinely grateful. "Do you, uh, want to dance?" he asks Sheri. "I mean, since Emily isn't here."

"I'd love to."

Brandon turns to Carol. "You want to dance?"

She blushes and nods.

My cheeks warm up. What if Jack doesn't want to dance with me?

Jack's chair scrapes against the floor. He stands and walks to me, holding out his hand, palm up. "Shall we?"

"I don't dance."

"Of course you do," he says, undaunted. "Fifth Avenue princesses always know how to dance."

I gasp. "What do you mean?"

"I confess. Brandon told me you're writing a book with that title."

A groan escapes.

"That book is not about me."

"I didn't say it was," he says, bending slightly. "Now, are you going to leave me standing here, or are you going to take my hand and dance with me?"

I take his hand, but I can't let go of the fact that he just called me a Fifth Avenue princess.

"If you don't think the book is about me, then why did you call me that?"

He leads me to the dance floor and takes me in his arms. "If I apologize and swear on the life of my firstborn that I don't believe the book is autobiographical, will you drop it and relax?"

"Fine. Consider it dropped. I'm totally relaxed."

He raises his eyebrows, and I know he doesn't believe me, but at least he smiles and begins to sway with the music.

"Dancy," Jack whispers against my hair. "You promised to relax."

The band is playing "When I Fall in Love," and I'm suddenly overwhelmed with the realization that I'm in Jack Quinn's arms. He smells like aftershave and a cool night wind. My heart does a somersault in my chest. "I'm sorry," I whisper. Taking a deep breath, I force myself to relax against him.

"Much better."

I close my eyes, swept away by the romance of the evening, the song, and the dance.

Jack doesn't speak, but I feel his palm against the small of my back, leading me around the dance floor. But all good things must come to an end, and I feel Jack moving back. I open my eyes to find Floyd cutting in.

I'm gratified to see reluctance move across Jack's face as he relinquishes his hold on me. He lifts my hand to his lips and brushes a soft kiss to my fingertips. "Thank you for the dance."

I nod and swallow hard, but before I can verbally respond, Floyd's sweaty palm replaces Jack's against the small of my back and he sweeps me away, leaving Jack with nothing to do but walk back to the table.

It's odd, reading my favorite author at this stage in the process. I'm still in awe and enjoying the book. But even great authors like Cate Able need to be edited. Clearly.

I think back to my own manuscript. I haven't written a word since going back to work, and I miss it. It's only been three days, but I'm getting close to the end of the book and I truly want to finish.

Valerie's dad is dying, and I haven't figured out yet whether she'll end up with John or Ben. Will she be happy, or will she have a tragic end? As much as I want to outline the book from start to finish, the twists of my own imagination keep surprising me.

My phone rings as I'm finishing up the edit of Cate's tenth chapter. Sheri? I sigh. She's been trying to get in touch with me for a couple of days. But what am I supposed to say to her?

I can't. I truly can't tell her about Kevin. It would just be too awkward, and I don't think she'd believe me anyway.

I force myself to take the call. "Hi, Sheri."

"Do you know I've been trying to get in touch with you for three days?"

"Yes, I'm sorry. I've been busy."

"Well, I wanted to tell you that Jack told me to get a proposal from you for *Fifth Avenue Princess*. Are you interested?"

"Jack wants my book?" What is going on here?

"It looks that way," she says, and I detect a note of smugness in her tone.

"I thought you were working on nonfiction."

She laughs. "Well, he knew you wouldn't give your novel to Fran, and he figured you wouldn't give it to him either. So I was the next choice."

"I don't know, Sheri. It's not finished."

"All I need are the proposal chapters and a summary. Surely you can do that."

"I'll think about it."

"Well, think fast. Because I desperately need to take something to committee."

"Again, I thought you were looking for nonfiction."

"Ugh," she groans. "You should see the garbage that ends up on my desk. Dating advice, diet books, and how to have great sex. I'm looking for something fresh, and there's nothing out there. I need you, Dan. I need your book."

"Sheri, what if it's no good?" I hate to whine, but after all of my editing experience, I'm terrified to show my own book to a decent editor. Especially Jack.

"It's good." She pauses. "If you wrote it, I know it'll be good. You can't do anything wrong."

I can't help but give a little laugh. "Flattery will get you nowhere, cousin."

"Seriously, I'm not above a little flattery, but in this case, I have no doubt that your manuscript is good. Please let me have a look."

"Like I said, I'll think about it."

"All right." She draws a deep breath. "One more thing."

Inwardly I groan. I know what she wants to discuss.

"Kevin and I broke up."

"Oh? I'm sorry, Sheri."

"I'm not. I heard what he tried with you."

"You did?" Surely Jack didn't . . .

"Trust me, you can't be engaged to a man like Kevin without having spies in the office."

"You didn't trust him?"

"Let's just say I was giving him the benefit of the doubt, but I had my suspicions. I'm just sorry you had to put up with his nonsense for me to find out he was a creep. Truly. I know he made passes at the other women in the office. I just figured I could tame him. But you know what they say, when the cat's away, and all that."

I hold my breath. Does she know?

I relax with her next words, but still I can't help but feel sorry for her. "His secretary quit after he asked her to work late and chased her around her desk as soon as they were alone in the office. Can you believe an editor would be that cliché? Anyway, she sent me an e-mail and told me all about it."

"I'm sorry."

"Oh, there's someone out there for me." She pretends non-chalance, but I know that inside she must be hurting. On a whim, I do what even I never expected.

"I'll e-mail you the summary and a couple of chapters by the end of the week."

"Really?" she practically squeals in my ear.

"Really. But you have to be honest."

"Don't worry. I will be. Brutally so."

I'm not sure whether to be worried or relieved.

18

The day of the funeral dawned with overcast skies and the threat of rain. Valerie's tears flowed freely. She didn't bother with makeup. There was no point. Ben stood firmly at her side during the funeral and burial, and Valerie clung to his strength.

Later, after everyone had gone and only Valerie and her mom remained, they sat on the porch swing, watching the rain fall, and shared their hearts. Valerie told her all about John, how he'd orchestrated her firing. How Ben had come along and she had fallen for him in spite of herself.

"He sounds so much like your father," her mom said. "Steady, reliable. Competent."

"Yes," Valerie said. "I've always thought he was like Daddy." She smiled. "I couldn't do any better, could I?"

"Not if you truly love him and want to build a life with him and his children. Just remember that you can't turn him into your dad. And it won't be fair to him or those children if you're with him for the wrong reasons."

—An excerpt from *Fifth Avenue Princess*
by Dancy Ames

At church on Sunday, I notice Brynn isn't acting like her usual self. She's almost sullen, and that worries me. I nudge Kale, who is sitting next to me. "What's wrong with Brynn?"

A frown creases his brow. "What do you mean?" he whispers back.

"Shh." Brandon gives us a fierce frown and we straighten up.

I've been attending regularly since Brandon came to visit that week. He's a good influence, and it gives me a chance to see him. Especially with his busy schedule. Not only has he started his junior year, he's also going to the Juilliard pre-college program until they move to Florida. I had to fight for it. Kale joined the effort, and Dad finally agreed to pay the money, even if Brandon had to leave before the end of the year.

I smile a little to myself as I think back just two months, before I found Granny's Bible and my new life verse. Learning to trust God really hasn't been all that hard.

What I'm nervous about now are the proposal chapters and summary I e-mailed to Sheri on Friday, as I promised. So far I haven't heard a word back, and I can only conclude that she hated every word of it.

I meet Brynn in the ladies' room after service. Staring at her in the mirror, I can't help but ask, "Brynn, what's going on?"

She bursts into tears and falls into my arms. "I can't marry him."

I feel like I've been punched in the gut. "What do you mean, you can't marry him? Did he do something?"

She shakes her head against my shoulder. "I can't live in New York."

Can't live in New York? I push her slightly away from me—just enough so I can look in her watery eyes. "Brynn, you need to calm down and talk to me. I'm guessing Kale has no idea you're having second thoughts?"

She shakes her head and grabs a tissue from the counter. "I haven't had the heart to tell him."

"Everyone gets jitters before their wedding. Tabby's so grumpy these days, we're about to toss her out of the apartment."

That brings a smile. "It's not that I'm having second thoughts about Kale. I love him more than ever."

"Then what's the problem?"

"That stupid condo."

Surely she doesn't mean to call my childhood home stupid. Does she? Of all the ungrateful brats.

"See? You don't understand. And I'm so afraid Kale won't, either."

"Are you saying you don't want the apartment my parents gave you?"

Fresh tears coursed down her pixie cheeks. "I know it sounds ungrateful."

To say the least. "Would you prefer a house?"

"Yes, but not in the city. I have to go home."

"To Oklahoma?" The shock I feel comes through loud and clear, but I can't help it. I adore New York. How could anyone prefer Oklahoma to New York?

"Seeing my parents and little sister last week just made me ache for the sight of my daddy's ranch."

"Can't you go for visits?"

"It's not the same. I want to raise my children the way I was raised."

"Tell me something, Brynn." I pause a second to gather my thoughts. "Why did you come to the city in the first place?"

A self-deprecating smile tips the corners of her quivering mouth. "I had a scholarship to NYU and, let's face it, what eighteen-year-old doesn't want to fly the coop and head to the big city when she graduates? I was ready to move home when I met Kale. And that's all it took for me. Only, I've grown up over the last eight years, and now I know I could never live here forever."

"All I can say is, talk to Kale. Give him a chance to try to change your mind."

She nods and gives me a hug. "Thanks, Dancy. I would have liked to have you for a sister."

Tenderness for this girl sweeps through me. She loves my brother. I have no doubt they'll work it out. One way or another.

The problem with freelance editing and writing is that there's no reason to get dressed unless you're going to the coffee shop. And, quite frankly, every time I try to work there, Nick wants to chat, or Emily shows up and shares her latest pictures or stories about Floyd, who is apparently quite the kisser. It's all I can do not to excuse myself and vomit when that happens.

I've been editing all night. I just can't bear to put down Cate Able's manuscript. So by the time Laini awakes, I haven't slept a wink. I'm sitting on the comfortable recliner, manuscript in hand, bug-eyed and desperately needing to get up and walk around.

"Have you been up all night?"

I yawn broadly and nod. "I couldn't stop. But I'm going to get some sleep after you and Tabby leave for the day."

"You're getting your days and nights mixed up. You're going to regret it." Laini *tsk-tsks*. "Maybe you ought to stay awake today so you can sleep tonight."

"I might."

"I'm going to make breakfast. How does a nice breakfast casserole and biscuits sound?"

Tabby stumbles into the living room. "We're getting fat, Laini. You're feeding us too well."

A grin tips Laini's lips. "Welcome to my world."

Laini is not at all fat. She's a little curvy, yes, but I don't care what my mom says. "A size 10 is *not* fat, Laini Sullivan, and don't you dare ever say that about yourself again."

She laughs and heads for the kitchen. "Size 12. I've gained, too. And don't worry, I'm trying some lighter dishes. Egg Beaters and tofu."

Tabby and I look at each other, trying not to make faces. Tabby pulls herself together first. "Sounds, um, fantastic. Can't wait." She heads down the hall. "I call first shower!"

Darn. She always does that. "Leave me some hot water, or so help me, I'll tell David how much your wedding gown is setting you back."

"Too late," she calls. "I already did."

"You're a disgrace. Mother says if a dress costs six hundred, you say two. If it costs two, you claim seventy-five."

Come to think of it, is it any wonder she and my dad struggled with their relationship? Maybe it wasn't all his fault, after all. Well, I still say it mostly was. He was the one who was unfaithful.

I slip into the kitchen, where Laini is pouring us each a cup of coffee. "I had a feeling you'd be looking for some caffeine."

"Hey, need any help?"

"Don't you dare touch a thing in my kitchen," Laini says with a mock New York-mother tone.

"Yes, ma'am." I laugh and sit with my coffee. "How long are you going to be around today?"

"I don't have class until noon." She shrugs. "But I have to

deliver some stuffed sandwiches and cinnamon rolls to Nick's. I could use some help. That way, you could stay up longer and maybe sleep tonight."

"All right." Laini cooks for us every single day. I know she loves it, but still, if I can help her even once, I have no right to refuse. "I'll help."

A wide grin splits her face. "Good, because I have to ask Nick for a favor."

"What's that?"

"I need a project, and I'm wondering if he'll let me decorate his place. He's going to need help, since they're buying the building next door and expanding the shop."

"They are?" I had no idea.

Laini nods. "It was Joe's idea. They're going to connect the two buildings with an outdoor café area. And they'll have two dining rooms. They'll also expand the menu and serve dinner. Italian foods mostly."

"Naturally." I grin. "I think that's a great idea. Nick's going for it, huh?"

"Yeah, he seems happy with the way Joe is working out."

Nick actually smiles when we walk in. "Princess! I ain't seen you in a while. That job keepin' you too busy to have a cup of that green tea you like?"

"I've been working at home."

"What do you mean?" He gives me a frown. "They let you do that?"

"I quit." I suppose there's no sense in keeping that information from him.

"You quit? Why'd you do that?"

"Because her boss was a creep who wouldn't keep his hands to himself," Laini speaks up.

Anger flashes across Nick's face. "It's okay, Nick. I have a new freelance company and I'm doing really well."

"Good for you. I always knew you had it in ya."

"She's also writing a book that might get published," Laini says. Her pride in me shows in her smile.

"Well, we'll see about that." This is a subject I'm not delving into. I turn the focus on Nick. "So, Laini tells me you're about to expand."

Nick's face flushes with pleasure. "Business is good, and my nephew is a real humdinger. He's turning this place into a gold mine."

"I'm so happy for you!"

"Yep, he's takin' over, and I'm going to live in California with my Nelda."

My heart sinks. "You're leaving?"

"Nita and my Nelda need me. It don't look like our girl's gonna make it, and I want to be there for the last few weeks or months."

"I'm so sorry, Nick."

"We're not givin' up 'til the angels take her. We're still prayin' for a miracle."

"So, when are you leaving?"

"I'm goin' out to visit for Christmas, and I'm not comin' back. We're puttin' everything in storage, and Joe's takin' over the apartment upstairs, too."

"Are you sure about this? You love this place."

He gives what I can only describe as a breath of surrender. "Not as much as I love my family. It's the right thing to do."

"I'll miss you, Nick."

He nods. "I'll miss you too, kid. You done good by me. I'll

always be grateful for the way you stepped in and helped me out during some rough spots. I'm proud of you like you was my own daughter."

My throat tightens. Nick's praise means more to me than I can express. Does he know that my own father has never once said he was proud of me?

19

The weeks after her dad died seemed like the longest of Valerie's life. And now that her mom was returning to Africa, she felt a heaviness with every waking moment. One day melted into the next until there was nothing but sameness. Even Ben and the children bored her, and she couldn't muster up enthusiasm for their presence the way she once could.

She found herself constantly thinking of John Quest. His eyes, his mouth, his kisses. Without thinking she picked up the phone and dialed his number.

"Hello?"

Her heart jumped, and she couldn't bring herself to answer. "Val, is that you?"

Still she couldn't say a word.

"I know it's you, honey. I saw your name on caller ID. Talk to me."

Without a word, Valerie burst into tears and slammed down the phone. John would never be the man she needed him to be.

—An excerpt from *Fifth Avenue Princess*
by Dancy Ames

'm looking right at my little brother, but I have to be honest—if I saw him on the street, I'd never recognize him. The spikes are gone, and his head is buzzed, but not in a geeky way. He looks very hip. Also, there's not a piece of metal sticking out of any visible spot on his body.

True to his word, he meets me in front of the concert hall where he will be performing in about an hour. He called me on the spur of the moment and asked if I wanted to go. "Yes" flew out of my mouth before my mind could form any other answer. I haven't seen Brandon since the night of the engagement party last Saturday, and I can't believe the transformation in my kid brother.

I grab him and give him a little hug, which he actually returns in a quick, pat-me-on-the-back sort of way. But that's okay. It's a start. I reach up and rub my hand over his fuzzy scalp. "Hey, what happened to you?"

He grins at me. "You mean my desperate cry for help?"

"Something like that."

A shrug lifts his shoulders. "I got over it."

"Let me guess—the thought of seeing a certain girl from Oklahoma helped you to mend your ways?"

"Not exactly. But it didn't hurt."

"Well, Brynn's little sister is going to be surprised to see you. I think you scared her a little."

"I scared a lot of people. Even my mom."

He looks so sad. I just want to wrap my arms around him and assure him that his mother would be here if she had any choice. "I don't think your hair had anything to do with your mom's need to take care of your grandma."

"Probably not. But she didn't exactly beg me to go with her."

"It's hard to concentrate on caring for a sick loved one and a teenager at the same time."

"I guess." His expression changes, and I know he's forcing

a smile. "You ready to go inside and face a room of musically inclined teenagers?"

"I'm not scared of any of you," I say with mock bravery.

"You should be afraid. Be very afraid." He laughs and steps aside for me to enter. I step in ahead of him, still grinning over his comment.

"Hey, Dancy," he whispers.

I turn to him. "What?"

"What's up with the weight gain?"

"How would you like me to slap you?"

"Don't blame me that your butt's gotten bigger. Must be Laini's cooking." He snickers; then his eyes widen. "Hey, how about inviting me over for a home-cooked meal?"

"After that remark? Why should I?"

He grins. "The more I eat, the less calories you'll consume."

"Brat."

"Chub."

"I'm not speaking to you," I say as we enter the hall.

"Wait, Dancy."

"What, cretin?"

Worry clouds his eyes. "You know I was kidding, right? If I really thought you were fat, I wouldn't have said anything. You look really good for a middle-aged chick."

Okay, now I'm torn. Do I let him off the hook and admit that I wasn't really offended? Or do I let him suffer for the middle-aged-chick remark? He looks so sweet and young and innocent with the new hair (or lack of it) and his equally new clean-cut image, I just don't have the heart to make him suffer.

"It's okay, Brandon. I'm not really mad."

Relief covers his face.

"Furthermore, I'll ask Laini when is a good time to invite you over."

"You don't have to."

Poor kid.

"Are you kidding me? Laini needs people around eating her food. It's where all of her self-esteem lies. And besides"—I nudge him with my elbow—"you were right. I need someone to help with all those calories. Heaven forbid I gain another pound." If my size 6 behind is noticeable to a teenager, maybe it's time I get back to the gym.

Squeeze, honey! You're not going to get back into that size 4 unless you work that butt."

Why did I ever agree to start working out with Tabby and her sadistic trainer, Freddie? I don't think I'm even supposed to be here. Freddie is on staff at the gym on the set of *Legacy of Life*. And besides, what's wrong with being a size 6? I mean, I don't want to hear the answer from my mom, but Tabby is a size 6, and she was nominated for an Emmy. And she looks amazing. And honestly? I don't think there's an ounce of fat on her.

"Nobody likes a chubby girl." Freddie's just a pain in my derriere. Literally and figuratively.

I stop my walking lunges and whip around to face him. "Lots of people like chubby girls."

"I'm not talking about chubby-chasing freaks. When was your last date?"

Okay, I can be smug about this one, because I just had one. "None of your business."

"Leave her alone, Freddie," Tabby says, as any true friend would. "Dancy is too good for all the jerks out there trying to date her."

Tabby steps off the treadmill, and I hear Freddie expel an

exasperated grunt. He's muttering something under his breath, but I ignore it. Tabby takes my hands. "I know I've been preoccupied with work and David and the kids, but nothing will ever replace our friendship."

"Thanks, Tabs." In my heart, I truly do know this, but sometimes when I'm lonely and Tabby is gone into her happy life that doesn't include me, and Laini is happily baking and whistling while she works, I wonder where I'll be when all my friends are married and I'm all alone. Because marriage doesn't seem to be in the cards for me.

"If you two start singing 'That's What Friends Are For,' I'm going to weep." Freddie's a pain. He really is. He claps his hands together. "Okay, enough bonding. Do you want to fit into that wedding gown you spent way too much money on, girlfriend? Or do you want to call the designer and tell her to let it out a few feet?"

I'm about to tell him to shove it when he turns on me. "And you, have you never heard of a thong, girlfriend?"

"What?"

"Those panty lines are downright scary."

"Believe me," I say, this close to punching him, "I'd rather have panty lines any day. So don't even go there."

"Fine, whatever. Do whatever you want."

"I will. I'm getting on the bike."

"Over my dead body, girlfriend." He steps in my path. "You get back to those lunges."

"Does *anyone* like you?" I ask through narrowed eyes.

"Did you call me, or did I call you?" he demands, hands on hips. Okay, he has a point. Mainly I wanted to spend time with Tabby, though, not be put through cruel and unusual punishment. I'm used to running, but lunges are in a painful league of their own.

"Okay, Freddie." I finally surrender. "You're the boss. Whip me into shape."

"Good girl. Now remember, when you're throwing up after the workout, you asked for it." Without waiting for an answer, he bends forward and presses a kiss to my cheek. It feels a little like the kiss of death.

I love November. The air is crisp, I get to wear winter clothes. The city is waking up to holiday decorations, and the Christmas stress doesn't start for a couple more weeks. Not until the day after Thanksgiving. Right now is the perfect time. The crowded streets are filled with smiling people, and we could experience our first snowfall of the year any day.

The wind whips around my legs and blows in my face, threatening to steal my breath, and yet I'm in a good mood. I'm almost to my apartment when my cell phone buzzes.

Sheri. My heart does a somersault. "Sheri. What's up?"

"Hi, I just had to call. I think we want to see the rest of the manuscript. Is it available?"

She said "I think." Which means, it could be okay, but it isn't wowing her yet.

"I'm not quite finished with it. But almost."

"All right. When you're ready, will you send it to me? ASAP."

"Will do."

Another call beeps in. "Sheri, my mother is trying to reach me."

"I'll let you go. But don't forget to get me that manuscript."

I promise and click over without saying good-bye. "Mother?"

"Brynn and Kale just called. They want us all to meet at your father's apartment."

She still calls it Dad's apartment, even though she's been living there for two months. "Did they say why?" Dread hits me as I recall my last conversation with Brynn. I pray they aren't announcing their breakup.

"No. Just that they need us all to be there."

20

Ben sat across from her at Sophia Lamour's, an exclusive dinner spot—ridiculously expensive and almost impossible to get into. They sat in a romantic little booth in the back of the dining room. Valerie had to wonder how much Ben had paid the maître d' to make that happen.

"This is just lovely, Ben." She smiled at this kind man, and her heart swelled with affection.

"You're lovely, my dear." He reached out his hand and she slipped her fingers into his palm. "Do you realize what day this is?"

There was no point in pretending. "You'll have to remind me," she said.

"Six months ago today, you came to work at the office."

"Oh! I can't believe you remember that."

"I'll never forget. That was the day I started living again."

—An excerpt from *Fifth Avenue Princess*
by Dancy Ames

've never seen my mother so upset. Dad's apartment is stunningly redecorated, but Dad looks absolutely miserable without his dead animals everywhere. I guess that's the price he's willing to pay to get Mom back in his life.

"Caroline, calm down," he says. Imagine—Dad, the voice of reason. He truly is growing up. "The kids have a right to live their own lives."

Kale and Brynn are sitting at the table, staring at a half-eaten Cornish hen, unable to meet Mother's tearful gaze.

"Mother," I say.

"Leave it alone, Dancy."

Why is she upset with me? I'm not the one who ran off and eloped. Kale is.

And that's not all.

"You don't want the condo?" Mother is losing her cool. "What are you two thinking? No one turns down a multi-million-dollar condo with a view of Central Park!"

Kale finally takes his wife's hand and stares squarely into my mother's eyes. "It was a great gift, Mother, and we truly appreciate it."

"Well, you certainly don't act like you appreciate it."

Brynn gives a barely audible sigh. "Caroline, please believe me. We love the gift, and there's no place we'd rather live . . . if we planned to stay in New York."

I gape as realization hits me. Brynn actually talked my brother into leaving. They're moving out of New York. My gaze swings to Mother, and by the utter horror in her eyes, I can see she's reached the same conclusion.

My gut clenches. Something is about to hit the fan.

"And just where, may I ask, do you plan to live, if not here?" Mother asks this not of Brynn, her frown squarely facing my brother.

"Oklahoma." He says the word simply as though it's a relief to get the revelation over with.

The thing is, Mother's not looking too relieved. Her lip

tightens, and she sits back in the chair, as though all words have escaped her. Which would be a first.

"What do you intend to do in Oklahoma, son?" Dad asks.

Kale's face brightens. "I've decided to go into family practice."

"And there are no families in New York?" Mother asks, her lips tight, her face void of all color.

"Brynn wants to live near her family. And you know I've always loved rural areas."

Poor Brynn. Did Kale really just pass the buck? Mother's glaring at her new daughter-in-law, and I know she's thinking Kale never would have thought about moving away on his own. But the truth is, I know he would have eventually left the city. I mean, maybe he would have found a suburb instead of a whole different state, but I can definitely picture him as a small-town doctor, making a modest living and raising dogs and chickens.

"Congratulations, you two," I say as I stand and walk around the table to give them both a hug. "How long before you move?"

"I've already left the hospital, and Brynn's parents are sending us to Jamaica on a honeymoon. We'll be back right before Thanksgiving and hope to be settled in by Christmas."

Mother gasps. "The groom's parents are supposed to pay for the honeymoon!" Okay, her son just told her he's moving across the country in less than six weeks, and she's fixating on the fact that she didn't get to pay for the honeymoon? I mean, if she really wants to send one of her children to a tropical island paradise . . .

"Mother," Kale warns. "You already paid for a lot of the wedding preparations and an engagement dinner. Brynn's folks wanted to do something special for their daughter."

"I suppose her parents knew you were going to elope, even though you didn't tell us?"

"No, Caroline," Brynn assures. "We only told them before you because we drove to Miami, Oklahoma, to get married. We stopped home to see them. And, believe me, they were just as upset as you are. Until they realized how happy we are."

"Well, of course, we want you to be happy as much as they do," Mother huffs. "But what was wrong with going ahead with your wedding? You couldn't wait three more months? So many people were looking forward to the event."

Event? When Mother says "event," she doesn't mean "blessed event." She means "party." Reducing the happiest day of Brynn and Kale's life to a party is just wrong.

Kale heaves a sigh. "Everyone was looking forward to it except us, Mother."

"Well, what are we supposed to do about all the arrangements? The flowers and the caterers? We'll have to forfeit our deposits."

A scowl darkens Kale's face, and I see he's about to blow a gasket. "We'll pay the deposits."

"That's not the point, Kale."

Poor Mother. She's getting more and more frustrated. I feel the need to step in. I mean, Dad's not taking up for her.

"Hey, Mother, I have an idea. Why not use Kale and Brynn's wedding date to renew your vows before you guys move to Florida?"

"That's a great idea!" Brynn's pixielike face brightens, and I know part of her effusive response is a result of getting off the hot seat.

"Don't be silly," Mother snaps.

"Why is it silly, honey?" Dad asks. "I like the idea."

She looks at him, surprise lifting her brow. "You do?"

And then my dad does something I never would have expected. He drops down on one knee in front of her.

"What are you doing?" Mother asks, her face suddenly red. Kale and Brynn exchange a warm glance and smile. My heart clenches at all this romantic love in the air. My dad takes Mother's hand and presses a kiss to it. If I ever doubted him—and I did—all those doubts flee with one look into his eyes. "Marry me again, my dear."

"Oh, Stuart. Are you sure?"

"I'd like to say the vows again, and this time, I promise I'll keep them."

Mother leans forward and kisses him. It's sweet.

There's one question rolling around in my mind. Since Kale and Brynn don't want the condo . . .

Well? Wouldn't you wonder the same thing?

I saw the movie *Misery* four times, and until this moment, I thought of Kathy Bates as a maniac and I completely sympathized with James Caan. But I have to say, I just read the end of Cate Able's book, and I'm livid.

She killed off Karly Rose. She killed off Karly Rose! I've been following this woman's life for six books. She's a hard-hitting reporter with a lot of intuition and no fear, and Cate Able has the audacity to kill her off?

I snatch up the receiver and dial Jack's number.

It takes four rings for him to answer. When he does, his voice is husky with sleep.

"Did you know she was going to kill off Karly?"

"Dancy?"

"Yes, and don't change the subject."

"Darling, do you have any idea how late it is?"

"What? No. I've been working. I just finished the edit for Cate's book. Do you have any idea what she did?"

"Of course I do. It was time to let Karly go."

"But why? Sales are as high as ever. Why on earth would Lane Publishing be stupid enough to let her kill off her lead character?"

"Perhaps she wants to move on." Jack's voice definitely sounds more awake now. And maybe a little annoyed. "Perhaps Cate is ready to stop being defined by the character she writes."

"But that's ridiculous. Why on earth would she stop a sure thing? This is a beloved character. Karly should not die. It makes no sense, Jack." I'm firm about this. I'm not going to back down. As a reader, I would be sorely disappointed. As an editor, I know this is a horrible mistake. The series isn't even close to dying out. And the lead character shouldn't be, either.

But Jack's having none of it. His tone is downright stormy. "Why on earth are you going on so? Cate has a perfect right to kill off her character."

"So you're going to let her do it?"

"Of course."

"Fine. You'll have the edit back tomorrow."

I hang up, so angry I could throw something. Why on earth say he is "fascinated" with my editing if he can't trust me on one of the most important issues I've ever taken to task in an edit?

You know what? Let him ruin the whole thing. Let him get millions of readers up in arms. Let Karly die. I really don't care.

My eyes are gritty, and I'm so tired I can barely move. I glance at the clock. Four a.m. I give a little groan. I called Jack in the middle of the night to yell at him about a book.

I dial his number again. "Hello, Dancy," he says.

"Hi. I just noticed the time. I wanted to apologize for calling so late."

"Or early, depending upon how you look at it."

"Right. Either way, I'm sorry I woke you."

"No worries, love. I'll talk to you tomorrow."

I hang up for the second time, but I'm disturbed by his defense of Cate Able. I wonder . . . are those two . . . ?

Mother insists upon throwing a reception for Kale and Brynn "at the very least." She hired a fast-thinking, fast-talking, exorbitantly priced party planner, and she's pulling out all the stops. The reception is in the elegant Loews Regency Hotel on Park Avenue the weekend after Thanksgiving. Right after the happy couple returns from their honeymoon. The hotel can accommodate up to two hundred, so Mother pared it down from five. I swear . . .

Once again, Brynn's parents are forced to fly into JFK and endure a night of Mother's pretension. At least she's forgoing the ice swans this time.

My legs shake a little when Jack walks into the room. For once, he isn't seated next to me, though. To my relief, I might add. Sheri's here, and Mother has seated Floyd next to her, so I guess she finally got the picture. I'm between Brandon and Aunt Tilly, and Aunt Tilly keeps burping. Brandon keeps staring over at the next table where Carol is sitting. Poor kid. He's absolutely pining for the girl.

"Why don't you go talk to her?" I ask. "Dinner hasn't even been served yet."

"You think it would be okay?"

"Of course. You're not a prisoner."

He gives me a crooked grin. "Okay. But if your mom yells at me for getting out of my seat, I'm blaming you."

"I'll take the heat. Now go."

"You've grown fond of the boy?" Aunt Tilly, the shrewdest person I've ever met, watches him go.

I nod. "He's a great kid. Too bad his parents can't see that."

"What's he going to do when your mother and father move to Florida?"

Oh. I wasn't really sure about that yet. I shrug. "I guess he'll go live with Nanny Mary."

Aunt Tilly's wrinkles scrunch together into a scowl, which is a little scary. "Would you stop calling her that? Makes you sound like a seven-year-old."

"I know. It's a habit."

"Well, stop it."

"You're right. I'll be more careful." Somehow calling her Mary feels wrong, sort of like calling Aunt Tilly, Tilly. Or Mother, Caroline. Oh, well, I should just get over it.

By the time the meal is served, Brandon's back in his seat and his eyes are glowing with the shine of new love. Aunt Tilly is having trouble staying awake after drinking a glass of champagne. And I'll just be glad to get this evening over with. Jack is seated directly across from me. I keep ducking behind the huge rose and carnation centerpiece. Every time I meet his gaze, I think about the fact that he defended the worst decision Cate Able has ever made in regard to her books. Does he even realize how badly my self-esteem has been hit because of him? He gives me the edit to do, and then won't trust my judgment in the end. Karly should not be dead. It's a horrible move strategically. They might as well have killed off James Bond or Sherlock Holmes or Miss Marple. It's stupid. And, yes, as a reader, I'm disappointed. But as an editor, I'm livid.

I'm relieved when the meal is over and Dad taps his fork against his crystal champagne glass to get everyone's attention. "First, Caroline and I would like to thank everyone for coming on such short notice. Next, we would like to propose a toast to our son and daughter-in-law. May you be as happy as Caroline and I are."

Is he kidding? My brother has a bemused look on his face, and I hear more than a few twitters of laughter around the tables.

"Moron," Aunt Tilly mutters. I find it hard not to burst into laughter at her remark, but I control myself as everyone lifts their glasses and toasts the new bride and groom.

Dread washes through me as I realize he's not finished. "We have an announcement to make."

Maybe it won't be so bad. Maybe all he's going to do is invite everyone to their vow renewal.

"As most of you know, Caroline and I have reconciled."

Clapping—mostly out of politeness I imagine, because why is he suddenly making this about them, when Kale and Brynn are supposed to be the center of attention?

"Thank you. But this isn't about us."

There's a relief.

"We offered the kids the home we bought when Kale and Dancy were children. But they've decided not to accept. So, we've decided to sell the condo and give them enough to buy a home in Oklahoma."

More clapping. This time sincere. Only, my heart nearly stops. Why didn't it occur to my folks that I might want to live in the condo? Am I really that much of a nonentity?

"Don't sweat it, Dan." Brandon's hand covers mine and I'm comforted by the warmth.

"I—I'm not. I'm happy for them."

"Dad should have given the condo to you. You're the one who cares about it."

Now how did he know that? I turn to him and search his wonderful brown eyes that are so like Dad's. He shrugs. "I know things."

"You're a smart kid, Brandon."

"Wish I was smart enough to figure out how to get Dad to let me stay in New York instead of moving to Florida."

"Don't worry," I assure him. "It'll work out the way it's supposed to."

Hope flickers to his eyes. "Think I could come and live with you?"

"And Laini and Tabby?"

"Tabby's getting married soon. You'll have an opening for a roommate."

"I know, Brandon, but Tabby shares a room with Laini. It's not like a teenage boy could just move in and take over her bed."

A rush of red floods his cheeks. "Oh, yeah."

"I hope you're going to say something to them about that condo." This from Aunt Tilly.

"What's there to say?"

"I could think of a few things."

I can imagine. I smile. "Don't worry about it. I have a great apartment."

"That's not what I've heard. According to your mother, it's a rat-infested sardine can of a place with holes in the walls."

"It is not!" There are no rats. At least, not for a few months. And the only hole is from when we tried to move the entertainment center and lost our grip. But we fixed it. And if she was really worried about where I live, maybe she would have thought about giving me the condo, or at least offering an affordable price and letting me buy it. But now it's too late. I've lost the beautiful prewar place. Tears well in my eyes. Has it been long enough since the announcement for me to get up and leave the room without being conspicuous?

It doesn't matter. If I don't go now, I'm going to end up crying in public and disgracing Mother.

I barely make it outside the banquet room before the tears flow. I walk down the hall looking for a ladies' room when I feel a hand on my elbow. I turn and look up into Jack Quinn's compassionate eyes.

"Dancy, sweetheart," he says.

Without a word, I melt into his arms and give in to my tears.

21

Valerie's wedding day dawned warm but not too hot, just the right temperature for a spring day in New York. She stared at herself in the full-length mirror. She wore her mother's wedding gown and a string of pearls, a wedding gift from her dad to her mom.

Mom hadn't been able to leave the orphanage in Africa to come to the wedding. She sent her love and a check and wished her all the happiness in the world.

Valerie knew she was making the right decision. She just had to be. Ben was a family man like her dad. Valerie knew she and the children would always come first. He would never betray her. Not the way John Quest had.

A tap at the door signaled it was time. Panic welled up for a moment. Could she really do this?

The tap sounded again. "I'm coming." She walked across the wooden floor and opened the door. Only instead of the wedding planner, she saw John kneeling on one knee, holding a black box.

"Don't marry him, Valerie. You know we belong together."

—An excerpt from Fifth Avenue Princess
by Dancy Ames

S o you cried all over him and went to the powder room and he was gone when you got back?" The outrage is evident in Tabby's voice.

Laini, Tabby, and I are sharing cheesecake around the table and rehashing the reception.

"It's odd. He seemed so sweet and kind and then . . . nothing." I give myself half a second to relive those moments of safety and warmth in Jack's arms. Then I get mad all over again. "He's just a jerk."

"You got that right," Laini says. "You know what I bet it is?"

"Hmm?" I ask around a gooey bite of cheesecake.

"I bet he knows you're right about that edit and he's wrong, and he can't face you."

They had overheard me discussing the book with Jack. I swear I didn't intentionally break the nondisclosure clause.

"You know what I think it is, girls?" My suspicions are stronger than ever. "I think Jack and Cate Able are an item."

"What?" Tabby says. "What makes you say that?"

"They're both English."

They look at each other and frown.

Laini shakes her head. "I have to tell you, I'm not following this train of thought."

"Well, okay," I say. "That alone isn't enough to prove anything. But they work together and he's extremely defensive of her. I mean, so much so that he can't bear for me to criticize her. I think they're a couple."

Part of me is convinced I only care because apparently Jack's feelings for Cate Able have completely robbed him of any good sense he formerly possessed. I'd say the last smart thing he did was hire me to do the edit. And he won't even let me do my job. I say, if she wants to be dumb and kill off a beloved and especially lucrative character, why drag Jack or Lane Publishing and now me into the chain of stupidity? Let her be stupid all by herself.

Oh, well. I'm putting it out of my mind. I'm finished with the whole thing. I have turned in my edit, and now I wash my hands of the entire episode. I couldn't care less if Jack is dating Cate Able. Seriously. It's of no consequence to me. None.

Shoot. I can't stand it any longer. I snatch up my phone.

Laini frowns. "Dancy, what are you doing?"

Kale answers on the third ring. "Kale, is Jack dating Cate Able?"

"What?"

"Come on. I know you're his best friend. But you're my brother and I have to know."

"Sorry, Dan," he says. "I agreed to nondisclosure where Cate Able is concerned."

"Have you ever met her?"

He chuckles. "Oh, yeah."

"Really? Tell me what she's like."

"Sexy. Real sexy."

I groan. "I figured. I guess that explains a few things. G'night, Kale. Congratulations again on your wedding."

"Wait, Dancy. Did you talk to Mother and Dad after the reception?"

"No. And I don't want to right now. I have to go." I click the off button and look up glumly.

"Did Kale say Jack's dating her?"

"No, but he might as well have. I have no chance in you-know-where with Jack Quinn." I turn to Tabby. "How are the plans coming along for your wedding, Tabs?"

Tabby's face takes on a serenity that, quite frankly, I envy. "It's all coming together." She frowns. "Remember you have one more fitting. Put down that cheesecake! And don't miss our appointment with Freddie tomorrow. You know we aren't going to have time to let out the dress again."

Heat burns my cheeks. We actually had to let it out from a size 4 to a size 6. Sigh.

I gasp. "Do you think Jack thinks I'm fat?"

"What?" Tabby expels. "Of course not. And I thought we were done talking about you."

"Well, what do you have to worry about?" I snap. "In three weeks, you're marrying the man of your dreams and becoming mommy to two adorable twins."

"But what if I ruin them?"

"Ruin what?" Laini asks.

"You know, the twins. They're such great kids. And I don't know how to be a mom. Most people get to grow into it from birth. But I've only known them for a year." She stabs a bite of cheesecake and crams it into her mouth. "I'm doomed to fail."

"Why do you say that?" I ask.

"I hated kids until I fell in love with those two. I don't deserve them."

I swear. What difference does it make, compared to my sad life? "You're just borrowing trouble, Tabs."

"Yeah," Laini soothes. "You're going to be a great mom to those two."

"You think so?" comes her teary and quite pathetic question.

"Of course." Laini speaks up before I can, which is probably just as well, because I happen to think Tabby should be past all this angst. She should just enjoy her life with the man she landed and his ready-made family. I mean, how lucky is she? But then, I guess everyone gets the jitters right before they get married.

My phone rings and I'm actually glad to remove myself from the current conversation.

My dad is on the other end of the line. "What is it, Dad?"

"Your brother."

"Brandon? What's up?"

"I think he ran away, hon. Do you have any idea where he might be? He's not there, is he?"

My stomach flip-flops as I remember telling him he couldn't live with me. What if he ran away for good? How many kids get swallowed up in New York City every day? Panic hits my chest.

"He's not here, Dad. When was the last time you saw him?"

"At the party. We couldn't find him when it was time to go."

"Did you look for him, or just figure he'd find his own way home?"

There's silence on the other end of the line. Silence that tells me a lot. "Dad! He's just a kid. What's wrong with you?"

"I know he's just a kid, Dancy. You don't have to tell me that. Not now."

"Do you have any idea where he might have gone? Did you check with Mary?"

"I called her, but she wasn't there. And she probably wouldn't have picked up the phone if she had been there."

"Good grief. What is it with you people that you can't be parents?"

"Come on. Surely I don't deserve that."

"You know what, Dad?" I'm bordering on what Nick would call disrespect, but in this case, it's time Dad got a dose of reality. "Yes, you do deserve it. I mean, I'm happy that you're doing right by Mother. But can't you think of your children a little, too? Especially the one who isn't grown yet."

"All right, hate me, but I need to know if you have any idea where he might have gone."

"I'm not sure." But I do have an idea. I say good-bye and disconnect as I slip on my coat.

"Where are you going?" Tabby asks, coming into the living room.

"Brandon's missing. I think he might have run off."

"Wait, you're not going out in this, are you?"

"In what?"

"It's snowing. Didn't you know?"

I didn't have a clue. But it can't be helped. I grab a scarf and slip my gloves from my coat pocket. "I'll be back."

"Wait! I'm not letting you go out alone."

Tabby grabs her coat.

"I'm coming too," Laini says.

"No. Laini, stay here, please. Someone needs to be here in case he shows up."

"Okay. I'll stay. But call me every thirty minutes, okay?"

Tabby gives her a quick hug. "We will."

I open the door and we head out. Lifting my phone from my coat pocket, I speed-dial Kale. He answers in just a couple of rings. "What is it, Dan?"

"Did Dad call you?"

"No. Why? What's wrong?"

"Brandon ran off. We think, anyway."

"Start at the beginning and tell me what's going on."

I do, and while I'm telling him the whole story, we leave the warmth of our building and step into the first real snowfall of the year. The sidewalk is blanketed, and the snow swirling around the streetlights reminds me of an old movie. Any other time, I'd walk slowly and take in the beauty, but not tonight. I raise my arm as a taxi sails past us.

Kale gives an exasperated huff on the phone. "What can I do?"

"I think I might know where he is. I think he went to be with his mom. Taxi!"

"Where are you?"

"I told you, I have a hunch about where Brandon might be and I'm headed down to the train station."

"Hey! You can't go out on the streets alone at night. Are you nuts?"

"I'm not alone. Tabby's with me."

"Okay, listen up, kiddo. Stay put and I'll come over there. We'll go together."

"Too late. We just got a cab. I'll call you when we get to Jersey."

"Absolutely not. Dancy, I mean it. Don't go there without me."

I hang up. Partly because I don't take orders well (just ask Nick), also partly because I'm mad at Kale. First he gets my condo, then he gives it back, then my parents sell it so they can buy him a new house in Hooterville.

My resentment runs deep right now. But mainly I'm not waiting because every second we waste is a second Brandon might be in trouble. "Can't you go a little faster?" I ask the driver.

"Look, lady, the streets are solid ice. The salt trucks ain't had a chance to get out yet. You shouldn't even be out here on such a night."

"You didn't answer my question."

"No. I can't go any faster. So sit back and don't talk to me. I'll let you know when we get there."

Sheesh. I wonder if he's one of Nick's brothers.

I'm about to tell him where to get off when Tabby's hand on my arm steadies me. "Take it easy, Dan. Let's just pray."

I'm not really one to make a public display of religion yet. But I happen to know that if anyone can bring Brandon back to us, it's God.

"You pray, Tabs."

"Dancy, God knows your heart and your mind. Just talk to Him."

I turn my focus heavenward. "Lord, we had a deal, remember? I would trust You, and You would direct my paths? Right now I need You to direct me to my brother. Please keep him safe. My heart breaks for him."

There doesn't seem to be anything left to say, so I stop. After a minute, the cabbie glances at me in the rearview mirror. "Is that it?"

"My prayer?"

"Yeah."

"I guess so."

"You didn't say amen."

"Could you just watch the road? It's pretty icy."

He mutters something, but I don't care. All I care about is that I see the train station up ahead. I reach into my purse and hand the cabbie some bills. He waves my hand away. "Keep it."

"Excuse me?"

"Just find your brother. Okay?"

Tabby places her hand on his shoulder. "Thank you, sir. God bless you."

"Yeah. Maybe He'll make the snow stop before they close down any streets. That would help."

"You never know," I say as I fling open the door and rush out into the driving snow. "Thanks again."

"You be careful."

"We will," I hear Tabby say behind me.

We catch the train into New Jersey and sit in silence until we reach the station. By some miracle, we find a cab and give the address. Brandon has been missing for the last three hours.

I'm beginning to panic. I pray he's with his mother. Otherwise, we'll have to call the police.

We pay the cabbie and climb the four steps to the door of Brandon's grandmother's house. I knock, and an older woman comes to the door. "Mrs. Cunningham?"

"Yeah, who are you?" she asks in a heavy Jersey accent.

"I'm looking for Mary Cunningham. I'm Dancy Ames. I'm sorry it's so late. But my brother Brandon is missing. We just wondered if he might have come here."

She pushes the door open, and I have to say, the woman isn't looking so frail. "How are you feeling?"

"Why do you ask?"

"You seem strong to me."

"Good. I am strong."

"Is Mary here, ma'am?"

The old woman waves me to a kitchen chair. "No, she ain't been here in a week. A real piece of work, that one."

"But I don't understand. She's supposed to be staying with you to help you through your cancer. Are you in remission?"

She scowls and shakes her head. Not in a negative way, but like she can't believe what she's hearing. "I don't have cancer, honey. And I never did."

I'm stunned silent. I honestly don't know how to respond to this. Tabby, however, has no problem. "Do you mean she made up a story about her mother having terminal cancer just to get rid of her son?"

She shrugs. "Like I said, a real piece of work, that one."

I hand her my business card. "If you speak with her, will you ask her to give me a call? It concerns Brandon."

"I'll give her your number, but don't expect her to call you. She's pretty much washed her hands of that boy. He's nothing but trouble. Just like her."

"That's where you're wrong. Brandon's a good kid. He goes to church, plays several instruments. How can anyone think he's nothing but trouble?"

She smiles. "I'm glad he has someone like you takin' up for him."

"The thing is, my father is moving to Florida in a couple of months, and my older brother just got married and they're moving to Oklahoma. I'm sort of wondering what Brandon's going to do. He wants to stay in New York so he can go to Juilliard."

"Like I said, I'll give my daughter your message, but I can't make any promises that she's gonna call."

"But what about you? Are you willing to let Brandon live here if Mary doesn't come back for him? He could stay with me on the weekends so he can still attend Juilliard."

She frowns, scowls really, as though she's deeply offended that I even suggested such a thing. "I'm an old woman. Too old to take care of a teenage boy. I can't do it. I won't."

We leave a few minutes later, my heart breaking for Brandon. Isn't there anyone out there who loves the kid? Besides me, that is. And my apartment is way too small. There's no way he can stay there.

On the train ride home, I find myself praying again. "Please, Lord. Please help Brandon."

Because of the weather, I suppose, I'm getting no signal on my cell phone, and neither is Tabby. She drops off to sleep as soon as the train pulls away. But I stare out the window at the wintry scene. Praying over and over. *Please, Lord. Keep my brother safe. Help us find him.*

The first person I see when we step off the train is Jack. And he doesn't look happy. "Are you quite mad?"

"Hello to you, too. What are you doing here?"

"Obviously I've come to take you home."

"But how did you even know?"

"Kale called me earlier, after you called him. I was closer than Kale, so he asked me to come straightaway and stop you from getting on that train. Of course, I was too late."

"You've been sitting here for four hours? Have you heard anything about Brandon? My phone went dead."

"He's safe and sound in his bed."

"What?" Relief washes through me. "What do you mean?"

"Seems he was in the tub when your parents returned home from the reception. But your dad saw the bed made and just assumed Brandon had run away."

"I'm going to kill that kid."

Tabby chuckles. "And less than four hours ago, you were bombarding the gates of heaven on his behalf."

" 'Bombarding' is a little strong."

"Fine. Praying, then."

"Well, he'd better start doing some praying of his own, because when I get my hands on him, I'm going to do some real damage."

"Now, Dancy," Jack says. "Be reasonable. All he did was go home. It isn't as though he ran away."

"No, of course not. You have that market cornered."

"I beg your pardon?"

Now that the adrenaline in my blood is starting to cool, I'm remembering why I was so upset earlier. "Too bad, because I won't give it."

"Are you angry with me?" He actually seems befuddled. We've reached his car, though, and Tabby is shivering.

"Let her inside before she freezes to death." He complies and then turns to me.

"If anyone has a right to be angry, it's me," he has the audacity to say. "And if anyone abandoned anyone tonight it was you who abandoned me."

"Excuse me? I went into the bathroom to wash my face, and when I came out, you were gone!"

"There's been a terrible misunderstanding, sweetheart."

"Don't call me sweetheart. And I don't see how I could misunderstand. I was only in the bathroom for a minute, and when I came out, you were gone."

"Only a minute? That's hardly long enough."

"I realized I left my purse at the table and I'd cried all my makeup off."

"Yes, I know. You should see my shirt."

"Sorry," I say with a scowl, sarcasm thick in my tone.

"I still maintain my innocence."

"Okay, then. Where did you go in the sixty seconds I was in the bathroom?"

"It's simple really. I saw Brandon leave the reception hall, quite upset, and I followed him, assuming I had at least ten minutes for you to compose yourself. He confided that another young man had captured the attention of the girl he admired, and he no longer wished to remain. I tried to persuade him to wait, but he wouldn't be convinced. I now see that I should have made someone aware, but I didn't want you to come out and find me gone."

"Which I did."

"Right."

"Well, what did you expect me to think? You obviously have a woman in your life already. Why do you keep letting me cry on your shoulder?"

My lips are quivering a lot, mostly from the cold. But also because I'm feeling tired and lonely and like I have no one who truly cares about me. Well, besides Laini and Tabby. But as much as I love those two, I don't want to grow old with either of them.

"What do you mean, I have someone in my life?"

"Who do you think?" I sigh. "It's okay, Jack. I know it's all secretive about Cate Able. But I've figured out that you have a relationship with her."

"Yes, I do, but—"

Tabby chooses that minute to open the door. "Guys, I hate to break this up, but I have to be at work in two hours. Could we move it along?"

22

Ben reached out. "Don't be fooled by him again, Val. Come and marry me. You know I'll never hurt you."

Valerie looked from John to Ben. She cared about both men in such different ways her mind was swirling in confusion. "I don't know what to do," she said. "I just . . . I can't think."

She swept past both men and began to run.

—An excerpt from *Fifth Avenue Princess*
by Dancy Ames

Tabby is snoring softly by the time we arrive at the apartment.

"I want to talk to you about Cate Able. To explain, really."

"Don't worry about it, Jack." I reach for the door handle. "I'm too tired to discuss it right now. Maybe some other time."

He gives me a sad nod. "I'm afraid I'll be out of town for the next few days. But when I arrive back home, will you have dinner with me? If you're to edit Cate Able's books, you have a right to know the truth."

I can't help but smile. Jack knows I won't be able to resist if he puts it like that. "Okay. Call me when you get home."

My mind is buzzing when I get inside, and I know there's

no point in trying to sleep. After Tabby drags herself out the door to work, I bring Laini up to speed, and then settle in with a cup of strong, hot coffee and resolve to finish my own manuscript so I can send it to Sheri as promised. By suppertime, I type the final word and click send.

I sigh and stretch out on the sofa. My head hurts and my nose is running. When I wake up a few hours later, my throat is sore and I can tell I'm running a fever.

For the next two days, I'm in and out of sleep. Tabby and Laini field all of my calls. By the morning of the third day, I have a long list of people to get in touch with. My parents have called several times, Sheri once, and the last name on the list from this morning is Jack.

I dial his number. "Jack Quinn's office."

"Crystal? This is Dancy. Is Jack around?"

"He's in a meeting with Mr. Kramer."

"Okay, I'll call back later."

I start to call my parents, but I realize I'm still hurt over the condo being sold. I need to let it sink in a little without any drama or illness to cloud my perspective. I know I'll get over it. But I need a little time.

I dial Sheri and she picks up. "Dancy! I've been trying to reach you. How are you feeling?"

"Much better."

"Great! I just wanted to let you know I see a lot of promise in the manuscript. I've sent it on to Jack for a read."

My heart skips a beat at the thought of Jack reading my work, but I try to play it cool. "All right. Thank you for letting me know."

The rest of the day, I play catch-up on laundry and e-mail. By the end of the day, I still haven't heard back from Jack, and I must say I'm a little nerved up by it.

I'm rehashing my conversation with Brandon's grandmother when I realize something. I can keep Brandon. There's no reason I can't lease a two-bedroom apartment. I have a trust fund that I'm old enough to break into. I can't afford luxury like my parents, but he won't go hungry, and as long as Dad pays his Juilliard tuition . . .

I jump up, shower, race out the door, and reach my dad's just as they're sitting down to supper.

"I'm sorry to interrupt."

"You're not interrupting, Dancy," Dad says. "Have you eaten? There's plenty. Amanda fixed enough for an army."

Brandon refuses to look me in the eye. Any other time, he'd have a good reason to avoid me, but after the afternoon I've had, I'm more than willing to forgive last night's wild-goose chase.

"How was school today, Brandon?" I slide into a seat while Dad pulls another place setting from the china cabinet.

A shrug lifts Brandon's shoulders. "It was okay."

"What brings you over, Dancy?" Mom cuts right to the chase.

"Actually, I need to speak with Dad privately." No sense in beating around the proverbial bush. "But it can wait until after dinner. I'm starving."

"Fine. The two of you can speak privately in your father's office afterwards." Mom presses her lips together, and I can tell she's annoyed. I suppose she wants to be included. And in most cases, I'd agree that she needs to be. But this isn't her issue. And I don't want her to be Dad's solution. I want him to do what's right for my little brother.

Dinner isn't quite finished when the doorbell rings. "What is this—Grand Central Station?" Mom grumbles with an uncharacteristic lack of grace—even the fake grace that befits the upper class.

Dad rises from his cushioned chair, re-covered in a pale green Italian silk brocade with small pink flowers. "I'll see who it is, darling."

"The reception the other night was nice, Mother," I say, trying to lighten the mood.

"You left early. Your father and I had an announcement."

"I was there for the announcement. It was nice of you and Dad. I'm sure Brynn will be able to find a great house for the amount of money she'll have to work with."

"Really, Dancy. Talking about money is vulgar. Where are your manners?"

"Somewhere in my rat-infested apartment, I guess."

Her eyes widen in alarm.

"I'm kidding, Mom."

"Thank goodness."

Dad returns to the dining room with Kale and Brynn. A real family reunion. Everyone sits. "Do you want us to set more places?" Mother asks after accepting Kale's kiss on the cheek. Kale shakes his head. "We've eaten. We just came by to drop off the deed to the condo. And to thank you guys again."

Mother takes a shuddering breath. "Well, as much as we'd like you to stay in New York, we can't live your life for you." Very mature. I'm proud of my mom. She's growing in character right before my eyes.

Kale turns to Brandon. "So, I assume you've apologized to Dancy for almost getting her and her best friend killed the other night."

Alarm flashes in Brandon's eyes, and anger shoots through me. "Leave him alone, Kale." I mean, Kale doesn't realize what Brandon's being faced with. A little compassion is in order.

"No." Brandon stands. "What's he talking about?"

Kale stares at our parents. "Are you telling me no one told him we thought he ran away?"

"What?" Brandon throws me a look of pure bewilderment.

Kale gives him a stern frown. "Dad thought you ran away because he couldn't find you after the party, Brandon. When Dad called Dancy, she was so worried she took the train all the way to Jersey looking for you."

"That's not safe at night!" Brandon appears a little shell-shocked.

"Well, as you can see, nothing happened, and I lived to tell the tale. And it's not your fault Dad didn't know you were home the whole time. If anyone needs to be held accountable, it's Dad."

"Dancy, really." My mother utters her first words in quite a while—and they're in defense of him? "Treat your father with some respect."

"No, darling." Dad presses his hand to Mom's. "Dancy is right. I should have looked more closely. To be honest, I should have known when he left the reception in the first place."

Well, then. I think that about sums things up, only who can wrap their mind around Dad taking responsibility for anything?

"Dancy, what made you look there?" Brandon asks.

"I was afraid if you were upset, you'd go find your mom. I was worried, and I wanted to be sure you were okay."

I see conflict in Brandon's face. He's obviously ashamed that he could have gotten me killed, and yet an odd joy lights his eyes. I push up from my chair and walk around the table. "This might not be a typical family, but we are family and we take care of each other."

"You have a lot of guts." Brandon's face splits into a crooked grin and melts my heart. I throw my arms around him and pull him close. And he doesn't even try to pull away. Instead, he grips my shoulders and clings to me like a beggar clutches a crust of stale bread. When we turn loose, we both wipe our eyes and grin.

I think now might be the time to talk to my dad. I turn to him. "Can we talk now?"

He looks a little dazed and gives me a wordless nod. "My office."

Closing the door behind me, I draw a deep breath. "I went to Jersey the other night to find Brandon's mom."

His eyes flash. "What happened?"

"I found her mother, who clearly isn't sick."

He scowls and pours himself a brandy at the wet bar (who needs a wet bar in their office?). After tossing it back, he meets my gaze. "I know. That was our story so Brandon wouldn't find out his mom didn't want him anymore."

I have to admit, I'm surprised my dad was in on the deception, let alone behind the whole thing. "Does Mother know?"

"Of course."

Of course. As if he's never kept anything from her. Okay, deep breath. This isn't the point. Brandon is what matters here.

"So what about Brandon? Don't you think it's time he knows the truth?"

Dad sinks into his brown leather chair. "I figured she'd be back by now and want him back."

"Okay, Dad, you figured that, but it didn't happen. As a matter of fact, even her mother has no idea where Mary is."

"I do."

I gape. "What? Where? And how did you find out?"

"She called and asked for money a few days ago. She's in California with some guy who is twenty years younger than she is."

"What about her son?"

"I'm taking care of him."

That's debatable, but I won't belabor the point. "What about in February, when you and Mother move to Florida? How can you take him away from Juilliard? He should have this chance, Dad." My hands are shaking, but I look him square in the eye. "I want him. I was thinking I could cash in my trust fund and find a place somewhere. If you could keep paying his tuition and buying his clothes, we should make it fine on what I can earn as a freelancer. And if I need to take on a part-time job, I don't mind doing that."

I'm not sure what I expect, but it certainly isn't "Wait here." Which is what Dad says to me. "I didn't want to tell you this way." He stands up and walks out the door, returning a minute later with my mother.

"Tell her, Caroline." Dad's face is practically glowing.

I look to my mother and wait.

"We've decided that since Kale and Brynn don't want the condo, we want to give it to you. We know you've always loved it."

What on earth is she talking about? "But you sold it!"

"Who told you that?" Dad asks.

"You did. The night of the reception you and Mother made that big announcement about using the money from the sale to buy the newlyweds their own house."

Mother shakes her head. "You misunderstood. We sold your *father's* condo. This one. It was worth considerably less than the one overlooking the park, of course, but housing is extremely affordable in Oklahoma."

My head is spinning. But I have enough clarity to realize what my parents have just given me. I let out a squeal. "Are you telling me the condo is mine?"

Dad smiles. "As soon as we get the deed signed over to you."

Then something dawns. "This is the perfect solution for Brandon and me."

"I don't understand." Mother's brow furrows. But Dad gets the point, because he averts his gaze as though he's ashamed. And in reality he should be, but that doesn't diminish my joy.

"Brandon's going to live with me."

"Ridiculous. The boy will come to Florida with his father."

The pleading in my dad's eyes touches a chord deep inside me. I realize something. He wants to do everything he can to be the husband my mother deserves, after all he's put her through. Sadly, that means Brandon doesn't have a chance at our father's attention. Even if Brandon did go to Florida with them, he would always be disappointed.

"It's the best solution, Mother. Brandon needs to have a chance to further his music, and you two need time alone. This is what I want to do for him."

"What are you talking about?" Brandon stands in the doorway, and I practically run to him.

"Mother and Dad gave me the condo. Do you know what that means?"

He shrugs. "You get a big place all to yourself?"

"Wrong." I take his hand. I know it's a corny display of affection, but I can't help myself. "You and I get a big place to *our*selves."

"I don't get it."

"If Dad agrees . . ." I stare at my dad and my heart lifts as he gives me a nod. "I want you to live with me in New York so you can go to Juilliard. And now that I have the condo, there's more than enough room. What do you say?"

Brandon lets out a whoop and lifts me effortlessly. "You rock!"

I can't stop smiling as I wander away from Dad's. He stuffed money into my pocket and told me to take a cab, so I hail one, and lo and behold it's the same cabbie from last night.

His face lights up at the sight of me. "Looks like you made it back in one piece."

I grin at him. "I did."

"Did the Man upstairs answer your prayer about the kid?"

"Better than I prayed for. I get to keep him when my parents move to Florida."

"What are you, some kind of saint or something?"

"Hardly."

"Where to?"

I open my mouth to give him the address to the apartment I share with my friends. But instead what comes out is, "988 Fifth Avenue."

He whistles. "Pretty nifty."

"Yeah . . ."

I pull out my phone and notice that Jack tried to call. Rather than call him back, I send a text. "Can you meet me at my mom's place?"

A minute later, I get a text back. "Better idea. Fifty-ninth and Seventh."

A smile touches my lips as I snap my phone shut.

"Excuse me."

The cabbie glances in the rearview mirror. "Yeah?"

"Can you take me to Fifty-ninth and Seventh instead?"

He shrugs. "You want to go to Central Park at seven thirty on a cold night like this one?"

"Didn't exactly remember it was Central Park, but yeah. I'm meeting someone there."

"A boyfriend?"

"I'm afraid not. This one's already taken."

My heart nearly stops when the cabbie pulls alongside the curb at the park. Jack is standing there, waiting. When he notices me in the cab, he walks over and opens the door, helping me out with his gloved hand.

"I'm glad you got in touch. I wasn't sure you wanted to see me again after our misunderstanding."

"You said you were going to explain. No matter what, I'd like to be your friend, Jack."

He keeps his hand wrapped firmly around mine. "I'm glad."

He leads me to a horse-drawn carriage under a streetlight. "Shall we?"

"A carriage ride through Central Park?" I give him a little nudge. "You could give a girl the wrong idea, you know."

I climb into the seat and he climbs in after me. "What idea?"

"That maybe you want to date me?" I know I'm being bold, but this is the new me. The me who owns a home and takes care of her teenage brother. It's time to go after what I want in life. And I want Jack Quinn. Cate Able is too much of a prima donna to deserve Jack. I mean, why does she have to be so reclusive anyway? Is she that important?

He turns to me and the look in his eyes steals my breath. "Then you wouldn't have the wrong idea. You see, I'd very much like to see you as a date."

"What about Cate Able? You said you two are in a relation-ship."

He turns to me and hesitates just a second before saying, "Dancy, you are looking at Cate Able."

I'm sure I must have heard him wrong. Surely he didn't just say he's Cate Able. I give a short laugh.

"It's true. Cate Able is my pen name."

I grin. "Come on."

"Seriously. And I'm tired of the secrecy. Which is why I killed off my lead character. I want to leave Cate Able behind and write under my own name."

I'm shocked. Jack is completely and utterly telling the truth. I sit completely still, trying to take it all in.

"Do you forgive me for my deception?"

"I suppose I have no choice. After all, you did trust me to edit your book."

"You did a fine job of it, too. Of course, I have a lot of work to do on the manuscript, thanks to you."

I can't help but laugh.

"And just for the record, I'm honored to hear that I'm your favorite author. I'm afraid your revelation went straight to my head."

"Well, Jack Quinn," I snuggle in closer to him and put my head on his shoulder. "You are an amazing writer."

"And you are a talent as well."

"How do you mean?" I ask.

"I've been reading your book today. Sheri sent it on last night. I was on the last chapter when your text message came."

"What do you think?"

"As a reader, or as an editor?"

"Either." I brace myself.

"I like the story and I believe we can get it past the committee."

"Really?"

"Editorially, we have some work to do. But that's to be expected." He turns me in his arms so I'm facing him. "Now, I must know which chap Valerie ends up with. I insist you tell me immediately."

A smile touches the corners of my lips. "You'll have to wait and see. Right now I'm much more interested in who I'm going to end up with."

"Would you care to hear my opinion on the matter?"

I pull back and look straight into his beautiful eyes. "Kiss me, Jack."

He's so close, our breath mingles.

"I thought you'd never ask." And his lips claim mine, warm and gentle and just the way I always dreamed our first kiss would be.

Riding in a horse-drawn carriage, kissing Prince Charming, suddenly I feel just like—and I know this is corny—a Fifth Avenue princess. But you know, if the title fits . . .

Epilogue

Peace swelled inside Valerie as she took in the beautiful African sunset. The children had been fed. And they ran in the dust, playing and laughing, their bellies full. In a few minutes, she and her mom would gather all of the children and begin the nightly ritual of washing, putting on pajamas, and reading a bedtime story. Maybe even reading two, if they were especially quiet and good during the first one.

As she rested against the side of the building and watched the horizon, Valerie smiled. She had chosen to be alone, but she wasn't lonely.

Here in Africa, her life counted in the way she wanted. She wasn't defined by her looks or her talent. But by her heart.

—End of *Fifth Avenue Princess* by Dancy Ames

Tabby's wedding day arrives on a beautiful sunny December Saturday, with snow blanketing the ground.

Last year, Tabby's sister got married, and David proposed at the wedding. I have no illusions that Jack will follow that example. As a matter of fact, I'm not ready for that step. After all, we've only been dating about a month. But what a month it's been!

My condo—can I just say that again?—my condo was finished last week. Thank goodness Brynn had only done a little painting, so there wasn't much to redo. And I thought the place nearly perfect the way it was. It didn't need much change, other than a cosmetic touch here and there.

And speaking of cosmetics, Laini and I are finishing up our makeup and staring in awe at beautiful Tabby. Today, she's beautiful Tabitha, the bride.

I have to say, over the last few weeks, I've made a lot of changes. Mostly to my manuscript. Under Jack's expert editing, I've revised and revised and revised. I even rewrote the ending so that Valerie ends up with—who else?—John Quest. According to Sheri, readers will want that happy ending with a man. I suppose she's right. Who doesn't want the fairy-tale ending?

Tabby is radiant as she walks down the aisle to her man, and after the preacher pronounces them husband and wife, I only have to wait a little while before Jack shows up at my side. "No fair," he says in that gorgeous accent.

"What?"

His fingers barely brush my elbow and he leans in, his lips close to my ear. "No fair to be more beautiful than the bride."

Reaching up, I touch his face. "No one is more beautiful than a bride."

"Then when that day comes for us, I'm not sure I'll be able to stay on my feet."

"For us, huh?"

"Don't you know?" He takes me in his arms.

"Don't I know what?"

"That someday I intend to ask you to be my wife."

Oh? I clasp my hands behind his neck. "Well, I think you should know, then, that I intend to say yes. Someday."

"Okay, my love." He dips his head and presses his lips to mine. "Someday."

With the promise of someday still tingling in my ear, I surrender to his kiss.

Author's Note

Dear Readers,

Thanks for joining me once again for a Drama Queens story!

Dancy Ames was born with the proverbial silver spoon in her mouth and took things from there—rich in a way most of us will only read about in books and see on TV, working at her dream publishing house, rooming with two best friends who were always on her side.

And yet . . .

Isn't that how it is? We look at the green, green grass in some-one else's yard and think, *If only I had that kind of grass, all my problems would be over.* Maybe it isn't that cut-and-dried, but how many women think, *I have a great husband, and yet . . . I have beautiful kids, so I should be happy, and yet . . . I have a great home, and yet . . . A great job, and yet . . .*

Dancy had to be stripped of everything that defined her in order for her to turn to God. And once she did, God was able to bring her to the place where He intended her to be all along. *You Had Me at Good-bye* was written during my own stripping-away time. Out of my release and surrender of my own will and my own goals, God remade me and this book. Sometimes I truly think God brings us low to raise us up.

Even though this book is meant to be whimsical and fun, I hope the truths embedded deep within the layers of the story came through and ministered in the way that I firmly believe God intended.

Until next time, may God bless you and keep you.

Tracey Bateman

READING GROUP GUIDE

1. Dancy struggles with an inability to confront difficult situations, even when she feels she's been wronged. What possible events in her past could have caused this? How do you balance the need to confront with the desire to be liked?

2. Why does Dancy find it necessary to buy in a larger size the same skirt as one her mother gave her so her mom won't know she's gained weight?

3. In spite of her mother's flaws, Dancy loves her. What keeps her from trusting her mother to do the same for her?

4. Jack's great at separating his personal and professional life. What are some ways we see this in the book? Is this ability a good thing? Have you ever seen someone carry this compartmentalization too far?

5. Do Kale and Dancy have the same perception of their childhood? How does this perception color their reaction to Brandon?

6. Laini cooks when she's upset or uncertain. What are other ways people handle life's ups and downs?

7. When she was young, Dancy gave up on God when she asked Him to help her dad to love her and she didn't see results from that prayer. Is that a valid reason to turn away from God? Why or why not?

8. When Dancy is devastated about losing the home she loves, she thinks Jack skips out on her while she's gone to the ladies' room. Why is she so quick to assume that someone

she trusts deserted her? Does our past make us more susceptible to certain kinds of hurts?

9. When Dancy's new boss acts inappropriately, she walks out on her job. What would you have done in her situation?

10. Jack has a hard time at first seeing Dancy as someone other than Kale's little sister. Why is it sometimes difficult for a relationship to mature beyond its initial dynamic? How can we open our minds to these possibilities, not just in romantic relationships but in family relationships as well?

ABOUT THE AUTHOR

TRACEY BATEMAN lives in Missouri with her husband and four children. She has been a member of American Christian Fiction Writers since the early days of its inception and served as vice president and president of the organization. Her hobbies include reading, watching the Lifetime Movie Network, hanging out with family, helping out in her church, and listening to music.

IF YOU LIKED *You Had Me at Good-bye* . . .

That's (Not Exactly) Amore

Book Three in the Drama Queens Series

When Laini Sullivan lands a job designing Nick Pantalone's coffee shop, there are two problems: one, Nick's nephew Joe hates all of her ideas, and two, Laini has to admit he's right—she's a disaster at design. Still, she can't risk losing the job. To compromise, Joe brings in help on the project, while Laini continues to bake the goodies that keep his customers lining up.

Their relationship is moving along, so when new guy Officer Mark Hall implies that Joe's family is tied to the mob, Laini doesn't want to believe it. But things spin out of control when she meets the family, including "the uncles," who seem to confirm Mark's suspicions. To make things worse, Nana Pantalone makes it clear Laini isn't the kind of girl she has in mind for her grandson. Laini's not sure if she should give Joe the benefit of the doubt or just set her sights on Mark and fuhgetaboutit.

CPSIA information can be obtained
at www.ICGtesting.com
Printed in the USA
LVOW11s1446231216
518584LV00001B/11/P